Matt has had a passion for storytelling from a young age. He was always inspired by the magic that came from reading fiction novels, the experience of escaping reality to find a world just between the page and reader.

He has studied at Macquarie University in Sydney to become an English teacher for secondary schools with hopes to reignite creative skills and allow students to embrace imaginative writing with an open mind. Since finishing high school 2015, Matt's goal was to write a novel that allowed readers of all ages to relate to within a fictional world.

I would like to dedicate this book to anyone who has been in a situation where they feel like they ain't enough.

Matthew Hayes

OKLEM

AUSTIN MACAULEY PUBLISHERS™
LONDON * CAMBRIDGE * NEW YORK * SHARJAH

Copyright © Matthew Hayes 2023

The right of Matthew Hayes to be identified as author of this work has been asserted by the author in accordance with sections 77 and 78 of the Copyright, Designs and Patents Act 1988.

All rights reserved. No part of this publication may be reproduced, stored in a retrieval system, or transmitted in any form or by any means, electronic, mechanical, photocopying, recording, or otherwise, without the prior permission of the publishers.

Any person who commits any unauthorised act in relation to this publication may be liable to criminal prosecution and civil claims for damages.

This is a work of fiction. Names, characters, businesses, places, events, locales, and incidents are either the products of the author's imagination or used in a fictitious manner. Any resemblance to actual persons, living or dead, or actual events is purely coincidental.

A CIP catalogue record for this title is available from the British Library.

ISBN 9781398482906 (Paperback)
ISBN 9781398482920 (ePub e-book)
ISBN 9781398482913 (Audiobook)

www.austinmacauley.com

First Published 2023
Austin Macauley Publishers Ltd®
1 Canada Square
Canary Wharf
London
E14 5AA

I would like to acknowledge the endless support from my family and close friends which inspired me to continue writing this novel.

I would also like to acknowledge Austin Macauley Publishers for accepting my work and providing a new author with an incredibly rewarding experience.

Prologue

1840: Isolated Field in the Earth Nation

The two lovers stood outside a hut. A field stretched out to either side of them, soft-lit beneath the low-hanging clouds, silvered in the moonlight.

"This will ensure that our future shall be everlasting, my love!" Jessani cried out.

Marvin shook his head vigorously. Everything had fallen apart.

"You will simply get yourself killed," he said. "They are sending me to the Supernatural Universe. Please, you must stay!"

"You are a doppelganger," Jessani said, crossing her arms defiantly, "you can protect me—"

"No, I cannot," Marvin cut her off. "I couldn't even protect my family."

He grabbed her arm and began to lead her towards the hut. Jessani pulled away, but her long black dress got caught on a root hiding within the luscious grass and she stumbled over. "You don't ever have to worry about aging," she said, ignoring Marvin's outstretched arm and standing back up. "You can live forever. We *could* live forever. Is that not something we both desire?"

Tears began to well in Marvin's eyes. A never ending future with the love of his life. It was something only imagined through dreams and poetry. Here stood an opportunity for this dream to become a reality, yet he could not allow it.

"You are talking about using unknown substances in another universe, Jessani. I do not know what I took. Nobody does. You know not what you plead for."

"I would rather take a risk and lose my mind than live a life without you," Jessani said through tears of her own. Marvin paused, taking in the beauty of his woman. There was a fierce determination in her eyes. She was willing to travel into another world to find a way to live forever with him. He took a deep breath.

"I still believe that you should have stayed with your mother and let your father's actions be dealt with. I now see you have his stubbornness. I cannot promise you anything, but—" he got no further as Jessani raced forward, throwing herself into his arms and kissing him passionately.

"We will find a way to live forever," she whispered.

Without warning, a raging wind swept over them, the moon vanished behind thick clouds and the fields unleashed a deafening roar. Marvin could feel his feet lift off the ground. He wrapped his arms more firmly around Jessani's waist.

"The Peacekeepers have opened the portal. It is time. Our fate now lies with nature and the Oklem."

With one final look at each other, the lovers were thrown into the air at a speed unlike anything Marvin had ever felt before. He lost his grip, and he was alone in the howling wind. Then there was darkness.

Chapter 1

Silence. That was the first thing Azar noticed. That and the painful constriction of his heart. He stood alone in the bush on a small dirt path leading towards his favourite viewing point. His horse, Starc, was grazing on the fresh grass by a lake back on the main trail. As usual, the ride had allowed his thoughts to spiral around aimlessly, just as the leaves that fell off the trees did. He closed his eyes. There were no more cannons in the distance, no more aircraft taking off from the landing docks. It was over. The war against Orven and his army of Pirates, hellbent on bringing a new order through forbidden portals, had escalated further than anyone could have anticipated. Everyone knew the story. That four centuries ago, Orven attempted to create a portal that would allow the most dangerous creatures of the Supernatural Universe, the Tychun, to enter the Nations. He failed that night, though nobody knows why. He then went into hiding before finally being captured in the year 1840, where he was sent on a one way trip to the Supernatural Universe with his closest followers.

Ten years ago, he suddenly returned and raged the longest war in history. The four Nations, Mortal, Fire, Ice and Earth had combined to end the threat by attacking the Pirates homeland, Skull, closing off all access portals to the Nations permanently, or so they hoped. But Orven was dead, and the city of Mintor was preparing to celebrate.

Azar continued along to the end of the path, which opened into a deserted park littered with old, rusted play equipment. The park was based at the top of a steep hill, where a broken fence had once stood to stop children from ploughing down into the dense bush. He sat down on an old, stone bench overlooking the city, watching as the sun began its descent on another cool winter's day. He remembered where he was when the Victory announcement came through. He was finishing his shift at Geminate, one of the many local cafes that flooded the streets of Mintor, capital of the Mortal Nation. The TVs, radios and every phone in the room buzzed with the news that the Nations had been successful. The war was over, although for Azar another one, much more personal, had just begun.

Still, relief had flooded through him at the thought of his parents returning home. As senators they had spent the last two years removed from the Nations in the only safe place there was for those of high status, the Trail of Tales. He had missed them, even more so now.

The sun's final rays of warmth glimmered off the peaceful city. The palace, tucked away in a side street, would go unnoticed to a traveller's eye. It was home to the leader of the city, Peacekeeper Drand. Unlike the other Nations, the palace did not dominate the city. Instead, it looked almost plain apart from the statues of past Peacekeepers standing tall at the gates. Next to it was the Whistle, the most advanced building in the city. It was also the tallest, housing senators, celebrities, special guests, soldiers, and politicians like Azar's parents. He was allowed to stay when his parents left, as he had no other family. However the political game had never captured his interest, so he rarely hung around the area. His thoughts were interrupted by his phone ringing. It was his mother.

"Mum! I heard the news. You can finally come home," Azar said proudly.

"Yes honey, the war is finished. But your father and I are not yet coming back to the Mortal Nation," Maree Geminus replied, her voice soft, almost as if she was exhausted.

Azar's heart sank.

"Why not?"

"The war did not end as simply as we would have liked."

Maree sounded hesitant, as if she wanted to say more, but couldn't. Azar wondered if there was someone else with her, listening.

"Orven held one final ritual as our forces descended on his position. Unfortunately, he was partially successful. It has enabled him to maintain a connection to the Supernatural Universe."

"Mum, Orven's dead. And you know I don't have any interest in the stupid war," Azar said. He thought about telling her what was really on his mind. Would she understand? Would she know what it was like to have her heart broken? Would she accept what he would tell her?

"You no longer have a choice, Azar," came his mother's stern response.

"Why can't you come home?" he asked, his voice barely holding together.

"I am trying to tell you, son." Maree lowered her voice—Azar had never heard her sound so…strange. "Orven appears to have used a blood sample to activate a portal. This sample is so rare it is almost non-existent. It's called Oklem blood. We cannot return home until we find out how he got it, and it is essential that we do. More than you know. I can say no more now—the walls have ears. But you must speak with Peacekeeper Drand."

Azar began to feel a mix of confusion and desperation brewing within his chest.

"Wait mum. Slow down. I don't understand."

"Honey it was you. Your blood was taken by Orven—"

Azar held the receiver away as if it might bite. After a moment, he held it back to his ear.

"How? What has my blood got to do with the most evil man in existence? I just wanted to know you were coming home."

"See Drand, Azar. Just do it," his mother now sounded frustrated, but urgent. Almost desperate. Azar hung up the phone. He grabbed a small stone, stood up and flung it off the cliff.

"How could today have gotten worse?" he asked himself, choking back tears. He sat back down, wrapping his arms around his legs and looked out to the city. Birds flew in an arrow formation over the Whistle. Azar tried to calm himself. His head was whirling as he began to break down the two major events of the day. And neither of them were good. His boyfriend had cheated on him and now his parents weren't coming home because Orven, the Pirate's leader, somehow managed to get Azar's blood which also has a connection to portals. It was all too much to take in. In this moment confusion of He felt a ripple come over him, and for a moment his vision blurred. Then the feeling was gone. He was completely lost, and realised that the only way he could find answers was to do as his mother had said. He must seek Peacekeeper Drand for an explanation.

"The universe has so many views to offer, doesn't it?" came a cool, crisp voice, "you just have to know where to look."

Azar turned around, startled. A boy, about the same age as him, was leaning against the rusted swings. He had dark hair slicked back, with a blond tinge running through it. He wore black jeans and his hands were shoved in the pockets of a brown coat.

"Nobody has been here for years," Azar said, subconsciously running his hand through his dark brown hair. It was supposed to be Azar's personal getaway place.

"Yeah I figured with the path being all, you know, hidden," the stranger said. Azar's guard was slightly raised. The boy looked clean, something that was pretty much impossible to be after travelling through the hills.

"So how exactly did you find this park?" Azar inquired. The boy spread his arms, seemingly unfazed by Azar's slightly suspicious tone.

"Well, what I assume is your horse gave it away. I guess he now has a new friend by the water." He had ridden a horse? In that expensive coat? Azar locked eyes with him, blue on brown, and decided he would give it the benefit of the doubt.

"My horse's name is Starc. I'm Azar." He got up and went over to the boy, offering his hand. A slightly longer than usual pause commenced before the newcomer removed his hands from his pockets.

"Jake," said the boy, extending his right hand.

"I ride around the hills quite frequently, and I have never seen you before," Azar said. Jake nodded, kicking the dirt with his foot.

"I'm new to Mintor. Moved here from the Earth Nation with my Uncle last week. The Pirates were getting a little too close. I guess if we'd known the war would be over a week later we'd have stayed."

"I've always been interested in that Nation," Azar said, "the bridge between our world of Nations, and, well, the one with planets I guess."

Jake laughed.

"Yeah there's quite a few stories I could tell you. But I'm sensing I interrupted your thoughts about something pretty serious."

"Nah it's just pointless drama," Azar replied quickly, hoping to divert from that topic.

"Got it," came the reply, although Azar felt Jake saw right through him. Silence followed, allowing the sound of wind in the trees and the call of the birds to take over. Just as Azar felt like things were getting awkward, Jake spoke.

"Well, I best be off. Probably not a good idea to be here after dark."

"Yeah it's a whole new place when the sun goes down."

"Any recommendations for good coffee in this town?" Jake asked.

"The Geminate Cafe has the best coffee. Plus I can give you a little tour. I work there." Immediately Azar thought he had been a little too obvious. But he couldn't help it. It was like something was taking over to try and salvage something out of the day of heartbreak.

"I'll keep that in mind," Jake said. He made his way through the park and disappeared into the bushes.

Azar turned back to the view, taking in the strange encounter. Maybe he was just over thinking things. He had gotten used to not seeing another person in the park for years. Though was it coincidental that this happened right after his mother's bizarre story? The sun had turned the sky into an ocean of pink and orange. He had to admit, Jake's timing temporarily held off the wave of depression he was planning to bathe in. Just then he heard a twig snap. He turned around, and laid his eyes upon another boy leaning against the old swing set, exactly where Jake had been. "You must be Azar," the boy said with a humorous gleam in his eyes.

He was dressed in black with brown boots and was adjusting a watch on his left arm. But the feature that stood out the most was his face. Azar felt gooseflesh prickle on the back of his neck. For a moment he was in his room looking in the mirror, for the boy looked exactly like Azar. Azar stood there in amazement, and fear. He wanted to run away but instead his own eyes nailed him to the spot.

Chapter 2

Azar didn't know what to do. He wasn't sure he could make it back to Starc, and was pretty sure he wouldn't survive the jagged, rocky descent down the hill.

"At last I meet the famous Oklem doppelganger. Doesn't this make things interesting," the newcomer said.

Azar didn't know what to say. Doppel-what? His bewilderment and confusion made speech impossible. This was the second time in less than an hour that he'd heard that other word. Oklem. What did this word have to do with him?

"You know it's rude to stare," the look-alike added, rolling his eyes.

"How do you look exactly like me?" Azar eventually stammered.

"That's a great question! We can get right on with business. First and foremost, however, I believe introductions are in order. Your name, your life, it's all just a little…average. I have a name, I like to be exciting, not easily forgotten. So you can be the sensible, drama-filled Azar, and I'll be Lux, the dashing lookalike who knows how to enjoy life and just let go."

Azar felt a slight pulling in his chest. Somehow he felt that Lux knew more about him than even he himself knew. His head was spinning from constantly having to deal with surprises.

However, this look-alike was controlling the entire situation, so Azar knew he had to speak. "Let's backtrack. A doppel what?"

"A doppelganger. You know, a freak event in nature where you have a look-alike but they're not a twin or result of some scientific experiment," Lux answered, waving his arm dismissively. Azar shook his head in disbelief.

"Why are you here?" he asked, folding his arms.

"We have got quite an adventure coming up. This meeting has been long overdue," Lux said. His voice carried a heavy dosage of sass, adding to his dominating presence. Azar spread his arms.

"Look, I have had a really bad day. And let's get one thing clear. Nobody ever "wants" to see me. I'm boring, a living example of disappointment. I have no idea what you are, but I think it's best to leave me alone."

"Always so dramatic," Lux said, stretching his words to mock his confused double. "I have had the opportunity to get a glimpse of your past. My arrival will certainly bring you a chance to achieve something that benefits yourself. We'll just have to see if you act on it. It's impossible to be normal in any of the four Nations."

"I'd like to think I've managed things pretty well, considering."

Lux snorted.

"Yes well I can assure you that a cheating boyfriend will be the least of your concerns when you decide to stop being a drama queen."

Azar had not had time to begin thinking about Brett. Now was certainly not an option.

"Not even five minutes in and I already don't like you," he said.

"Is it dislike or fear of the unknown?" Lux challenged.

"I don't know what is going on, but I'm leaving," Azar said. He made his way past Lux, glancing back only to see Lux was gone. Suddenly he ran into someone, and realised Lux was standing in front of him again, holding an arm across Azar's chest.

"I low…?" Azar started

"I am faster, stronger, and a hell of a lot meaner than you," Lux said. "I'd hate for us to get off on a bad start. I am not on any sides here. You're off to see the "oh so mighty" Peacekeeper Drand, aren't you? Send him my regards."

"It's none of your business," Azar snapped, still reeling from the speed in which Lux had moved. "Only…It's just that the Peacekeepers and the senate are not exactly innocent people," Lux added.

A little shiver shot down Azar's spine.

"What are you talking about?"

"There are always three sides to a story. In this case of the war, there's the Peacekeepers, the Pirates, and the truth. I highly advise you to be cautious of what your leader has to say. I too am searching for some answers."

"Then," Azar replied, pushing Lux's arm aside, more roughly than he meant to, "search elsewhere. I have no interest in all of this, but somehow I seem to have a role in this Nation that I did not audition for. Leave me alone, for I'd hate to think of what could happen if there's two of us involved."

Azar made his way to the bushes, stopping to look backwards once more before he left the park. There was nobody there. For the first time in years, there was a part of him that wished he was not alone.

****

Azar returned to his room in the Whistle, still trying to figure out what the appearance of his double could possibly mean. He knew the Supernatural Universe had many different creatures lurking within its realm, but it wasn't possible for them to travel to the Nations. The path had been sealed a long time ago, he had been told. He realised it was late evening, but knew that he could not sleep until he found some answers to what was going on. Azar had never privately visited the Peacekeeper before, so he made sure his attire was a little more fitting than a shirt and jeans. He found a buttoned shirt and black pants neatly folded at the back of his wardrobe. Avoiding the mirror as he got ready, he thought about the past year and his relationship with Brett. Azar knew Brett was a little hot headed and they had, on occasion, argued over small things. But the one thing Azar thought he knew for certain was the love they had for each other. To have that core part in his heart shattered by Brett's cheating nearly overwhelmed him. What made it worse was that he had nobody to talk to about it. There was not much going for him at the moment, and the thought of giving up was slowly becoming a more frequent consideration. But if there was one trait he had inherited from his parents, it was stubbornness. Azar didn't give up easily.

He made his way out to the hallway. The Whistle had ten operating lifts. As there were sixty floors, people were travelling up and down all day and night. The sun had long set by the time Azar was leaving, so he decided to take the underground passage connecting to the palace rather than walk the streets. It was not a quiet trip, however. Doorways lined the corridor leading to brightly lit labs, training rooms and offices, all buzzing with people. Azar continued through, eventually coming to an elevator. Two security guards monitored it. They quickly recognised the visitor, for everyone knew the son of Maree and Steve Geminus, and allowed him to enter. The lift opened into a lobby. Unlike the exterior, the walls within the palace were covered in bronze and silver. A woman with short dark hair and dressed in a grey suit made her way over to Azar.

"Good evening Azar. Peacekeeper Drand is expecting you. If you'd like to follow me," she said warmly. She led Azar up several flights of stairs and entered a doorway. It opened into a small waiting room. Azar sat down patiently as she went through another door. On the wall was a small screen, with a news report playing. An image of Orven, the feared leader, was displayed above the caption "DEAD". His stringy grey hair, crooked yellow teeth, wrinkled skin; all sent shivers down Azar's spine. The assistant returned a short time later, beckoning him to come through.

After the whirlwind of a day he'd had so far, he wasn't sure if he should be surprised by anything he was about to be told. This was the first time in his life that he was entering Peacekeeper Drand's quarters. Taking a deep breath, he stepped through the doorway. The first thing he noticed were the large golden drapes across the windows. Apart from a few lounges and a small table in the middle, the room was essentially empty. Azar laid his eyes upon Peacekeeper Drand, who was sitting on a white lounge, drinking tea. It was then that Azar realised there were four lounges and they were all different colours.

"Welcome Azar. It is good to see you at last."

"The honour is mine, Peacekeeper Drand," Azar said, suddenly becoming shy.

Azar made his way over and shook Drand's hand. The Peacekeeper did not stand, nor was he wearing any of the formal robes Azar had only ever seen him in. Instead he was in a buttoned blue and white striped shirt and black pants. He had short black hair and a round face, and was holding a cup of tea in his hands.

Drand was in his mid-twenties when he became the leader of the Mortal Nation. Part of becoming such a powerful figure included halting any further growth or aging. The process of becoming a Peacekeeper is a secret only those chosen can know, so how they become immune to aging was another mystery. This invincibility ensured that the chosen individual would live as long as the wonders of life allowed. Despite leading the Nations, Peacekeepers were very secretive beings. They are not elected by the people of their Nations. It was rumoured that angels appeared in the capital of the required Nation to choose a new Peacekeeper when the time came. But it had been centuries since the last Peacekeeper was killed, so nothing was confirmed. Azar knew that all the staff were personally chosen by the Peacekeeper, and that, at least in the Mortal Nation, they simply worked until they retired and passed away. The other current Peacekeepers were around forty to fifty years old when they were sworn in, so Drand was a frequent topic of debate by civilians. Why did nature choose someone so young? Was it a sign of evil?

Azar's thoughts were interrupted by Drand, who signalled for the young guest to take a seat.

"No need for formalities here, my boy. I know you must be disappointed that your parents are not yet returning despite the war being over. But we do have a dilemma which must be addressed. Before I begin, however, I must ask what you know so far?"

"About the war?" Azar asked, sitting on the blue lounge.

"Perhaps, or anything out of the ordinary really," Drand replied. Azar sensed the Peacekeeper was almost willing him to explain Lux's appearance. But how could he know? Just now, Lux's warning about trusting the Nation's leaders radiated through Azar's mind.

"Not much," Azar said eventually. "I've never really taken an interest in the war or anything."

"So there hasn't been any strange encounters?" Drand pressed. Azar tensed a little.

"You tell me," he replied, sounding a little more icy than he intended. Drand smiled and gave a slight nod of his head.

"I realise you may be frightened to talk about it, so let us discuss your doppelganger."

How did Drand know that Azar had met Lux? The Peacekeeper gently put down his teacup. "What is a doppelganger?" Azar said.

"Put very simply, a doppelganger is a living look alike. A double. The catch is they are a supernatural creature."

"I'm supernatural?" Azar asked, his heart rate increasing slightly.

"No, you are not," Drand replied. "Which is why I cannot understand why you have one here. I have never heard of two mortal people from our universe looking exactly the same but being born by two completely different sets of parents, and at two very different times in history. "Then who is Lux, how did he find me?" Azar asked.

"So that's the name he has chosen," Drand said thoughtfully. Azar's stomach turned. But why? Did he not trust Peacekeeper Drand?

"I must admit, I do not know very much about him, he holds the missing pieces to this bizarre puzzle. I believe that seeing as he sought you out, you can find the information we need," Drand replied. Just then the door opened and a waiter came in with a glass of water. He placed it in front of Azar.

"Oh, uh, thank you," Azar said slowly.

The waiter smiled and turned, taking Drand's empty tea cup with him. Only once the door had closed, Azar continued.

"You want me to interrogate him?"

"Nothing so sinister, my boy," Drand laughed. "See what he wants, and maybe in exchange he can tell you who he is. Now are you aware of Orven's story? The events leading up to the great war which has finally come to an end?" he asked. Azar was not sure why Drand dismissed Lux so easily, but he decided to stay on track with what Drand was interested in discussing. "Admittedly, I've never been interested enough to care about the political scope," Azar replied. He thought about what things would be like if he had shown a little more interest in his parents' political careers.

Drand sat back in his chair and looked intently at Azar.

"Politics is certainly not for everyone, there is no shame in that. I shall start there. Four centuries ago, Orven commenced his first attempt to open a portal to the Supernatural Universe and bring forth dangerous creatures known as Tychun. He failed, although I have never known what went wrong. The Peacekeepers weren't there, so all we know is the report we got back from a spy. After that, Orven went into hiding for nearly two centuries. In the year 1840, Peacekeeper Serain eventually captured him in the Fire Nation, and together the four Peacekeepers sent him along with his biggest followers through a portal into the Supernatural realm. Then, with our special powers which I cannot disclose to you, we sealed the path preventing anyone from travelling to or from that universe."

Azar slowly took in the information. It was mostly just more details to what his parents had told him, before they went into hiding. He had many questions, but there were two outstanding ones. "How did Orven survive for so long?" he asked, perplexed.

"Orven immersed himself into the dark depths of the Supernatural Universe. A place where everything is possible, but at a price. Invincibility is a very popular desire, and he found the right ingredients to create the potion which kept him and many of his close circle Pirates alive. Before we sealed the path, travel between the universes was allowed. Though there were limitations on who could come through, as some creatures, like the Tychun, are meant to stay away from our world."

Just then a beeping sound echoed across the room. Azar turned his head to the back wall as Drand sprung up, darting over to the machine and pressed some buttons.

"Apologies for that interruption. Just a video message. I will check it later," Drand said.

As the Peacekeeper started back towards the lounges, it allowed Azar to ask his other burning query.

"When and how did Orven come back to our world?"

"Orven returned ten years ago," Drand answered. "Peace had resumed in our Nation's for so long. Nobody could have anticipated Orven's rapid and destructive return. A portal was opened—how is still a mystery to this day. Orven came with those we banished and the ten-year war began. The ferocity of the attack almost overwhelmed the Earth Nation, with three quarters of it being captured by the Pirates. So that is the story, and you can see why it is a relief that Orven is finally dead."

Azar nodded in agreement. How could somebody be so intent on a goal so horrible that they would waste centuries trying to achieve it? Another knock sounded at the door and the female assistant stepped into the room.

"Pardon my intrusion, but your guest is arriving shortly," she said, then turned and left without awaiting a response.

"The final topic to discuss is you," Drand went on. "Unbeknownst to us until a few days ago, you have a very special blood type. It goes by the name of Oklem blood."

"My mother mentioned the word. I have no idea what it means," Azar said, folding his arms. "Having Oklem blood means you are an Oklem, a very rare creature created by nature to counter the Supernatural forces. The catch is that only nature decides who and when they shall arise."

"So I have been an Oklem my whole life?" Azar asked. He had never thought of himself as being anything more than normal.

"Well, this is the part where it gets interesting, the reason I wanted to talk to you. As a Peacekeeper, we have the ability to distinguish a Nation-born citizen from a Supernatural creature. We can also determine the exact creature as well without even thinking, we just know. We have this remarkable ability to ensure we can never be blindsided. An Oklem is not a naturally born creature, however you are still classed as being different because you are not like a normal citizen from one of the Nations. Therefore, Peacekeepers can identify you as being an Oklem. To become one, you must be given a dose of Oklem blood."

Azar felt the hairs on the back of his neck stand up.

"I think I'd remember that happening," he replied, although even he wasn't convinced by what he was saying.

"Even if the blood was slipped into a drink or something so innocent and mundane? It's unlikely you even suspected foul play. Keep in mind that normally being an Oklem has absolutely no impact on you as an individual," Drand stated.

"Normally?" Azar asked, raising his eyebrows.

"You decide whether or not to act on being an Oklem. But you do have a doppelganger, so I do not know if that changes the game. An Oklem has a gift, and that gift is your blood. It can be used to create portals across the Nations, and to universes," Drand said.

"But portalling already happens," Azar pointed out.

"Not to places that are forbidden," Drand replied softly. "Portals in general only stay open a short while before their power runs out. An Oklem's portal lasts until they choose to remove it." Azar was intrigued at what he was hearing, but he couldn't help but feel like he wasn't being told everything.

"So I have portal powers. What aren't you telling me, Drand?" Azar said, getting nervous.

"If I can tell a mortal from a supernatural being, I would have known about you from very early on in your life. But today marks the very first time I can see you are an Oklem. As soon as you entered, my senses acknowledged that I was in the presence of something that was not human. The blood in your body is electrified, but you feel no difference. Now I saw you two weeks ago at the public meet and greet day, and you were very much a Mortal Nation citizen." Azar felt a pulling from the pit of his stomach as he began to understand what the Peacekeeper was saying.

"Which means I was given this Oklem blood recently," he said.

"Correct. You can see the obvious concern. Now our sources led us to believe that Orven gained a dose of your blood with the intent to create a personalised portal direct to the dark depths of the Supernatural Universe. He was killed before he could activate it, and the entire ritual was destroyed, including your blood dose."

"Well, that's a relief," Azar said, taking a deep breath.

The door opened again and the same waiter returned with a full cup of tea.

"Your guest is here," he announced. The Peacekeeper took the cup slowly, bowing his head.

"Thank you, we will conclude our conversation."

Azar took a sip of water as the waiter left the room. Then he got up, preparing to leave.

"If my blood is gone, it doesn't really matter what Orven was trying then," he said.

"I wish that were the case. Orven has a very large network of followers, which is why I do not believe your doppelganger has coincidentally showed up today," Drand said, a very stern expression on his face. Azar wondered how many dilemmas the Peacekeeper must face all the time. He could see the mental toll it was taking on him, the dark bags under his eyes.

"Before he seemingly vanished, Lux told me that he wasn't on any sides. Is it possible he is here for his own purpose?" Azar asked.

"As I mentioned before, I feel it is best for you to discover how your doppelganger functions yourself. Create your own unique bond with him."

Again Drand was avoiding any discussion about Lux. Azar let out a sigh. "All this sounds really…interesting. A little scary, to be honest, but before I go, I want to know why this means my parents can't return home."

A sorrowful expression flashed across Drand's face for just a moment before he composed himself.

"They will return when we know the Nations are safe, and that there will be no further uprisings," he said.

Azar did not believe Drand, which terrified him. Could he trust anything he had been told?

"I think you need some time to reflect on everything, and I need to prepare for my guest," Drand continued quickly, standing up also.

Azar was not entirely satisfied. There was still too much left unanswered. Where were his parents? But he was also aware of a small warning flaring at the back of his mind. Maybe he could ask Lux for the information he was after? As well as that, Azar was tired after the day's events, and there was nothing more Drand was willing to discuss. As he did not want to disrespect such a powerful figure on his first visit, he simply bowed his head and left. But walking down the hallway, he wondered if he should tell someone else. Was the Peacekeeper to be trusted? He needed to start investigating himself. Azar wished for the second time that day that he could call Brett, who always had the right answer.

Chapter 3

"How are those toasted sandwiches coming along?" Wendy's voice was raised, demanding as always.

"Almost ready," Azar said.

It was lunchtime, and the Geminate Cafe was buzzing. Azar carried the plate of toasted sandwiches past the counter and placed them in front of the hungry customers. The three gentlemen murmured their thanks before digging in. Azar returned with their drinks. For the moment, everyone appeared to be satisfied. Another family nearby got up, leaving a mess across the table. Azar rolled his eyes as he grabbed a bucket and got the cleaning gear.

It had been two days since his meeting with Peacekeeper Drand. Apart from work, he realised that he had no commitments. He knew he would have to face his ex at some stage, he just didn't feel ready to yet. He felt like he was almost non-existent. With Brett gone from his life nobody needed him. As he started stacking plates, the doors opened again. He glanced at the newcomers, then stopped as he recognised Jake's face.

"The stories are true. This place is full as," Jake said with a smile.

"Glad that you didn't get lost," Azar replied, shaking his hand. Behind Jake stood a girl with blonde hair down to her lower back, two golden earrings and blue eyes.

"I'm Emma, Jake's sister," she said. She had a much more mature presence about her, her posture elegant as she extended her arm. Jake hadn't mentioned a sister the night before. Azar glanced at his watch. He still had two more hours to go.

"We don't mean to interrupt you," Jake said. "We were just passing through and decided to drop in."

"No, it's fine. I need a short break. Wendy I'm taking five," Azar called out.

Wendy, who was almost like a second mother to him, was a short, chubby woman with curly grey hair. She had started the cafe twenty years earlier, and the building of a nearby station ensured a constant flow of customers throughout the day. Azar had been working there for five years, and he could always tell Wendy whatever was on his mind. She was the only person Azar trusted with his sexuality. It was, admittedly, one of the things that kept him sane. The high customer demand also allowed him to be distracted from the drama he had been involuntarily plunged into. What made the business so successful was the delicious and vast range of products and energetic service. Behind the counter Wendy looked fierce, but in the kitchens she had a heart of gold.

"No worries," she called back.

Azar sat down at the now clean table. The two siblings joined him.

"Did you guys want anything?" Azar asked.

"I'm fine," Jake replied.

"I'm a big chocolate lover. Got any brownies?" Emma asked.

"Always looking for sweets," Jake mumbled, earning a punch on the shoulder.

"Fresh batch will be ready anytime now," Azar said, eyeing the siblings. There was a very clear distinction of formalities between the two.

"So did you both move here last week?" he asked casually.

"No, Emma has been here for five years," Jake replied, though his gaze was fixed on the table. "I'm a private investigator for Peacekeeper Drand," Emma added.

"Oh wow, I didn't know he needed one," Azar said thoughtfully.

"It's not as exciting as it sounds, mostly just internal matters," she replied.

"So what do you do, Jake?" Azar asked.

Jake opened his mouth slowly. "Well." Just then another worker came up to the table.

"Hey Azar, sorry to interrupt," she said.

"It's fine, Sophie. What's up?"

"I'm having a twenty-first in a few days' time, just giving you the invite," Sophie replied. She handed Azar a small piece of paper.

"Look at you having a house party," Azar said lightly.

A shy smile crept across Sophie's face.

"Just thought I would do something different," she said, her cheeks beginning to flush. Then, stealing a quick glance at Jake, she turned around.

"She seems rather strange," Emma observed.

"She's had a very tough life," Azar explained. "Her mother passed away a few years ago, and her brother is in jail. She was quite lonely and depressed when Wendy hired her. So this party is making positive progress."

He looked across the cafe at Sophie, who was talking to a girl with black curly hair. Azar read the invitation.

"Hey, we can bring friends. Want to come and meet some locals?" he asked.

"Parties are not really my thing," Emma said. She didn't seem embarrassed to admit it, stating it matter-of-factly.

"Well, I am the social one here, so I'll come," Jake replied.

"Trust me—opportunities for new friendships are very much wanted," Azar said, briefly making eye contact with Jake.

Azar heard the oven ding.

"Sounds like the brownies are done," he said. Just then another wave of customers came in. "Azar!" Wendy called out.

"I'm so sorry," Azar began, getting up. Jake did too.

"Don't be. You've gotta work. We actually came by to ask if you wanted to come to the Brinx Club tonight?"

"Oh, uh sure. Just leave your number here and I'll message you when I'm done. One brownie coming up, my treat," Azar replied, leaving his notepad on the table and darting back into the kitchens. As he went through the door, he saw Wendy in the back corner, whispering into a phone. She suddenly hung up and came over to him, nudging him in the back. Azar looked at her suspiciously.

"Who was that?" he asked.

"Oh, just a customer complaint," she replied dismissively. Then she looked at him with a cheeky grin.

"What?" the Oklem asked as he filled a jug with cold water.

"He's hot," she said with a wink. No more was needed to be said.

Azar put a brownie on a plate, grabbed the jug of water, stuck his tongue out at Wendy and went through the door. He couldn't disagree with Wendy. There was something appealing about Jake's smile that Azar couldn't ignore—if only he could forget Brett long enough to appreciate it.

****

After his shift, Azar returned to the Whistle and prepared to go out. There was a nervous excitement bubbling inside his stomach. Maybe tonight would be the start of a new social life, he thought. He put on his coat and made his way through the now dark city streets. The city teemed with nightlife, with clubs pumping out music, drunken teenagers stumbling aimlessly, and people flooding the streets. Azar had never been clubbing. He heard what it was like, had seen it through TV shows, but had never had anyone to go with. Brett was never interested in going out. He'd always opt to stay home where he felt it was safe. Friends had been a loose term, many falling under that category simply because Azar saw them daily when he was at school and now at work. Going clubbing alone wasn't even something to be considered. He was about to cross the street to the Brinx Club when a hand grabbed his shoulder. He turned around, startled, and froze.

The nose ring, messy blonde hair, the sweet cologne. Memories flooded into his mind. Their first date, New Year's celebrations, the heartbreak.

"I need to talk to you," Brett said.

"It's too bad I don't want to talk to you," Azar replied sharply. Immediately he raised his internal walls, the ones that prevented any emotions to seep through, the ones that blocked everyone out. "I need you back, Azar. I want you back. You don't understand what is really going on."

"If I had never walked in on you, would you have ever told me?" Azar demanded.

Brett paused, his eyes appearing to well up.

"What do you think?" he eventually asked.

"How could you do this after so long? Was I not…"

"Shhh," Brett said, holding a finger to Azar's lips. Azar shook his head in disgust.

"Forget it Brett. Forget everything."

"You don't understand, Azar. It's not safe here."

Another person came up behind Brett. He wore a long silver coat and had curly red hair. Azar recognised him immediately as the boy that Brett had been in bed with.

"You must be Azar," the boy said. "I'm Jordan. Heard quite a bit about you, including some pretty hot stuff-"

"Shut up Jordan," Brett snapped.

"You know you've made me realise how foolish one can be when they desire love," Azar said. "There were so many signs I ignored. I mean you are a part of the criminal underworld, but I was too stupid. And if you were even slightly genuine, Jordan would be gone. You're as good as dead to me. End of conversation."

"You cannot abandon me now, Azar. We are needed now more than ever," Brett called out as Azar stormed across the road. The heart ache was desperately trying to break through. He felt like he wanted to cry, like he wanted to turn back and run into Brett's arms but just then a limo pulled up outside the club. The doors opened and a woman got out. She wore a silky red dress and had her blonde hair tied in a bun. Azar realised it was Emma. And she was so beautiful that for a moment he forgot about his ex.

"My sister always knows how to arrive in style," came a familiar voice. Azar turned to see Jake standing behind him. Unlike Emma, he was dressed in a plain white shirt which pressed against his chest and skinny black jeans. Azar felt his heart rate begin to increase. He forced himself to turn back to the limo.

"She looks stunning," Azar replied quickly, watching as Emma made her way up the stairs. He noticed a golden bracelet wrapped around her right wrist three times.

"Ready to have some fun?" Jake said.

Azar couldn't help a slight smile creep across his face. Looking at who he was about to walk into a club with, he suddenly never felt so ready. The more he thought about Brett cheating with that incredibly unattractive piece of work Jordan, the more he wanted to show that he could move on too.

Chapter 4

"When am I getting my payment?" Brett asked impatiently. He had returned to his flat and was lying across his bed. Jordan sat on the edge of the mattress typing at a laptop set up on a chest of drawers.

"We're not done yet," Jordan said. Brett yawned, stretching his arms in the process.

"What do you mean? You saw Azar. There are two doppelgangers. We had a hot session which was not planned and Azar walked in. I need to patch things up with my boyfriend," he said sternly.

Jordan snorted.

"You think Azar will ever look at you again? He loathes you. To be honest I'm rather surprised you so willingly agreed to breaking up with that boy."

"It might surprise you but there is more reason to what I did than your role in it all," Brett replied. "Besides, the money is worth it. Our bond is strong enough to get past this. He'll get over it, then I can take him wherever he wants to go."

"Probably to court," Jordan laughed.

"Where's my money?" Brett snapped.

"Currently in the process of being stolen," Jordan said, moving to reveal his computer screen. It was split into four sections, each showing a part of what looked to be the inside of a club. Brett hopped off the bed and went over. He could see a dance floor full of people. On the bottom right screen was a door being guarded.

"Always making things difficult, aren't you?" Brett asked. "You couldn't just get the Pirates to rob a jewellery store or something less complicated?"

"Well, let's just say I have far more reason in this matter than the part you play," Jordan said darkly. Brett crossed his arms and was about to reply when there was a knock at the door. He made his way over. As he looked through the peephole, his stomach turned as he opened it.

"Azar? How did you get here so quickly? I thought you were at the Brinx…"

"We need to talk," Azar said.

"Before you go off at me again I need to explain what happened," Brett said, stepping aside.

"None of what you saw was real. I was helping Jordan in return for some big pay-outs. We can get away from Mintor. We can get out of the Mortal Nation if we want to."

"Stop," Azar said, holding his hand up to enforce this command. He made his way into the bedroom. He had a very confident stride, Brett observed, not like the Azar he knew.

"What are you doing?" Brett asked. He noticed Jordan was nowhere to be seen, the laptop no longer on the drawers.

"Just making sure there's no red hair sticking out from the sheets," Azar replied coldly.

"I told you it wasn't real."

"And you expect me to believe you? Who cheats on their partner in order to reward them, Brett? I want to know exactly what Jordan promised you."

"I can't tell you that. You wouldn't understand anyway," Brett said, folding his arms.

"Perhaps you can answer that, Jordan," Azar said, turning his head towards the bathroom. His voice had changed. A moment passed before Jordan slowly emerged from the bathroom, laptop in hand. He had a lethal look on his face as he faced Azar. Did they know each other?

"This is a bold move coming from a doppelganger," Jordan said. Brett froze. It was only now he realised that the visitor was not wearing what Azar had been wearing earlier outside the Brinx Club. He was dressed in black and wearing brown boots. The newcomer placed his hands on his hips.

"I prefer Lux to doppelganger. It's even more bold for one of Orven's closest circle members to be blocks away from a senate which is hunting you down," he said.

"Lux?" said Brett. "I'm so confused…"

Brett had to admit that the smile on this boy's face was nothing like Azar's. Even though Brett knew Azar was a doppelganger, he could never have prepared himself to be looking at a face he was so familiar with, yet see so much difference in every action and word. Lux tapped his foot impatiently.

"Answer my question, Jordan. What is the real reason you're here?"

"Times are changing, and don't play games, we all know your real name is Marvin," Jordan replied darkly.

"That name died with the old me centuries ago," Lux said venomously. Jordan snorted.

"You may have stopped Orven's plans all those years ago, but in doing so you created the mortal doppelganger who is also an Oklem. Even in his defeat, Orven will be successful."

"Orven has failed," Brett said. "His armies lost, and Azar is not an Oklem. There hasn't been one of those since Orven was sent away to the Supernatural Universe."

Brett could feel Lux's eyes piercing into him. Would the doppelganger expose him? He controlled his breathing, keeping his gaze fixed on Jordan.

"I find it hard to believe that Orven would have had any interest in me after all this time," Lux said.

"Then everything is going to plan," Jordan observed.

"Right," Lux said distastefully, "I don't suppose it'll bother you that your current operation at the Brinx Club is about to be foiled?"

Jordan shrugged.

"It's not my money being stolen. That's not my priority anyway, I don't really care how it goes." Jordan made his way to the bed, sitting back down at the drawers and placing his laptop on them. "Well, I care," Brett said, "and what do you mean it's not your priority? Why are you stealing from the Brinx Club anyway?" he asked. Then he started thinking. Jordan had insisted on coming with Brett to visit Azar, who as Jordan stated is a mortal doppelganger. Realisation dawned on him.

"Were you just using me this whole time to get to Azar?" he asked.

"No," Jordan replied. "I genuinely like you, but I could never date you. You can't be trusted."

"You don't need Azar for anything else, Jordan," Brett said. "You saw him. You don't need to harm him—"

"I won't be harming him, Brett. Somebody just wanted me to give him a visit. You'll get your money, relax."

"I'm not going to relax," Brett said aggressively. He turned to Lux, who was watching the two young men bickering with a humoured gleam. "What are you doing here?"

"You really should get your priorities sorted, cheater," Lux said. "As Jordan knows, working for Orven locks you in for life. Once you're not needed, he disposes of you. Unless of course he doesn't know about you," Lux added. Brett looked him directly in the eyes. After a moment, Lux sighed.

"But there's nothing special about you, so why would Jordan say anything?" Jordan took a step towards Lux.

"Perhaps it's time you explained why your first appearance since returning is here in the Mortal Nation of all places?" he said.

"I'm glad we can get to that. I don't like to involve many people in my schemes. Too many loose ends, and let's be real, you are hardly one to trust. I apologise in advance for this." In a split second Lux closed the gap and grabbed Jordan by the head, then smashed him into the set of drawers, knocking him out. The laptop fell onto the floor. Brett took a step back in alarm.

"I am disappointed in you, Brett," Lux said, turning to him as he dusted his hands.

"What do you want?" Brett asked, this time his voice trembling.

"I am stronger, faster, and all round a better individual than yourself. I have one question that has been burning inside of me since I came to this pathetic city and met my doppelganger. How did you do it?" Lux asked. A burning anger suddenly raged within Brett. Why was he being tormented in his own home? He glared at Lux.

"You think I am going to tell you because you have supernatural abilities? You're pathetic," he hissed.

In the blink of an eye Lux darted forward, grabbed Brett by the shirt and slammed him up against the wall of the corridor outside the bedroom.

"You have put everyone's lives at risk. None more so than Azar's. The one person you claim to be protecting," Lux said.

"I had to!" Brett snapped, struggling against the powerful grip.

"No you didn't. You did it for yourself. You knew his love for you was wavering so you've made sure you can keep him in your life forever. I do not know who you are really working for, but now Azar is gaining attention from dangerous villains. Do you honestly believe you can protect him? Look at you now, and I am hardly trying. You've made your choice. If you truly want to protect your ex-boyfriend, you will be spending all your energy on watching Jordan's every move."

"What? Why him?" Brett asked.

"Because if Orven is dead, who is Jordan working for?"

And then Lux was gone, so fast that the only sign he had actually moved was the front door being thrown open.

Brett slumped to the floor, gasping for air. He fought back tears as he reflected on the scene. Had he done the right thing? Everything he was doing was for Azar's protection. He couldn't turn back now; he had to trust that his plan was going to work. But he had one question that he needed an answer to. Why was Lux so fixated on keeping Azar alive? A few minutes later Jordan walked in, rubbing his head with one arm, his laptop tucked under the other.

"Well, after that rude intrusion I think it's time for me to leave. Make sure your people are ready to move at a moment's notice. It's best to stay one foot ahead of the opposition, especially when there's more than one," he said, glancing at the open door.

Chapter 5

The music blared out onto the street as Azar followed Jake into the Brinx Club. Nineteen years and this was the first time that Azar had ever entered a nightclub. The club was crowded, sweaty arms and chests bumping into the two boys as they made their way across the dance floor. "Right! You want a drink?" Jake asked, rubbing his hands together. Azar blushed, realising yet another part of him was now coming to light.

"If you haven't yet, I'm pretty lame. I don't really know any drinks."

If Jake wondered why, he was too polite to ask.

"My policy with drinking is to have whatever you want, as long as you consume alcohol," Jake replied with a grin.

"Sounds good," Azar said. He looked around, then frowned.

"Emma's upstairs. She likes the VIP section," Jake said.

Azar liked how Jake could tell what he was thinking without him having to say anything. Brett never seemed all that interested in what Azar really wanted.

"Now that you've moved to Mintor," Azar shouted to be heard above the pounding music, "what are you doing? Studying? Working?"

"Well, I guess you could call it working," Jake replied, running a hand through his hair. Azar could see the hesitance in his eyes. "Save the D and Ms for another time," Jake added. "What?"

"Deep and Meaningfuls. You know, the convos delving into our darkest secrets."

"Oh, right. I seriously need a life. Go get me a drink! Whatever," Azar said, laughing helplessly.

Jake came back with two cocktails. They toasted, and drank. The sweet mango sent ripples across Azar's body as it made its way down his throat. He didn't know what it was, but he felt a sensation come over him. The drink, the atmosphere, the company. He felt free. Just then the DJ cut the music.

"Good evening all and welcome to the Brinx Club on this beautiful night. It is now ten pm so let's start the mashups!"

The crowd erupted as the music began again. Jake turned to Azar.

"Let's dance!"

Azar followed Jake to the dance floor in the middle of the room. But he couldn't dance. His self-consciousness always prevented him from doing anything that would gain attention. Whilst Azar did his best to remain anonymous, Jake had let loose, dancing in his small place, nudging people with every movement. Just then Azar felt something. The feeling of being watched. He glanced to his right and his eyes came upon a girl with long black hair. She wore a black dress and her makeup was obvious even to Azar across the room. Her stare was both mean but curious. She tilted her head slightly, indicating for him to follow her.

His initial instincts were to ignore her, dismissing it as some drunken act on her behalf. Besides, women were not his thing. He soon tired of the dancing, but Jake showed no sign of slowing down. Azar went back to the bar for another refreshing drink. As the barman gave him his glass, he leant forwards.

"That woman wants you to stop avoiding her," he said, glancing upwards. Azar followed his gaze to a second level of the club, where the same woman with black hair stood, looking directly at him. Azar began to feel like there was a further purpose to her. Should he tell Jake? His mind went back to the strange encounter on the hill, where Jake's random visit was immediately followed by Lux. And where was Emma? Why wasn't Jake allowed in the VIP area? Peacekeeper Drand had urged Azar to be cautious. Maybe this woman knew who he was, or maybe even where his parents were.

Azar pushed his way through the crowds and went up a flight of stairs running along the back wall. The music was not as loud off the main floor. He saw the woman seated on a lounge which overlooked the dance floor. Azar sat across from her. After an awkward silence, the girl spoke. "Why are you here?" she said, her gaze remaining fixed on the DJ.

"Heard of a good night out?" Azar replied.

"From what I remember, you weren't much of a party boy," she said. "I've been looking for you for so long. I wasn't sure you came back when the portal opened ten years ago."

"I'm sorry. Do I even know you?" Azar asked.

This brought her eyes to lock with Azar's. Hers were dark, cold.

"I don't have time for your games, Marvin. I mean Lux. That's your new name now right?"

Azar froze. Who was Marvin?

"How do you know that name? Who are you?" he asked.

A slow realisation spread across the girl's beautiful face. She ran black lacquered fingernails through her hair which up close was so silky it looked like water.

"The doppelganger," she said softly. She grabbed a wine glass off a passing waiter's tray. It was now as Azar quickly scanned the area that he realised this club did have waiters weaving through the chaos. Strange, he thought. Then he turned back to the woman.

"How do you know Lux?" Azar asked again.

"So demanding. Why don't we start with some polite introductions. I'm Jessani," she said, taking a large sip.

"Azar. Unfortunately for you, I'm getting sick of half answers. What do you have to do with Lux?"

Jessani laughed, placing her now empty wine glass on the small table separating the two. As she leant forward, Azar saw she had a necklace. On it was the symbol of Skull, the Pirate's homeland. The symbol was a human skull, circled in red with a line going through it.

"You really need to spend more time with Lux," she said. "Your deliveries are so dull. Where's the sass? The attitude? I suggest you find your doppelganger and send him my regards. I'm sure we'll meet again."

"You're a Pirate," Azar said, his heart racing. She was not what Azar had mentally depicted a Pirate to look like. His mother's warnings rang in his ear. Jessani raised a hand to her chest.

"I'm insulted. I suggest you stop trying to figure out the world so quickly, Azar. All you'll find is heartbreak and let downs."

Azar said nothing. She stood up, tossing her hair back. Azar glanced back down to the dance floor. He searched for Jake but couldn't see him anywhere. He looked back to Jessani but she had disappeared. Something was not right here, he thought.

"Ditching me already?" Jake said as he appeared in front of Azar and slumped onto the seat Jessani had occupied moments ago.

"I'm not much of a dancer," Azar said, peering cautiously around the room. He still had not seen Emma the entire time. The night was starting to make him suspicious.

"Are you expecting someone?" Jake asked, breaking through Azar's daze.

"I don't think so," Azar sighed. Then he decided to test his new friend. "Just some girl. You wouldn't happen to know a Jessani would you?"

Jake almost toppled off the lounge as he sat up. "Where was she? What did she say?"

"Who is she?"

"Azar don't play games," Jake warned.

"I am not the one playing games," Azar replied coldly. "With all that has happened recently I was stupid enough to believe that maybe you and Emma would turn out to be friends. You want something from me. What is it?"

Just then the doors to their right flew open. Azar hadn't even noticed there were doors there before now. A small figure dressed in a black suit emerged, clutching a black briefcase to his chest. He had a shaved head and a large golden earring on his left ear. Jake leapt off the lounge and tackled the man from behind. The case slipped from his grip and landed on the ground, bursting open. Gold coins spilled across the floor as people nearby moved away from the scene. Azar stood up in a stunned silence. Jake wrestled with the man on the floor before he was pushed off with great force. The man sprung to his feet and sprinted towards the stairs. Ignoring him, Jake ran through the open doors. Azar wasn't sure if it was the alcohol or the night's events that made his head spin, but he decided to follow Jake. As he neared the doors Jake had entered, he heard a small cough. He looked to his right and saw Jessani standing a few metres from Azar, a fascinated expression on her face.

"Mintor really is the place where the party is at, isn't it?" she said.

"Is it Mintor or myself?" Azar replied, unsure of what his next move would be. Why had Jake been so afraid of her?

"Good question. Oh and do tell the Flare twins to stay out of this, especially Emma. I'd hate for Jake to lose his sister" she added icily.

Then she turned on her heel and made her way back towards the staircase down to the ground floor. Jake and Emma were twins, Azar thought. What else were they hiding? Hesitating for a moment, Azar cautiously walked through the doors. As he made his way down a dark passage, he could hear cries of pain and sounds of…combat? The passage opened into a large, round room. In the centre sat an unopened bar. Poles stood in various places around the room. However the scene that lay before Azar was surely not the room's intended use. Emma stood to the right of the bar, holding what looked to be a golden whip. Four figures in black moved in on her. Azar felt his heart in his mouth. She whirled the whip, connecting with the man closest to her and sending him flying into the wall.

Azar saw a flash of steel from one of the men. It was a huge broadsword, the kind that Orven's army used. Then he heard a cry behind him, and wheeled around to see Jake in combat with one of the attackers, a woman this time. Emma took out another with her whip, and the sword clattered to the floor. Azar lunged at it, but he collided with something. Suddenly a hand grabbed him, lifting him off the floor with ease. As his legs kicked wildly, he looked at his attacker, taking in a rough, scratched face. He was thrown back onto the ground. The large man towered over him with a thick, black beard, wearing armour and raising an axe. It was a Pirate, one of Orven's soldiers. Fear encompassed Azar as the Axe came down at him. But a sudden charge of adrenaline shot through his blood, and Azar rolled to his left just in time. He kept rolling, but the Pirate charged at him. There was no way Azar could move fast enough as Orven's soldier raised his axe again. With the Pirate's muscle combined with momentum, Azar wasn't going to avoid the weapon. Emma's whip snaked out like a golden flame, curling around the Pirates neck. Azar could see it tighten quickly, forcing the Pirate to drop his weapon and attempt to loosen the tension. Jake suddenly tackled the large man, plunging a knife through the Pirate's armour and into his chest.

A silence filled the room. Azar looked around at the bodies in horror. Then at Emma, then Jake. Azar knew that the entire night was never intended to be a social get together with friends. "Azar wait—" Jake began, but Azar took off out of the room, down the stairs, shoving people aside, his exit nothing but a blur to himself. He had hoped that Emma and Jake, especially Jake, might have been some new friends, real friends. But now he knew that no one would ever want him for himself. Not Brett. Not Jake. His parents have been lying. He just wanted to disappear, to give up. And that thought terrified him.

Chapter 6

Azar slammed his bedroom door shut. The thud was so loud he half thought he'd shaken the entire Whistle, but he didn't care. He stormed over to his bed, punching his fists into the mattress. Then he lost all his energy and crashed down. The one positive thing he had hung on to. The possibility that he could actually have a normal life with normal friends. But again he had been let down. He wasn't sure why he was surprised anymore.

"You know this is a lovely place you have here," came a familiar voice. Azar sat up, startled. Lux stood across the room, arms folded.

"How did you get in here?" Azar asked, momentarily distracted.

"I was watching you a long time before you knew I even existed," the doppelganger said, "I've figured out a few tricks."

"I really don't want to be around anyone so can you please just leave me alone," Azar said, then reburied his face into his mattress, feeling like he could cry.

"I am so intimidated," Lux said.

Azar was about to order Lux out again when he thought about his meeting with Drand. Perhaps he could probe some more information out of his stalker doppelganger. Something to give him a reason to hold on.

"Why is Jake here now? What does he want with me?" Azar said, sitting back up on the bed. "Same thing everyone wants. You."

"Because of my blood?"

"For some that is the reason. Others are fascinated because you are both an Oklem and a doppelganger. Jake, however, has more personal reasons. Ironic, really, considering his initial orders."

"Orders?" Azar queried.

A genuine look of intrigue flashed across Lux's cold face.

"He hasn't told you? I assumed that's why you're so emotionally distraught. Interesting," he observed. "Do you think Jake stumbled across your secret spot in the hills?"

Truth be told Azar hadn't really considered that. But after the night's events it made sense that it too was not coincidental.

"I'm starting to think not, but why would he be looking for me in the first place?"

"It wasn't you he was looking for," Lux said, rolling his eyes. "Maybe ask him for the truth, then you'll stop being so whiny."

Azar was getting annoyed at Lux's attitude, so he decided he would press for some answers. "Is this why you've come back? To judge my lifestyle? You told me on the hill that there are three sides to a story. If we break those sides down further, what's yours?" Azar asked, tucking his legs up under his chin. Lux looked at him.

"Mmm, he does have a brain. Perhaps one day you will know "my story". But for now, I'd rather focus on you. Firstly, you really need to find a boy," Lux sighed, making his way over to the window.

"Excuse me?" Azar said, raising his head. It was almost a natural instinct to become defensive when the topic led towards homosexuality.

"You're so starved of pleasure you've become a brick wall. Certainly not the personality I was hoping to see from my doppelganger."

There it was, the window of opportunity.

"Yes Lux, I am boring, you know that already. We're completely different. It does make me wonder how the hell Jessani thought I was you," Azar said, staring at the ground. In the blink of an eye, Azar felt himself rolled onto his back and the weight of Lux on top of him.

"What are you doing?" Azar asked, caught off guard.

"What did you say?" Lux fired back. Azar looked deep into Lux's eyes in surprise. It was like looking into a living mirror. They were both terrified.

"You're.... afraid? Like Jake was. Now we're getting somewhere," he said slowly.

"When did you meet Jessani?" Lux said.

"At the club," Azar snapped, pushing Lux off him. "She thought I was you and said that she wasn't sure you'd come back through a portal ten years ago. I can only assume that was Orven's portal. You are supernatural, why else would you have been in their universe?"

Lux stood back up, breathing deeply.

"I am not supernatural. Jessani was one of Orven's most important members in his circle. She scares even the Peacekeepers," Azar's doppelganger explained.

He went back over to the glass wall overlooking the city. Azar stood up, keen to continue pursuing some answers.

"If she's so dangerous, how is she wandering the streets of Mintor? And how do you know her?"

"Long story," Lux said, wiping the sheen of sweat off his forehead with his sleeve.

"I have time."

Lux turned back to him, the fear he had displayed moments before now completely masked.

"No Azar, you don't. Figure out your life. Are you going to become a slave to the Peacekeepers? Are you going to remain an overly depressed rock who can't even trust himself anymore? Maybe you should go and ask Jake why they didn't tell you before jumping to the conclusion that you're nothing more than a tool ready to work on request. Maybe you should find a guy who is worth your time rather than linger on Brett who you know was never going to be a permanent boyfriend. You're an Oklem for goodness sake. Start taking the initiative. And please don't get yourself killed in the process," Lux added.

"How can I take the initiative when I'm not told anything?" Azar demanded.

Lux turned away from his double and made his way to the door.

"Do what I do. Improvise, be spontaneous. Take the power and use it to your advantage. Always make a statement from the moment you enter a room."

Lux exited, leaving Azar to sit alone in total astonishment at what his life had become. One minute he was just an ordinary, heartbroken young man, the next he suddenly had a supernatural double, and he had almost died from a Pirate in the heart of Mintor. Despite this, he wasn't sure he wanted to be what Lux said he should be. He hated drawing attention to himself. But his doppelganger had been right about one thing: Brett was gone, Jake was not. Maybe there was an explanation. For once in his life, he was going to take the initiative. Tomorrow he would demand answers, and his first target was Peacekeeper Drand.

Chapter 7

Azar burst into Drand's quarters, the doors almost flying off their hinges, determined to find out the truth. It was late evening the following day. Azar had spent the day going over what he knew, and he couldn't stop wondering about the look of fear in Lux's eyes after he mentioned the girl who called herself Jessani. After a sleepless night, he had tried numerous times to call his parents, but they never answered him. So he decided to be spontaneous. Drand's assistant had told Azar to wait in the small foyer until the Peacekeeper summoned him. As soon as she had left, Azar sprung up and entered the same room he had last met the Mortal Peacekeeper in. But this time Drand was not alone. He wore a white gown with diamonds sparkling off his shoulders from their reflection of the large chandelier above. He was holding a thick, green book, and looked as if he was in the middle of reading something out of it at Azar's arrival. Azar didn't recall the chandelier being there last time. Then he realised there were only two lounges in the centre of the room. Across from Drand, on the orange lounge, sat a woman with blazing orange hair. She turned to Azar and fixed fiery red eyes on him.

"Oh my god," she stated, standing up with a horrified expression. An orange mist surrounded her, swirling gently in lazy circles.

"Sorry to interrupt," Azar said slowly, his bold act faltering slightly.

"Remarkable," the woman said softly, "you look just like him."

"Yes he does Serain, but he is not Lux," Drand said, standing up.

Serain! The Peacekeeper of the Fire Nation! Azar had never seen a Peacekeeper from another Nation before. He was never allowed to be with his parents at gatherings of the Nation Leaders. "Drand, how does a mere mortal manage to plough into one of the most sacred rooms in the Mortal Nation?" Serain demanded. Her voice was deep, and she had a posh accent. She was wearing tall orange heels, and was in a mesmerising orange and red dress. She immediately presented herself as being of high class, ensuring that it wasn't just her literal glowing that captured people's attention.

"Well, I think we both know he is not an ordinary person," Drand answered, "you can also see he is an Oklem."

What more did Drand know about Azar that he had been withholding? Azar took a guess with his next comment.

"You did not warn me about the Pirates at the club, I almost died," Azar said. His heart pounded in his chest. He was speaking to a Peacekeeper, and he also had no idea if Drand even knew about the previous night.

"It was a necessary risk," Drand answered. Azar's instinct was right.

"Why is my life being so controlled? What is with all the secrets? I seem to be the centre of everything that is imploding in this city yet am kept out of the loop," Azar said heatedly.

"And it shall stay that way," Serain cut him off. "The less you know the better. The last thing we need is to have the Oklem doppelganger going off and trying to help when all it will do is make things more complicated."

Azar turned to Serain, the oldest of the current peacekeepers.

"Madame Peacekeeper, I'm sorry to break it to you, but I'm not leaving until I know the truth.

Drand, you can't expect me to just keep living my life as if nothing's wrong when my parents are missing, I have some know-it-all double wondering about the city, and now the Fire Nation's Peacekeeper has come to visit. You know what happened last night, meaning Jake and Emma are obviously working with you in some way. This is all obviously related to me and probably some scheme of Orven, so I want to know what is going on."

Drand's face drained of colour, and Peacekeeper Serain's flames lashed around her head. Even Azar surprised himself with his defiance.

"Have you no respect at all? Do you know who you are speaking to?" Serain demanded, placing her hands elegantly on her hips.

"Azar, I can't tell you the truth because we are still trying to figure it out. There are layers of complexity to this that you could not imagine. I need you to trust me that I am doing what is best. Would you have agreed to go if I had told you that you may be killed meeting Orven's most vile follower?" Drand asked, raising an eyebrow.

Azar shook his head.

"But why did I have to be there?"

"You didn't die," Serain added harshly, eyeing Azar closely, "and Drand required you to confirm something."

"Which would be?" Azar asked, crossing his arms.

"Jessani is here. She came out of hiding—presumably because she saw a face she knew and acted upon it," Serain answered.

Azar realised what that meant. "She thought I was Lux. She was a little bit disappointed when she realised I wasn't him."

Azar made a mental note that Jessani and Lux know each other well enough for her to want to see him at a time when she should be in hiding.

"Jessani would not make an appearance so soon especially in Mintor unless there is a very important reason," Drand said.

"Any ideas on what that could be?" Azar asked, hoping to get something.

"If we knew, I can assure you we would be responding to it now," Drand answered.

"So Jake and Emma are your spies?" Azar continued, jumping straight into the next topic. "Is that how you know Jessani was there?"

"Emma is my private investigator, Jake is a spy. They are here to discover if there are any lingering threats to both the Nations or their Peacekeepers, and if there are, they must deal with them."

Azar turned away for a moment. He was hurting. Jake had lied to his face. He quickly shut his emotions down, realising both Peacekeeper's were looking at him.

"Okay so what do we do? Just wait for the enemy to reveal their plan?" he asked.

"No, we must work with what we know. Our best reference is Lux. You need to get close with him so we can learn what his true intentions are," Serain said.

"Only if you want to," Drand chipped in. Azar saw a genuine look of concern on the Peacekeeper's face. Azar wanted to refuse, but he knew he would only be left out even more if he did so. He was an Oklem, whatever that truly meant was still a mystery, but he knew he needed to be involved. If anything, it would be a distraction from his never ending loneliness. "Of course I don't want to. But I need to. I'll see what I can find, although it may be a little difficult. We may or may not have just had an argument. And he is stubborn. But that takes me back to my first question," Azar said, directing his gaze to the Fire Nations leader. "How do you know Lux?"

A silence followed.

"Azar, come and have a seat, all this standing makes it difficult to have a civilised discussion," Drand said, indicating for the boy to join him as he sat. Serain too sat down. Azar noticed the lounge was vibrating softly, and also glowing. It was like a physical sign that it was somehow charging the Peacekeeper. Azar could see Serain was choosing her words very carefully, a slight frown on her forehead.

"Lux has been around for a lot longer than the defeat of the Pirates," Drand began, cutting through the growing tension.

"He's been a pain since the seventeenth century," Serain said.

"The seventeenth century? Did you know this?" Azar directed his question at Drand.

"I did know," he conceded, "but we didn't know he had returned. And more importantly, I didn't know what he looked like."

Azar wasn't sure why, but he was inclined to trust the Mortal Nation's Peacekeeper.

"Being alive for so many centuries, I of course know," Serain said, "but I have never seen you. The identical image is a very helpful tool I'm sure Lux has been acting on since his return. I do not wish to discuss any more of the doppelganger for the time being. I must say I am eager to be informed of how you are an Oklem?" she observed.

Azar shrugged.

"I know as much as you. I have somehow been given a dose of it recently, that's all I know," he said.

"As much as I hate to acknowledge this, it does lead to our concern that your parents have been conspiring with somebody on Orven's side," Drand said.

Azar's heart sank. Where had that come from? He also noted that Drand had once again averted from Lux and was bringing the conversation back to Azar and his parents. Before he could respond, Drand continued.

"Initially I suspected that your parents had somehow given you a dose of the Oklem blood, but you have confirmed you have not seen them in two years, and they could never have trusted it to get to the right person if they sent it through a messenger. But I am left asking why have they been hiding if they are innocent?"

Azar hated himself for understanding the reasoning behind Drand's theory. But there had to be a reason. If only he could just talk to his mother again and clear everything up.

"We are certain that Orven was killed," Serain commented, "so even if they did vanish in order to stay hidden, that would no longer be necessary. The remaining Pirates now live under Mintorian control in Skull."

Azar was not convinced at how anything could be certain. Drand sighed.

"I hope you see that I am not trying to leave you in the dark. But we must be careful who we talk to. I want you to see if Lux can tell you any more about Jessani or Orven or anything that might allow us to understand what happened when Skull was defeated, and what is happening now. If he is not on Orven's side as you have told me in the past, it shouldn't take much for him to tell you information. Perhaps it can lead us to your parents. Just don't get yourself into trouble. Now leave us, it is getting late and I have duties to attend to."

Azar did not want to leave, but he knew there would be no more said for his ears if he stayed. He certainly didn't plan on disobeying an order from the Peacekeeper. He did know one thing for sure. Lux had been around for a long time, and Azar wanted to know what he had done to make the Fire Nation's peacekeeper so hostile to him. Maybe if he found out what Drand wanted to know, they in turn could help him find his parents.

When he got out of the Peacekeeper's office, it was almost midnight, but Azar needed some fresh air. The footpaths were well lit—the city never slept. He was about to cross the road to the Whistle when a voice caught his attention, coming from a shadowy alley behind him.

"Maree and Steve Geminus. Your missing parents. Positions available for a visitor's trip to the Trail of Tales."

Azar froze. The voice sent ripples across his skin.

"Bet you weren't expecting to hear that," Brett said, stepping into the light. Had he been following Azar? Brett's association with the underworld meant he knew the alleys and underground pipes like they were his home. In a way, they were. Brett was wearing a black overcoat and dark jeans. His green glow-in-the-dark sneakers had been a present from Azar for Brett's last birthday, and made the Oklem forget for just one fleeting moment that they were no longer together. Not wanting to show weakness, Azar cleared his throat.

"Is there a stalking issue in this city?" he asked, thinking about how Lux, Jake, even the Peacekeepers seemed to know where he was all the time. "What are you talking about?" Despite being mad at Brett, he had to admit that his heart skipped a beat to see him.

"Well, your parents don't appear to be coming back here anytime soon. We'll have plenty of time to discuss this. I'm going to the Trail of Tales to see them. Care to join me?"

"I'll pass, why don't you take your new boyfriend," Azar said, turning to go. As he did so, he heard an engine approaching. A motorbike rounded the corner ahead, racing towards Azar. Then more bikes followed. Suddenly Brett's hand grabbed Azar's right arm, and for the briefest of moments, the Oklem felt a light buzz in the back of his head. Like a transmission.

"Funny you should mention that," Brett said, snapping Azar back to earth. By now the bikes had stopped, forming a semi-circle around Azar and Brett.

"You brought your gang along. You know I'm not intimidated by them," Azar said coldly. The Whistle was literally across the road. Could he run fast enough? One of the bikers removed their helmet, revealing the smug face of Jordan.

"You need to listen to your boyfriend, Azar," Jordan said.

"I am done with him, meaning I am done with this whole gang thing as well. Now move," Azar demanded, intending to shove his way past the human blockade. But the bikers swarmed in, holding him still. Jordan raised a small bottle and pointed it at Azar. The last thing he was aware of was the spray in his face.

Chapter 8

Emma Flare burst into the briefing room of the palace, her brother Jake hot on her heels. The previous night at the Brinx Club had been a disaster, and they hadn't spoken to each other since then. Peacekeeper Drand had summoned them randomly, however, so here they were. Emma had been in bed, and so only managed to throw a purple sweater and black tights on. Jake was still dressed in a blue buttoned shirt and white pants. Where had he been on a Wednesday night? They had quickly travelled from their small apartment three blocks away on Emma's pink motor scooter. She had received it as a twenty-first birthday gift from the Mintorian Police Department (MPD) for her continued efforts in fighting crime.

Upon entering the room, Emma was surprised to see Peacekeeper Serain standing beside Drand. In the centre of the room was a table, with a small holographic layout of the city of Mintor. Against the back wall stood three large, black stools. These were the pedestals used when Peacekeepers or special persons made contact through holograms.

"Azar was not impressed," Jake said. Emma glanced at him. That was a strange note to start off with, she thought. "We are aware. He left not more than ten minutes ago, seeking answers to things he could not understand," Serain said, her eyes glowing fiercely.

"Stubborn just like his double," Emma observed. She had been studying Lux's past, trying to find whatever she could. But information was scarce, even for someone of her level.

"We must draw our attention to Jessani's arrival. What could possibly bring her here?" Drand asked.

"Perhaps it was just a scare stunt, letting us know she's still around," Jake said. This new problem just added to the growing list the two faced. Emma knew that Jake did not like going behind Azar's back the way they had—his desire to be honest was unfortunately what made him lack the ability to become an investigator like her.

"A member of Orven's circle would not take such an unnecessary risk if that was the intention," Serain said. "I fear there is political motivation. Tomorrow they are holding elections to replace Maree and Steve Geminus as senators in the Council of Mintor. She must have some role in it all."

"What do you mean elections?" Emma asked. "Surely Azar's parents being kept in hiding does not call for their replacements."

"We don't have proof that his parents have done anything unlawful," Jake added. This time his face began to flush slightly. Emma raised an eyebrow at him but said nothing. She noticed the two peacekeepers exchange glances.

"You have not informed them?" Serain said.

Drand looked uncomfortable, his skin chalky.

"Azar's parents are suspected of aiding Orven during the war. They have been missing for over a year in the Trail of Tales."

"Impossible," Jake said.

"Does Azar know?" Emma asked.

"He knows that they have disappeared, but not where they are. I refrained from telling him they are wanted because we all know what he would do if he found out where they were."

"He would try and get there," Jake replied gravely. "I need to go and make sure he is back at the Whistle."

"I can send someone for that," Drand replied.

"No," said Jake. "I think Azar needs to see someone that he knows."

Emma made a note to talk to her brother. Being twins and inseparable since birth, she could tell Jake's heart was beating quicker than usual. He was also starting to blush. Jake had been lonely all his life. But it wouldn't do for him to get attached to Azar—the last thing Jake needed was to fall in love with an Oklem. Drand sighed.

"Very well. Now…" just then the centre hologram podium along the back wall sprung to life. A man appeared, wearing a long robe.

"Peacekeeper Blizzard? An unforeseen appearance indeed," Serain commented, bowing her head in respect.

Peacekeeper Blizzard, the Ice Nation's leader, was the second youngest of the Peacekeepers. His appearance however contrasted this fact. He had a long white beard, and wore an ice crown. "Unfortunately I come bearing bad news," he said. "The winds have been talking, the mountain peaks rumbling. There are strange things happening above the Trail of Tales."

"Above?" Drand said.

"Indeed, the winds are suggesting that something is trying to portal in. Something that does not have the access."

"The Supernatural Universe," Drand said slowly.

As far as Emma knew, the link that allowed the Supernatural Universe to portal into the Nation's universe had been sealed. Orven's return came from a separate portal that had been created in the Pirate's homeland of Skull. Because of its physical connection, it allowed Orven to leave the Supernatural Universe alongside Jessani, Lux, and many of his Pirate followers. It sounded like someone, or something, still over there was now trying to portal in.

"I will make a suggestion of who may hold key information," Blizzard said, pressing his palms together. "There is only one other being we know of that also appeared ten years ago through Orven's portal. One that is not a Pirate. I think you need to find the original doppelganger," Blizzard said, looking at the Peacekeepers.

"Indeed, it is time to face him again," Serain said. Jake and Emma glanced at each other, both noting the "again". What business did Serain have with Lux? Emma assumed they were referring to Azar's doppelganger.

"Thank you Peacekeeper Blizzard, we shall make contact in a few days," Drand said. Blizzard bowed his head before vanishing.

"I will visit Azar and see if he knows anything about Lux's location or plans," Jake said.

"And I will focus on tracking down our mystery man from the Brinx Club," Emma added. Drand nodded.

"As Peacekeeper of the Mortal Nation, I do not like being in such ignorance in my own home. We must remain vigilant. Jake, do not let Azar leave this city. I fear Orven's ultimate goal stretches far beyond our current knowledge."

"I'll find out what I need to," Jake said, making his way out.

Emma followed him back down to the palace's front cobblestone entrance where she had left her bike, and as soon as they were alone, she grabbed her brother's shoulder.

"What are you doing?" he said.

"What are *you* doing?" Emma shot back. "Volunteering to go to Azar when he's furious at us."

"He has had a lot to deal with, but when it comes down to it, he will help me," Jake said. Emma raised her eyebrows again.

"Help you?"

"Us. Drand. You get what I mean," Jake snapped quickly, blushing again. Emma stamped her foot.

"Jake this has gone on for far too long. It's no secret to me. You like boys. You like Azar, that's fine," Emma said, putting her arm around his shoulder.

Jake shook her off, but didn't deny what she was saying. Emma continued.

"I mean you only mentioned him every five seconds in the meeting, and you can barely say his name without your face turning red-"

"Okay nosey, what's your point?" Jake said.

"Are you sure this is wise? To get involved like this with *a*...Oklem?"

"You think I can't protect myself," he said accusingly. Emma had rarely seen him on the verge of tears, but she needed him to know that she would always care for him.

"It's the opposite. You want to protect everybody. And that's a great way to be, Jake. But you have to ensure you don't put your own safety on the line without good reason. We don't know anything about Azar. He seems genuine, but don't let your guard down."

"You know, I would have hoped after twenty-one years that my twin sister would know that her brother would never risk leaving her to live alone," Jake said, turning on his heel.

"Um, where are you going?" Emma asked him as she grabbed her pink helmet.

"To check up on our doppelganger, remember?" Jake replied.

"It's the early hours of the morning. I don't think he'd appreciate being woken. Come back home—you can visit him tomorrow."

Her sisterly voice carried a hint of authority in it. After a moment, Jake took a deep breath and turned to her.

"Fine, but don't say another word about me and my life. You don't know everything," he warned.

He clambered on behind Emma, and they began the short journey back home. Emma had been given the option to live in the Whistle once she became the Peacekeeper's agent, but she preferred living away from her work area. It also allowed her to keep an eye on Jake, who in times like these could allow his emotions to interfere with his duty as a spy. On the way, Emma caught a whiff of a cologne, a herbal scent, something Jake would never own.

Chapter 9

Jake awoke the following morning, glancing at his watch. 7 am. He was tempted to go back to sleep when he remembered that he needed to go and see Azar. He got out of bed and went to the kitchen, which tucked itself into the corner of their small unit. He got out some cereal and poured himself a glass of orange juice. Emma's bowl sat unwashed in the sink, her way of saying she had eaten and already left for work. Her salary was decent, Jake's not so much. He relied heavily on Emma, and he hated that he couldn't provide equally for the two of them. He sat alone at the small, round dining table, which was in between the kitchen and living room. To one side were the two bedrooms and bathroom, the other was the front door. His eyes glanced to the fridge, where he saw an old picture of their family. The only picture they had of the twins with their parents. Neither Jake nor Emma knew the real reason for being abandoned. All they remembered was being dropped off at a youth training centre somewhere in the Earth Nation. A few years ago, Jake had attempted to track them, but the Flare name seemed to no longer exist. At the training centre, which doubled as their home, Emma's skills were soon recognised, but she always made sure Jake was moved with her. He knew he wasn't as good as his sister, but he was determined to try.

As he scraped the final crumbs of his breakfast into one last mouthful with his spoon, he thought about the argument he had had with Emma after meeting the Peacekeepers.

He was aware that Emma knew he was gay. And despite the fact that the majority of those living in Mintor were accepting of homosexual people, the law was not so friendly. Politics as well remained what anti-gay followers called "purified", and Jake was convinced he would lose his job if people were to discover his secret. He didn't mind that Emma knew, he just hated having to talk about it, and worried about who else may hear. He felt like it was something very private. His phone buzzed, and he remembered who it was. Before Emma had rung him to meet at the Peacekeeper's quarters, he had been in the middle of making out with a guy he had met online. The secrecy was both frightening yet enticing. Anonymity allowed him to explore his sexuality without judgement. He slammed his fist on the table, rattling his now empty bowl. Why was being gay so difficult? It was something he couldn't control but also couldn't display.

Sighing, he got dressed and made his way out onto the wet streets of Mintor. It was mid-morning, and the city was buzzing under the cover of umbrellas. As he entered the gates of the Whistle, he was ushered into one of three small boxed rooms sitting outside the main building. He went through security screening and was quickly cleared. Being a spy, his work tag allowed the process to take little more than a few minutes.

He knew where Azar's room was. Emma had quickly found out everything about Azar and his family when the Oklem became a mission of theirs. It's how he had first found Azar on the hill too. He made his way up the elevator to level fifty-eight. The doors opened into a quiet corridor. He made his way to room 58F. Azar had his own apartment, with his parents right opposite him in 58E. Jake knocked lightly on the door, and a few seconds later it opened slightly.

"What do you want?" Azar asked. He was in a dark blue dressing gown.

"There's a lot to talk about," Jake replied, spreading his arms, "but firstly I want to make sure you're alright."

Azar reluctantly stepped aside, allowing Jake to enter. There wasn't much to the room. A queen sized bed sat against the furthest wall opposite to the door. The blinds were down behind it, but a second glass wall to Jake's left revealed a beautiful view of the city. A perfect view to wake up to, Jake thought. To the right was a door which presumably led to a bathroom.

Jake realised Azar was looking at him expectantly, so he began.

"I wanted to tell you who I really was, why I needed you to go to the club with me, but Drand feared it would have ruined our intentions. If you were expecting Jessani, you would have let on to her very quickly. But she thought you were Lux, and because of their history, she revealed herself."

"History?" Azar scoffed. "That's what you call it?"

Jake looked at Azar's eyes. A little shiver shot down his spine. There was something off, and then it dawned on him.

"Lux?"

"I really am getting good at being Azar, aren't I?" Lux replied with a grin. Jake looked at the double in amazement. Now that he knew it was Lux, he could see a coldness in the look-alikes' eyes. He had only seen Azar a few times, but he made a mental note to never mistake the doppelganger's again.

"What did you do to Azar?" he demanded, taking a step closer.

"Nothing. It's nice to see you care though. I've been awaiting his return from your precious Peacekeeper since last night. Thought I'd have a quick nap," Lux said, stretching.

"What an invasion of Azar's privacy," Jake said.

"Oh please, spare me the over protective lover talk," the doppelganger murmured, making his way back to Azar's bed. Jake's blood turned cold. Where had that come from?

"Excuse me?" Jake said, his heart rate increasing.

"Denial, denial, denial. That's all you people do," Lux said with a flat tone, bored almost.

"Azar left the Peacekeeper's last night," Jake said, bringing the focus of the conversation back to the real issue.

"Well, he must have gotten lost. The good thing about being an exact look alike is that I fit perfectly into his clothes. This gown really is gorgeous," Lux replied, looking down at himself.

"What are you doing here? In Mintor?"

"Oh Jake, surely after all these years you'd know that you will never just be handed an answer."

"What plan of Orven's are you carrying out? What does Jessani have to do with it?" Jake pressed. In the blink of an eye Lux had moved from the bed and was standing inches from Jake's face. Jake took a slight step back in surprise.

"Let me make one thing clear," Lux hissed, "I am not working for either side here. The Peacekeepers can't be trusted. Orven is dead, Jessani is nothing to me."

Lux made his way over to the window, peering down into the streets. Jake saw Lux tense slightly. Something wasn't right, and it wasn't just the fact that he was standing in Azar's room talking to a supernatural creature wearing Azar's gown.

"If you are not with the Pirates, what do you think is the meaning of Jessani's arrival?"

Lux did not answer immediately, instead shutting the blind, then walking across the room and into the bathroom.

"Well, I know the gangs have been busy in the dark hours of the night," he eventually said, his voice echoing off the tiles. Jake slowly paced towards the door as he heard a toilet flush and the sink taps turn on.

"What have the gangs been doing?" Jake asked.

The doppelganger emerged with a small hand towel.

"Entertain me for a moment," Lux said, ignoring Jake's question. "What is stopping you from telling Azar the truth?"

A bewildered look flashed across Jake's face.

"What do you mean?" he stammered. Lux sighed, tossing the towel onto the floor.

"If you want Azar to trust you, you need to be honest. Tell him why you were really on that hill when he first met you. And then tell him how it was only your feelings that stopped you from plunging your knife through his chest."

A sudden fury shot through Jake and he aimed a punch at the doppelganger. Lux met the fist with an open palm, completely stopping Jake's momentum with ease. Then he pushed back, hard, sending Jake sprawling to the ground.

"You're not your sister, Jake. She wouldn't have missed," Lux said.

"You don't know anything about me," Jake said through gritted teeth, standing up. "Why do you always change the topic after revealing a crumb of information? How do you know so much?"

"I thrive on chaos and confusion," Lux answered. "And on the contrary, I know far more than you would be comfortable with me knowing. I'm sure Azar will understand, you disobey direct orders because of your feelings. They're so obvious. I mean why else would you have come to see Azar? I don't understand why you people are so afraid of loving the same gender. There are actually real problems to worry about in life."

Jake clenched his fists. What Lux said hurt, because Jake knew it wasn't that simple. He opened his mouth to respond when multiple bangs echoed from the streets below. Gunshots.

"What's going on?" Jake asked. Lux shrugged, then went to the entrance, opening the door.

"I suggest you go and find out. Good luck."

Jake despised how easily Lux had gotten under his skin. And now he was concerned about Azar's whereabouts. But his primary duty was to protect the city. He pulled out his phone and called Emma. She didn't answer. Remaining calm, he knew had to get to the Palace's communications centre. That was where he always received his missions. Taking one final look at the doppelganger, Jake left the room and headed for the elevators.

Chapter 10

Azar woke slowly. He could feel a vibration running through him. As he opened his eyes, he realised he was looking at clouds through a window. He sat up, startled. He was in an aircraft. Then he remembered how he'd been rendered unconscious. What had Jordan sprayed him with? He felt groggy and a little bit dizzy as he looked around. The aircraft was small, with four rows of soft, golden lounges. Then a speaker crackled to life.

"Ladies and hotties," came Jordan's cold voice, "we shall be arriving at the Trail of Tales in approximately one hour. If you look out your window in five minutes, we will be crossing the border of the Mortal Nation."

Brett emerged from the cockpit, looking at Azar.

"He's awake at last!" he stated with exaggerated enthusiasm.

"How could you do this?" Azar asked. He noticed he wasn't restrained, so he stood up and reached for his phone. It wasn't there.

"You were being stubborn," Brett replied, showing little care for what he had done. "I left your phone in Mintor. You shouldn't worry, you have all the company you need. This is your parents we're going to see, remember."

"This is my freedom which is being taken from me. You know I have never left the Mortal Nation before," Azar said. "I would have liked to be given a choice."

Azar was only now realising the seriousness of the situation he was in. He had quite literally been kidnapped and had no way of contacting anyone. But who would he call, anyway? Brett made his way to a lounge, lying across it on his back.

"Also, you're leaving the Mortal Nation with me. Azar, you haven't heard the full story. I love you and this journey is the start of my redemption to get us back to what we were." By making Azar a hostage apparently, Azar thought. A silence filled the plane.

"Is there anybody else on board?" Azar asked, looking for an emergency door.

"Besides the pilot, Jordan, no. He managed to pull a few strings and give us a luxurious trip," Brett said, folding his hands behind his head. He did not seem too concerned about Azar being free. Azar's eyes darted behind Brett, where he saw a seatbelt clipped onto the side of the lounge. He could attempt to knock Brett out by suffocating him. Azar slightly reeled back in horror at what he had just thought. Brett had also been in numerous fights with the underworld, and Azar knew he would be no match. Brett probably did too, which is why he let Azar be free.

"I get the feeling Jordan isn't just some random person you picked up from your local gang community," Azar said, sitting down as far from Brett as possible. Brett looked at him.

"Worse. He works for Orven," came the brisk reply. Azar stared at him in astonishment.

"So you're a traitor to the Nation's," the Oklem concluded.

"Azar, you don't *know* the whole story. It was a moment of weakness to sleep with him. He played his cards perfectly and promised me cash which I was going to use to travel the Nations with you."

"You shouldn't have had a moment of weakness, Brett. That's the problem," Azar said, wishing he was anywhere but in this aircraft. He was really starting to regret Lux's advice to be bold. So far it had gotten him into a minor feud with two Peacekeepers and his own kidnapping.

"Come on Azar, you've held the "I hate you" act for too long. I would never do anything to harm you."

"Why should I believe you?" Azar demanded, standing up again, barely able to contain his emotions. At that moment, the aircraft hit some turbulence, and Azar almost lost his footing, instead stumbling into one of the walls. A rising panic was also swelling inside him. Brett stood up as well.

"Because I made a promise to your parents," he snapped back, equally as heated.

"What?"

Azar was thrown off.

"I promised to protect you through thick and thin. I never meant to fall in love with you, but I did. It certainly made it easier. Why do you think I immersed myself into the underworld? To have people to protect you."

"Protect me from what?" Azar said, exasperated. "You mean to tell me that my parents hired you? That I've been some mission?"

The hostility between the two was simmering, and suddenly Azar's heart rate started to increase. There was so much going through his head. Was any of the romance between the two young men real? What relationship did Brett have with his parents? Why? Maybe Azar was being taken to see them, but if Brett was working with the Pirates, where does that leave Maree and Steve Geminus? Brett made his way over to Azar, who stood his ground.

"You're not a mission. You're an Oklem. I'm not working for the enemy. Everything I did was for you," Brett murmured, barely louder than a whisper.

"What are you protecting me from?" Azar said. This is what had been the base of their relationship. They'd fight, then turn the anger into passion. Before Azar realised what was happening, they were kissing, Brett moving in quickly, smoothly, and suddenly it was like Azar was watching a memory.

The first time they had kissed was two years ago. They had just finished a movie, and were walking back to Brett's apartment.

"That chick near the front was so desperate for that guy's attention," Brett laughed.

"It was almost more entertaining than the movie," Azar agreed.

"Yo Hefty," came a deep voice. The boys turned to a side alley where a man dressed in black emerged.

"What do you want, Jay?" Brett asked, dismay plastered on his face.

"Our products," Jay replied. Jay was bald, but tattoos covered the little skin exposed. Azar looked at Brett.

"What's happening, Brett?" he asked.

"It's complicated," Brett replied. He turned back to the man apparently named Jay.

"I'll bring it tomorrow. Now go," Brett said. Jay stepped in front of Brett and straightened his back.

"Don't disappoint," he warned, turning around and heading back into the shadows.

Azar suddenly stormed off, consumed by shock. Was Brett a gang member? Had Azar been set up for a crime? He could hear footsteps approaching from behind and picked up the pace. His breathing intensified.

"Azar,' Brett said, catching up and grabbing Azar's left arm.

"How could you not tell me?" Azar asked.

"I was going to, but I was scared you would judge me. Yes, I am involved in that stuff. But I entered that world when I was going to give up. And do you know what has since given me hope? You."

Azar stopped outside the Geminate cafe, a large, glowing billboard sitting above it.

"You gave me hope," Brett repeated.

"How?" Azar asked, crossing his arms.

"You have shown me that there is a purpose in life. You have hopes and aspirations, you want to be an author, set up a supporting charity for scared gay boys and men just like we were when we met. I am going to support you through everything."

"Then why are you still working with god knows what criminals that live in these alleys?" Azar said.

"They're like my second family, Azar. They will not hurt you."

Azar looked into Brett's eyes, and he believed what he saw in them. Then they leant in and kissed. The kiss now was as passionate as it had been that night, almost as if Brett was reliving the same memory. For a moment Azar didn't intend to pull away, consumed in how vivid the memory was. Then the memories of walking in on Brett and Jordan came through, him being knocked out, kidnapped by the very people Brett promised would protect him. He pushed Brett away and stepped back, breathing heavily.

"I can't," he said, turning his back on his ex. As soon as they landed, Azar was going to make a run for it. He had no idea where he was going, and whilst he was alone, he also realised that he only needed to worry about protecting himself.

Chapter 11

Emma took a sip from her hot chocolate as she tried to keep her fingers from turning into ice cubes. The winter rain was hammering down into Mintor, but unfortunately her work didn't cater to the weather. She was sitting at a sheltered bus stop, wearing a shiny red coat with a large black scarf wrapped around her neck. Jake had been fast asleep when she awoke, so she did not disturb him. She was waiting for a suspect to emerge from a small dry-cleaners across the busy road. Her whip was gently wrapped around her wrist, ready to be unleashed at her will. Ever since she had been recruited from the training centre in the Earth Nation to work as the Peacekeeper's private investigator, her life had been filled with hunting down key Pirates helping Orven's cause. Her natural skills with her whip led to it becoming her primary weapon, which she was allowed to customise gold upon her arrival in Mintor. More often than not, she had been successful in tracking her targets down. Although her work gave her access to any information she required, she was still fairly unfamiliar with the Nation's Peacekeeper's. She knew who they were and how long they have reigned, but everyone knew that. Drand had allowed her to learn who he was, and she knew his intentions were always good. But she couldn't help a slight instinct of suspicion when it came to doing any form of business with the Nation's. It was as if they each held dark secrets, and she did not like that.

The second bus since she had arrived at the stop pulled in, temporarily blocking her view. When Emma did not stand up to board, the driver leant forward from her seat.

"Are you okay, honey?" she called out.

Emma didn't reply, instead smiling and bowing her head slightly. The driver closed the doors and the bus pulled out. Emma was waiting for the man whom she had allowed to escape at the Brinx Club. Before the battle had occurred, she had managed to place a tracking device on his blazer. Since then, he had been visiting the dry cleaner's across the road almost every day. Now Emma wanted to know why.

As the bus cleared her view, she saw the doors to the dry cleaner's open and a man in a brown suit emerged, his face hidden under an umbrella. It didn't matter, Emma knew he was a decoy. "Go," she commanded into a hidden microphone attached to her scarf. Just then a Mintorian police vehicle came roaring up the road, its purple lights a beacon of justice and security. The man took off on foot, the vehicle pursuing it, its siren wailing like a child who lost their mother in a crowd. Emma stood up, grabbing her pink umbrella and making her way to a nearby pedestrian crossing. She needed to ensure she looked like every other civilian in order to get close enough to her suspect. She knew he was about to emerge, assuming the police had been led astray. Emma was right, as just now the dry-cleaner's door opened again, and another man emerged in a suit identical to the first. But this man wore a black cap with dark sunglasses. He buried his hands into a dark leather jacket and made his way down the road in the opposite direction to the decoy.

The light sequence changed and Emma began crossing the road, her umbrella battered from side to side as other pedestrians raced across the soaked asphalt. Using the rush to her advantage, she closed her umbrella as she stepped onto the footpath. The man was almost at the same corner. As he approached, Emma feigned a sneeze. She doubled over and watched as the man's legs came into view. Then she swung her umbrella with force at his groin. As he cried out in alarm, she then pushed him up against the wall of the corner supermarket. He offered no resistance, almost losing his balance as he tried to double over to ease the pain. Emma pulled out a pair of handcuffs from her jacket as another police vehicle pulled up on the corner. She locked them tight before removing his cap. His shaved head was all the proof she needed.

"I need to have a little chat about the Brinx Club," she whispered into his ear. Suddenly the sound of multiple gun shots echoed across the city. It was coming from near the palace about three blocks away to the south.

"You're too late," he said.

"Gunshots are hardly a surprise as we clean up the scraps of Orven's army," Emma said. Her earpiece crackled to life. It gave her a direct link to the communication's centre at the palace. "Emma Flare we have a code red at the Bank of Mintor. Initial reports suggest a Pirate attack. Peacekeeper Drand has ordered you to resolve the matter immediately."

Emma's blood turned cold. She was rarely summoned to an active crime, but clearly there was a major issue if Pirates were involved. They should be running for the hills since Orven's death. She left the suspect with the officers who had pulled up alongside her and ran back across the road to her motorcycle which was parked in a small car park behind the bus stop. The rain intensified as she keyed the ignition. She tossed the umbrella aside, immediately feeling the water starting to penetrate her clothing layers.

"And this is such a nice coat," she said to herself in dismay. She revved the engine and sped away, heading towards the palace. As she wove in and out of traffic, she saw two police vehicles race across an upcoming intersection. Assuming they were headed to the same place, she followed. As she rounded the corner, she found the target. The Bank of Mintor.

The white stairs that led up to the entrance was a scene of carnage. Even from a distance she could see bodies lying on the stairs. As she neared, she saw officers engaged with…Pirates? Their large broadswords and heavy grey armour could not be mistaken. The Pirates were joined by other local gang members, who each had leather jackets with logos on them that Emma had learnt to recognise over the last few years. There was a constant barrage of gunshots from both sides that continued to echo through the rain as more police vehicles raced past Emma, who pulled up on the curb. As she hopped off her bike she wondered, what exactly did Drand want her to do? Joining the havoc would not be of much use, she decided. Besides, she could see that the numbers were growing in favour of the MPD. She decided to think differently. Why on earth were Orven's soldiers attacking a bank?

She suddenly felt the hairs on the back of her neck stand up. She knew the feeling; the feeling of being watched. But from where? She was so deep in thought she was oblivious to the charging Pirate coming from her right. Only when she was crash tackled was she snapped back into reality. She landed heavily on the ground, but immediately sprung up. Her whip uncoiled like a snake, ready to strike. Whilst part of being an investigator involved her needing to fight, she never liked to engage in hand to hand combat alone. One error of judgement and she could be dead. The soldier swung his sword at her. She darted back then swung her whip at his legs. The whip was much stronger than it looked, and for a normal target, it would easily have brought the enemy down to his knees. But this Pirate was much larger. He grabbed the whip and held it outwards, bringing his sword down in the other hand to sever Emma's prized possession. But Emma had prepared for this. On the handle of her whip was a small black button. She pressed it and suddenly the whip became electrified, energy surging down to the Pirate. The electrical shock blasted through his hand, and he dropped both weapons with a startled cry, his sword clattering to the ground. Emma stepped forward as she pulled her whip back, no longer electrified, and kicked his stomach with the sole of her black steel cap boots, forcing him to his knees. She slashed him again and again with her whip until the giant finally succumbed to the merciless golden bombardment. She crouched over him.

"How did you know who I was?" she demanded. "Everyone else is at the bank."

The Pirate laughed. His voice was gruff.

"I do not take questions from children," he said.

Emma was going to pin him to the ground when she noticed a white van rounding the corner. A news vehicle. It was now she realised that the gun shots had ceased. As much as she wanted answers, she could not break her most important rule. Do not be seen by the media. It could blow her entire cover. The cuts from her whip would ensure the Pirate was too immobile to escape. But to be certain, she aimed one final kick at his temple, knocking him out. She raced back to her bike, setting it onto its wheels. The engine roared to life and she headed for the palace. If the Pirates were still strong enough to launch a surprise attack, then everybody in Mintor was in danger. She had left her phone in her locker at the palace, so she could only hope that Jake was safe.

Chapter 12

The aircraft descended through the clouds. Azar peered out the window to catch a glimpse of the Trail of Tales. All he could see was a large open field lined by a forest. There was no grand airport buzzing with thousands of people. In fact, he could see no movement at all as the aircraft hovered then descended horizontally into the field. When it had come to a stop, the airstairs opened from under the walking platform down onto a dirt path that disappeared into the dark shadows of the trees. Azar made his way to the clamshell door. A slight breeze was all that disturbed the silence.

"This is not the usual way to enter this land. But I need you to trust me," Brett said, appearing next to him. Trust? That was gone and never coming back. But Azar just needed to get to the treeline and he would escape. He had not said a word since the kiss.

"No thank you to the pilot?" came Jordan's cold voice. Azar turned to see him standing in the doorway of the cockpit.

"I don't know what scheme of Orven's you are playing out, but I won't stop until I find the truth. The whole truth," Azar added, looking at Brett also. Then he began to descend the stairs. Before stepping onto the dirt, he took a minute to think over a few things. This would be the first step he took in what felt like another world. The air was incredibly fresh, the clear blue skies reminding Azar of perfect Summer days on his hill overlooking Mintor. Brett could be leading him into a trap, or his parents could be perfectly fine. His life had been turned upside down; he had no idea where his decision to leave home would take him, but maybe Lux was right, and there was only one way to find out. He stepped off.

Azar turned to ask what direction when he saw something at the end of the trail. Standing out against the green forest, someone in a black robe.

"The See-er, this should be fascinating," Brett murmured.

"See-er?" Azar asked.

"You know, a fortune teller, but a real one," Brett said.

They made their way along the path. The isolation combined with the silence was nothing short of off-putting. There were no birds chirping, almost as if nature itself were holding its breath. As they approached the See-er, he turned, moving into the trees. Azar glanced at his ex.

"He's not very social," Brett said, indicating for Azar to continue.

"Then we should get on just fine," the Oklem replied. Azar's plan to run now seemed like a feeble option. The forest was very dense, and there were probably dozens of ways he could injure himself if he leapt into the shrubs. For the moment, he chose to stay on the path.

They walked in silence. Eventually the forest opened out to a stream. Two wooden canoes sat waiting, appearing to hold themselves against the current. The See-er turned around. His face was concealed by the hood of his black cloak. He raised a bony finger at Azar.

"You come with me," he ordered, his voice croaky, old.

Brett grabbed Azar's arm, making him jump.

"The Trail of Tales is not like the other Nations. There's a reason that no one, including Orven, has ever attempted to take control here. Listen to what he has to say," Brett said quietly.

"How do you know so much about everything? Literally nothing has made sense to me since the war finished. Isn't the opposite supposed to have happened?" Azar asked.

"Just because the war is finished, it doesn't mean the story is," Brett replied. "I'll see you in the city."

Azar frowned, dissatisfied with the answer, but followed the See-er into the first canoe. Azar sat in the bow, the See-er sitting higher up at the stern. Azar looked around for paddles, but the canoe suddenly began moving on its own, as if someone had released its invisible restraints. They continued downstream in silence. Azar was about to talk when a bubble-like shield wrapped itself around them.

"Why does the Oklem leave the Mortal Nation?" the See-er asked.

"How did you know I am an Oklem?" Azar replied, not hiding the suspicion in his tone.

"I know many things, boy. For centuries I have watched armies collide, heroes fall, Nations develop. Do I need to repeat my question?"

Azar was a little taken aback at the aggressive tone in the See-er's voice.

"I was taken against my will. But for two years I have wanted to see my parents. I only just found out they have been missing and are under suspicion of being traitors. My captors believe my parents are here. I guess I will find out soon enough," Azar said.

The See-er didn't reply immediately. Again silence consumed the area, broken only by the trickle of water echoing through the trees. There was a strange blue mist swirling around the stream, and Azar almost felt like he could hear whispers.

"You are not the first Oklem here, however you are the most intriguing," the See-er eventually replied.

"But why?" Azar asked. "What am I supposed to be?"

"That is the remarkable beauty of your kind. Nobody knows what your purpose is. Your life is your personal mission," the See-er said slowly. "You have only very recently been turned, which is why it is fitting you should be here now. Oklem are more powerful than Peacekeepers. But each one in the past has had a different need. A need that Nature felt could not be resolved by those of us that dwell in this universe. It is not my place to tell you what the past Oklem have done. I am here to guide you as you begin to discover who you truly are."

Azar noticed the stream went into what looked like a cave up ahead.

"Where are we going?"

"There is much you do not know, some things you never will," the See-er replied. "We are headed into the Fortune Caves, a place where spirits of the past, founders of the Nations and supernatural worlds can lurk. Here you will find answers, and you will see things visible only to your mind. But you must remember that the most important thing to do is listen, for the truth is not always in what you see, but what you hear."

As soon as the canoe entered the cave, darkness surrounded them, as did total silence. Not even the sounds of the forest penetrated the atmosphere. The bubble suddenly lit up, electrified. Then it cracked and broke apart, little shards of light slowly drifting towards the water. Suddenly a burst of pink light shot from a wall, exploding across the cave. It created the sense of a meteor shower. On either side of the stream were flat rock ledges. Apart from the light, there were no other features to look at. Soon the pink was joined by orange, then green, soon an array of colours. Azar watched in awe as the cave lit up.

Then the colours slowly faded, and an image appeared on the right-hand ledge. He was looking into a courtroom from above. Azar's parents sitting with their heads down. It was as if he was there.

"Guilty. Guilty. Guilty," came a continuous chant. That was all Azar saw, before the image disappeared. Was this the truth? Were his parents traitors? Then Azar saw something to his left. Turning he saw Brett standing there, in a suit, his arm outstretched.

"Come back to me," he repeated. Azar wasn't sure if this was another vision or reality.

"Come to me," came another voice, and then Jake was there, standing next to Brett, holding a purple flower. For a brief moment a third boy appeared. Unfamiliar. Silent. A voice echoed around them.

"There are always three sides to a story."

Azar only had time to see the third boy had blue hair and a sly smirk before the vision vanished. The canoe continued through the cave, the colours re-igniting and continuing to bounce off the walls like rockets. Things were happening so fast that Azar could hardly take in what was going on. He turned back to the ledge on his right and gaped. He was standing there, making out with a woman. He watched as her long, silky black hair blew back gently as she parted, revealing the face of Jessani.

"Oh Marvin," she said softly.

The collective noises from the three scenes continued to echo over and over, though they slowly became more distant. Suddenly the canoe sped up, racing through the cave, the light show maintaining an equally fast pace overhead. Then, as if he had delved into another consciousness, Azar was no longer in the boat. In fact, he wasn't anywhere. He was watching a scene unfold. A tall man with his back turned was facing a blue hologram. Azar's parents stood together in the hologram. "It is done?" the man asked.

"Yes Orven," Maree Geminus answered, "he is an Oklem. Our son will be unlike anything that has yet been seen."

"You have been most loyal, Maree. Your son will be the change, and you will be known as the mother of a hero. Now keep your child safe until it is time. For if anyone knows about this—" he was cut off as a door burst open. Azar's parents vanished. Soldiers bearing the arms of the Fire and Ice Nations swarmed in. Orven turned around, smiling.

"You caught me," he said. Suddenly the room was blinded by a large white light, but Azar could see through it. In the space of seconds, what looked like a portal opened behind Orven and he fell through, vanishing. Gunshots rang out by the blinded soldiers, and the light faded. Orven's body was lying on the floor. Cheers erupted. A sinking feeling intensified deep within Azar's chest. That was not Orven's real body.

Orven was not dead.

Darkness again covered everything. Azar could feel a pulling within him, a calling. This strange sensation filled his mind, and for a moment, he left his consciousness. He heard one word, '*Oklem*', being repeated. An image of a cave appeared, bare of any features apart from glowing green walls. The image widened to reveal large snowy mountains, found only in one place. The Ice Nation.

Azar woke up back in the canoe. Although had he ever really left?

"Oh my god!" he exclaimed. The chants had gone but the lights remained above him. In the silence, Azar could hear another voice, a woman's, talking in his head. The See-er had told him to listen, so he closed his eyes and trained his focus into the sounds:

The war has ended, but the enemy lives on. Be warned, for everything is not as it seems, and everyone is not as they claim to be. The moment where you are so frightened is the moment when courage will lead you to the truth.

Azar opened his eyes. He could see daylight ahead. The lights started breaking off, crashing into the wall and disappearing. The canoe exited the cave, and Azar gaped in awe. The stream opened into a wider river, which led straight towards a large golden wall.

"We have arrived at Lisarow, ancient city and capital of the Trail of Tales," the See-er said. Azar jolted, startled. He had forgotten he was not alone. The canoe drifted to a small wooden dock and stopped.

"Can I talk to you about what I saw?" Azar asked, his mind racing over the visions.

"If that is your desire. However I only speak of Fortune Cave events in my lodge. You will find it in the city when the time is right. For now you must be cautious, for even the safest house in the universe is home to unexpected troubles."

****

Azar clambered out of the canoe, not surprised at how wobbly he was, but surprised to find tears on his cheeks. He turned to help the See-er before realising that he had disappeared. Apparently a common aspect of being supernatural, Azar thought. Brett emerged from the caves moments later. He looked at Azar, who avoided his gaze.

"Well, how was that?" Brett asked as the canoe came to a stop.

"Guess you'll never know," Azar replied, turning to the walls of a city he was hoping would hold the answers he so desperately sought.

Chapter 13

There was a sense of mystery to Lisarow. Surrounding the city was a wall made of solid gold, however the buildings within were made of wood. At first Azar was unsure of how a golden wall which could so easily be plundered could protect what was such an ancient city. It appeared that the Trail of Tales was a place of magic. Brett had told Azar when they had arrived that there was a reason nobody had tried to take over this land. It protected itself. The place left him in a state of awe. The days were hot and the nights perfectly mild. He had arrived the previous day, and learnt that the locals spoke the same language as himself. Brett informed him that they had to lose their native tongue and speak the same as the Peacekeepers in order for the Nations to trust them. This allowed them to maintain their independence. The Trail of Tales had no political grounding. There was no "leader" as such, rather the land created its own rules. What these rules were however, Azar wasn't sure. He had left Brett and began to explore on his own, but soon discovered that answers were scarce. He had immediately started asking about his parents whereabouts. Nobody seemed to know anything apart from that Maree and Steve Geminus were rumoured to be missing for over a year.

Another element which added mystery to the city was that whilst the buildings' exteriors were made of wood, the interiors were designed with the most fashionable materials and layouts. Some had coloured carpets, some marbled floors. The "shops" themselves were very basic compared to the standard that Mintor operated at. Here there were bakeries, blacksmiths, fortune tellers. He even stumbled across a small stall where you could exchange currency. Needless to say, things were far cheaper than back home. There were no fast food outlets, no shopping centres, no expectations to spend. Azar found the people to be friendly, but could feel there was something they withheld from every conversation. They would avert their eyes when talking, would shy away from any topic relating to the war or even Azar's parents. The sun had started its descent, the sky a glorious shade of orange, so he returned to the small inn they had found and prepared to go and find somewhere new to eat.

Azar was cautious of Brett, because as much as he wanted to forgive him, he knew deep down that he couldn't. He hated the predicament he was in. The sooner he found his parents, the sooner he would leave, with or without his ex's help. When checking in, he made sure there were two separate beds in their room. He had considered telling someone that he was technically a hostage, but after what he had seen in the Fortune Caves, he realised that maybe he could find some answers whilst here. Besides, if Brett thought Azar was working with him, he would be less inclined to be suspicious. As Azar was about to leave, the door opened and Brett returned, carrying a fully packed bamboo bag.

"I figured we should probably change clothes, Lisarow doesn't exactly have the climate for jeans and jackets," he said, placing the bag onto his bed. He pulled out a range of buttoned shirts, many representing the tropical theme of the city with palm trees and beaches.

"Where did you get all this from?" Azar asked. He certainly hadn't seen any clothing stores during the day.

"On the outskirts of this city, there are four small complexes representing each Nation. Gives a little taste of home to travellers. Fortunately I know your fashion sense, so let's get changed and head out," Brett replied.

Azar put on a light blue buttoned shirt and white denim shorts. It was a relief to have a change of clothes. Brett wore an orange shirt and black shorts. As Azar opened the door to leave, he stopped. For a moment his vision blurred, and he felt a ripple through his…mind? He could hear a very distant echo, barely a whisper. Then, just as quickly as it had come, it vanished. He took in a deep breath, and could feel drops of sweat running down his back. He turned to face Brett, whose eyes remained fixed on the ground. Had he noticed? What was going on? The sky was still bathed in beautiful tropical colours. But what made it so noticeable was the lack of lights from the village. Instead, large fire beacons lit up the town. Azar stepped out onto the street, the warm air suddenly suffocating. He needed to be alone.

"Hold up I forgot my wallet," Brett said, turning and going back into the room. Now was Azar's chance. He ran as fast as he could, weaving around corners, clueless to where he was headed. After a few short blocks, he stopped, panting. What was he doing? He wasn't going to find any answers here. He wanted to go home.

"You look like you're new here," came a soft voice from behind, cutting through Azar's train of thought. He turned around to see a lady with short grey hair and a purple blouse standing there, her feet bare.

"Very new," Azar replied, attempting a weak smile.

"Well, you picked a good night to visit. Down by the water they are having carols and a feast, free for all.

"Sounds like a plan, thank you," Azar replied. The woman returned a smile and continued her way along the path at a slow hobble. Azar wandered through a few more streets before he caught an unmistakable scent. The ocean. At least that was something familiar, he thought.

He followed the scent, staying on the path lit by the fire beacons. Music became clearer and voices grew louder. He eventually came over the top of a sandy hill and looked down at the scene. People lined the waters' edge, dancing, singing, sitting around large fires. The scent of seafood and fresh meat drifted up, making Azar's stomach grumble. Perhaps that was why he was feeling light headed. Since he had met Lux, he hadn't eaten much at all. He was too worried about everything. Shoes and sandals were spread out across the top of the hill. Azar decided to leave his there as well. He descended into the crowds. It was near impossible not to be consumed by the energy and atmosphere. He went around to the many roughly made huts eating plate after plate, experiencing a variety of flavours from sweet to sour, plants to meats. When his stomach refused to take any more, he went further along the beach where he found a thriving market place. Locals sold jewellery, toys, even some small furniture like cabinets. Azar made his way along, his feet gliding through the soft and warm sand. He came to a stall where some very unique jewellery caught his eye.

He picked up a necklace. It was coloured black, but a dreamy mixture of green and aqua that glistened out of the centre was what really drew his focus. Azar glanced up at the stall owner. A woman with a blue bandana on her head sat there, staring at him with intrigue. Movement behind the stall caught the young man's eye. A little girl stood with her hands tucked behind her back. She had long red hair tied in a braid, and wore glasses. She looked away shyly.

"How much is this?" Azar asked the woman in front. "Whatever you think it's worth," she replied. He pulled out some coins and handed them to her. Her eyes widened.

"So generous," she murmured. Azar took the necklace. As he turned to go, the little red-haired girl stepped forward.

"You can take the other one for free," she said.

"That's very kind, but I don't need another one," Azar replied.

"Perhaps not at this moment. But they are meant to be together. Please," she replied. She reached down below the table and pulled out another necklace. It looked the same, but the centre colour was a combination of light purple and yellow.

"They are gorgeous," Azar muttered. The girl handed it to him and he took it graciously.

"These were made by my great-grandfather. We have never ever given them away. For he always said that they must travel together, not necessarily physically, but emotionally."

"Then why do you give it to me now?" Azar asked in fascination. The girl looked at the other woman and they smiled. Then she drew her gaze to him.

"I just know that you have an exciting adventure ahead," she answered.

The older woman stood up, joining the little girl.

"Our family has passed these down believing that they bring with them a sense of security and well-being. So keep one, and give the other necklace to someone who does this for you, whom you have an emotional attachment to. Someone who not only makes you feel safe and loved, but alive."

Azar was momentarily speechless. That was all he wanted. It was as if something shifted within him. His sadness had lifted just enough as he could resonate with their words so personally. He had not been feeling alive for a long time, he conceded. And now he finally accepted the truth. Brett was not the right one for him. Deep within he felt this sense trickle through him. Hope? The possibility that there could be a future love so consuming that every touch, every moment, would electrify him and make him feel alive again.

"Thank you, if only you knew what this means to me," he said, holding back the sudden impulse for tears.

"We do, for it is what brought you to our stall," the little girl replied. Her eyes were wide with excitement.

"This might be a very strange request, maybe it's this place, but can I give you a hug?" he asked the child. Her face beamed as she made her way around the stall. Azar crouched down and held his arms out as she raced into him. She was so fragile, yet so full of life. The hug was perfect; it was real.

"What is your name?" he whispered into her ear.

"Fayre," she replied. She stepped back and stood in front of him. Azar looked into her eyes.

"I'm Azar. I want you to promise me that one day we will meet again, and we will both be exactly who we want to be. Do you promise?" he asked. The girl leaned in forwards and kissed him on the cheek.

"I promise," she giggled.

Azar bowed his head and stood up. He left the stall, tucking the necklaces into his back pocket. He returned back to the centre of the night's gathering as the music was turned up and everyone started to dance. Feeling far more positive, Azar joined in. There was no shame, no judgments, just laughter and peace. For a moment he let go of everything and just had fun. Then the music became slower, and couples began to dance. Opting to avoid an awkward moment, Azar turned to go. As he did, he realised a woman was standing in front of him, her ankle length dress swaying gently above the sand, her arm outstretched. Azar froze. Her curly brown hair shimmered around her shoulders, and an orange flower garland hung around her neck.

"Azar?"

"Mum?" he murmured in astonishment.

"My sweet child, it has been a while," Maree Geminus said.

"Mum, where have you and dad been?"

"Shhh. There is much to say. But first, will you take this moment and dance with me?" Maree asked, holding her right hand out.

Chapter 14

Maree refused to let Azar say a word as they danced. Azar's emotions were in disarray. There was a slight hostility between the two as they pressed their palms together and slowly waltzed. Azar didn't know what he was going to say afterwards. Eventually the music began to shift back into a more celebratory style, forcing the mother and son to part.

"I know you have so many questions burning on the tip of your tongue. Come along and we will talk," Maree said.

Maree made her way along the beach, eventually coming to a quieter stretch of sand away from the noise. Azar immediately embraced her, more forceful than intended, which almost made them lose their footing. Maree gripped him tightly, tears flowing down both of their faces. Azar had been starting to wonder if he would ever get to see his parents again. Eventually he took a step back but continued holding her hands.

"Mum, what is going on? The war finished, you should have come home," he started.

"I wanted to, baby," Maree replied, "but we could not return."

"Peacekeeper Drand said you and Dad were missing. Where were you? Why did you cut contact with him?"

Maree's face darkened slightly at the mention of Peacekeeper Drand.

"Your father and I came here two years ago for our own protection. But we realised that we were in no danger here. Lisarow is not plagued by laws and rules and political status. We saw it as an opportunity to be free, rather than being kept hidden from sight in some dull room. We did our best to keep in contact with you, but we had to be cautious."

Azar let go of his mother's hands. The vision he had seen in the Fortune Caves kept probing at the forefront of his mind.

"So are you against the senate? Are you against the Peacekeepers?"

"We are not against anybody, we simply have changed our views on the world."

Maree sat down on the sand, looking out towards the ocean. Azar did not know how far the waters went, how far the Trail of Tales stretched. He sat down next to her.

"The day the war finished, you called me, saying you could not return home until you found out who took and delivered the Oklem blood for Orven's ritual. Peacekeeper Drand told me that I was recently turned into an Oklem. It cannot be a coincidence that you called when you did. I don't know how my blood was taken, I certainly don't remember offering to help Orven, but the blood was mine, wasn't it?" he asked, his voice wavering slightly. The thought that he had a part in aiding Orven horrified him, even if he did not have any knowledge he was doing so.

"I see Peacekeeper Drand has told you what you are. You must be proud," Maree said.

"Proud? Mum what are you talking about, I'm a freak," Azar said.

Maree shook her head, and Azar's stomach lurched.

"You're a hero, my sweet child," Maree said. "Your father and I organised everything."

Azar felt sick. His own parents had made him an Oklem?

"That doesn't make sense. You haven't been in Mintor," he eventually said.

"No, we haven't," Maree conceded. "We needed somebody to get close enough to you. Despite it making us sick that you like boys, your sin can be forgiven when you pledge your loyalty to Orven."

"No," Azar whispered in horror, standing up. Brett had turned Azar into an Oklem. He had also brought Azar to Lisarow. Tears began to uncontrollably race down Azar's cheek as the reality of what his mother just said hit him. His sexuality had been exposed by Brett, and his parents believed that being gay was a sin.

"Brett has done nothing but ensure you have been safe at all times. He has been immensely loyal to us and to you," Maree stated, rising to her feet also. Azar could feel the rage seeping through his veins, but he also wanted to run away.

"I saw it in my vision, you talking with Orven. You made me some freakish creature just to help him gain access to the Supernatural Universe."

"Azar, it is far more than that," Maree argued, raising her stern voice.

"Oh mother I wish you had a valid reason but I cannot see that being the case," Azar said, turning to go.

"Being an Oklem gives your life a new meaning. Your blood can reopen the path. The Peacekeepers cannot be trusted and the only ones who can truly oppose them are stuck in another universe. The Oklem are the key to bringing forth a new order. You will be worshipped!" Azar was shell shocked. His mother was acting nothing short of delusional, and it scared him. "Lux was right, there are three sides to every story," he said.

"Who?" Maree asked, a slight hint of confusion flashing across her face.

"My doppelganger. I'm sure you know all about him as well."

Azar saw Maree's face delve into a genuine expression of horror.

"Your what?" she whispered. Suddenly she let out a cry of fear and fell to her knees.

"As if you didn't know," Azar said, standing over her. But something told him her response was genuine. That only made him more sick, more worried.

"I, I didn't," Maree stuttered, shaking her head vigorously. "Azar if you have a doppelganger it means your blood was never purely mortal. That means mixing it with Oklem blood would not have the same outcome for the portal. Orven's plan cannot work."

Azar hated every word he was hearing. He hated that his parents betrayed the Nations. He hated that Brett had turned him into an Oklem. He hated everything. It was too much. He stormed along the sand, heading up the slope to avoid walking through the celebration. The shadows from the fire pits were long and danced up the trees and across the huts as people were leaving the party. But his emotions began to overwhelm him. Still barefoot, he darted into the city and collapsed in a dark corner between a hut and wooden fence. As he slumped against the wall, he felt a sudden ripple through his consciousness. He gripped the sides of his head.

"Get out of my MIND!" he yelled. The feeling vanished, and he was left feeling completely vulnerable. His biggest fear was true. His parents did not accept him for something he could not control. It was worse than anything else that was happening, worse than him being an Oklem, worse than the loneliness he faced every day.

Soon after he felt footsteps approaching. Azar focused on his breathing, trying to be as silent as possible.

"Azar I know you're here."

It was Brett's voice. How did he know? Azar was going to remain silent, assuming it was a tactic to draw him out. But he realised that he needed to face Brett, if anything just to punch him in the face. So he stood up and emerged back onto the dusty path. Brett stood a few metres away with Maree next to him.

"I understand you are confused, Azar," Maree said. "Just let me explain what your father and I have chosen to do."

Azar stood still, avoiding eye contact. He knew whatever his mother was about to say would not justify her betrayal of the Nations and Azar's trust. But understanding her point of view could help him inform Peacekeeper Drand. The Peacekeeper was clearly the only person he could trust.

"Orven is our only hope," Maree began. "If he fails, the Peacekeepers will descend unchallenged into a dictatorship so powerful that not even nature will be able to find a way to break it. Why? Because it already gave us a tool. The Oklem was created centuries ago not as a weapon against the Supernatural Universe as everyone has been led to believe, but to counter the Peacekeepers. Yet each time, the Oklem have been manipulated and weakened by these so-called leaders. I am going to make sure my son is different. Despite the fact that your blood is not purely mortal, it is still powerful. So you can hate me, Azar. You can hate your father. But you will not follow the same path the other Oklem have taken. One day the universe will see why we are risking everything, and because of us, you will be alive to see it as well."

Azar was stunned. Maree was so certain of what she was saying that he knew it didn't matter if she was right or not. It didn't matter what sacrifices she had to make. She would continue to fight for Orven until she either succeeded or died. Azar had nothing else to say to her, so he turned his attention to Brett. "All the lies. Deception. Making me an Oklem. The criminal world. Nothing in that could ever make an argument that you were doing anything to protect me. You used me. For what purpose?" Azar asked, spreading his arms out.

Brett shrugged.

"To be honest it could have been anyone," he said. "But your parents were persistent that it had to be you. They want some of the glory. I didn't want to, Azar. It's why we were together for two years before I had no choice."

"There is always a choice," Azar said.

Maree stepped forwards.

"The best way to ensure there will be a universe without political corruption is to be the leaders of the movement," she explained. "There is a dinner that you *will* attend here in three nights time. There you shall witness the beginning of the change. You are my son, a Geminus, and I will not let you disgrace our name which has become something far greater than what could ever have happened in the Mortal Nation."

Azar's anger began to subside. Now he was only going to work on protecting himself. He needed to threaten the two people standing in front of him. People that weeks ago he loved. He looked at his mother with a loathing he had never expressed onto another being in his life.

"I hope you gain everything you expect to receive," he replied, his voice filled with so much coldness Maree took a step back, "but just like every attempt by Orven and the Pirates, you will fail. You are right. I am a Geminus. I am a doppelganger. I am an Oklem. I will be the greatest challenge Orven has ever faced. If I truly am stronger than the Peacekeepers as you stated, then you, Maree, have already lost."

Azar turned on his heel and made his way back along the beach. His knees felt weak, his heart was pounding. Before tonight, the old Azar would have spent the next week crying, hating himself, then convincing himself that things will change, only to be left alone again and again. Not this time. His mother's betrayal made him realise something. He was different. He was part supernatural. It was finally time for him to see exactly what he was capable of doing. It was time to visit the See-er.

Chapter 15

Emma very slowly opened the heavy, wooden door, ensuring every creak sounded like a long and excruciating squeal of pain. The attack on the bank had ended two hours ago. Emma had met with Peacekeeper Drand, Jake and various enforcement commanders to understand what had taken place. There was no definitive answer. Seeing as Pirates had attacked, Emma believed there was one person she could get answers from. The bald headed man from the Brinx Club was associated with Jessani in some way. Emma had him brought in to the cold and dark interrogation rooms that were located under the palace. She was not going to leave until she found a motive. The man did not look at her as she made her way into the room. He was sitting on a steel chair, hands intertwined in front of him on a metal table. The effect this room had was perfectly suitable, Emma thought. She made her way to the opposite chair and sat down, looking into the man's beady black eyes.

She had since changed her clothes, now wearing a black coat, red skirt and black stockings. "How about we begin with a name?" she started, maintaining her stare at the man's diverted gaze. The man sitting before her had been caught using a number of different names as he had carried out numerous ploys for Orven and the Pirates. But he had always managed to evade police. Emma was aware that this was the man's first interrogation, and she intended to leave a mark on him. Her question was left unanswered.

"I thought you Pirates were always vying to be at the top of the leaderboard," she continued.

"I'm not a Pirate," the man retorted.

Emma clicked her tongue.

"Working with Jessani, leaving a meeting full of Pirates at the Brinx Club. The evidence cannot be refuted," she said matter-of-factly.

The man's hands separated and he looked calmly at Emma. His face was covered in wrinkles. "My name is Robert Johnson. I am a delivery man. I take packages from point A to point B without asking what it is, as long as I get paid. I am not a Pirate, I simply took up an offer." Robert Johnson was a name on the file Emma had read before entering the room. Emma was not so sure that anything he said could be considered true. Nonetheless, she decided to give him an opportunity.

"You knew about the attack on the Bank of Mintor. That information would not have been shared with you unless you played a part in it," Emma replied, her voice becoming slightly more threatening. "Your life is over. You will spend the rest of it in a cell whilst others you worked with are free. Is there anything else you'd like to say? Perhaps attempt to make a bargain?" Silence again.

"Have fun in prison," she said, standing up and making her way towards the door. As she did so, she heard a sharp intake of breath. Then a soft…giggle? She turned back to Robert, whose body was shaking from his bottled laughter.

"You act so tough yet you did exactly what she said you'd do," he said with a grin.

"What did I do?" Emma asked, cocking her head but keeping her tone relatively disinterested.

"You "caught" me," Robert replied, waving his hands in the air.

"You weren't hard to follow," Emma said, slowly stepping back towards the table. Robert shook his head.

"I was caught because I wanted to be. I knew I was a goner when you caught me at the Brinx Club. So I used my last few days of freedom to make sure I didn't go down without giving something in return," he sneered.

Emma slammed her hands down onto the table.

"What did you do?" she demanded, her voice filled with malice.

"I have made my mark in this universe," he replied, lowering his voice.

Emma could see a loathing in his eyes. She needed to get him to talk, to fuel his growing ego. "Or," she said, "maybe you don't know anything because a delivery boy isn't high enough on the food chain."

Robert leapt up, his chair falling back and crashing onto the floor. His legs were tied to the feet of the table, meaning he could not move any closer to Emma.

"I *freed* her," he announced, pointing a finger at himself. "Me. Jessani, Orven's most dangerous assassin. I went to her asking what I could do. She had everything planned. The attack was ready to go. But there was just one problem. You," he said through gritted teeth.

Emma unleashed her whip and lashed out at Robert, sending him and the table crashing into the wall. His cries of pain soon led into yet another fit of laughter.

"What about me?" Emma asked, her voice slightly breaking.

"This right here!" he cried. "You! You are dangerous. Intelligent. A threat. We had to keep you away from the Bank. I allowed you to follow me for days. Now here we are, and in this city of betrayal there is now one more foe that is *free*."

Emma stood over the man, who was not shying away from her. His face was alive. He had been successful in whatever plan he was acting on.

"Who?" she pressed.

"You do not need to threaten me anymore. The Pirates want me to tell you. You may have taken out the Pirates great King Orven," he said, his voice going quiet once again. "But every king has a queen."

Emma's mouth opened in surprise. Who was the queen? Why had she never heard of this before now?

"Your faith in those that lead the Nations will be your ultimate downfall," Robert concluded. Emma made her way out of the room, slamming the heavy wooden door shut. She burned at the turn of events. Regardless of whether there was a queen, Johnson believed wholeheartedly that he had released someone. The fact that she had never heard of the Pirates queen from the Peacekeepers concerned her. So much so that she was going to go straight to Drand's quarters, with or without an invitation.

Chapter 16

The See-er stayed in what appeared to be a large brown hut along one of the golden walls surrounding Lisarow. Azar made his way into the hut. He could feel an energy in the room, vibrating through the walls. Upon entering, a light mist wafted through the opening corridor. There was no door so much as a thick black curtain blocking out the natural light and buzz of the town. The hallway opened up to a large round room, lit by candles spread around at uneven spaces. There was almost no furniture, the walls were bare.

"You have come," the See-er said. Azar turned to his left. A bean bag sat in front of a small table. Behind that, the See-er sat on a chair, unmoving.

"I don't really have anyone else to turn to," Azar said, "so I have decided that I need to know who I have become."

"I see," the See-er replied. Was he making a joke? Sighing, Azar sat down opposite the strange being.

"What do you want to know?" the See-er asked, his voice rough, as before.

"I...don't know," Azar shrugged. "Everything has happened so quickly. Orven's defeat was supposed to mean freedom."

"But he isn't defeated, is he?" the See-er said.

Azar's eyes narrowed. "If you know this, why haven't you told anyone? Orven is the most dangerous person to exist—"

"I see many things, boy. Nature is something that I cannot interfere with. It is not my place to warn the world of every threat to their existence. I have played my role. Life brings challenges we must overcome by ourselves."

"Even if it means the end of us?" Azar asked.

"We're still here now, are we not? Orven is far from the most dangerous being to live. If you knew what creatures lurk in the Supernatural Universe, you would find it a challenge to leave your home each day. Orven has used his name to strike fear into all the Nations, but in reality his forces were unable to overthrow any Nation in its entirety."

"So we should ignore him?"

"You must start thinking like an Oklem, boy," the See-er snapped, his vocal chords straining. Instead of being taken aback, Azar replied immediately.

"There is so much mystery to that term. How did the Oklem ever come to exist?"

"I could sit here and narrate to you like they do with a child's story time, or I can show you," came the reply. A moment of silence swept over the room.

"Show me?" Azar said, full of doubt.

"The biggest strength an Oklem has is the mind. Now draw your attention to this." The See-er put a clay bowl on the small table. "Close your eyes. Now put your hands on it and allow your mind to emerge into the object."

Sceptical, Azar did as he was directed. Putting his hands on the bowl, he closed his eyes. He felt nothing. He pursed his lips. Then he felt it. At first it was barely more than a slight twitch in his mind. He drew his focus towards it, and suddenly he could feel himself moving. Almost like he was in a dream but conscious of it. This feeling's intensity increased, and soon, like he had in the Fortune Caves, he was watching a scene unfold.

1461: Ice Nation Cave

The See-er was sitting on a mountain, watching an approaching storm in silence. A bolt of lightning struck a nearby boulder, and in the blinding light a figure emerged, swamped in a blossoming yellow cloak. They had a shaved head, and grey fingernails twice the length of their fingers.

"Be warned," it said in a deep female voice, "for a time approaches where man from the Mortal Nation will work with the darkest of creatures. A common objective to be the sole rulers of all shall see an unchallenged shadow grip the universe. To oppose this, all the Nations must be unified. You have been warned."

The creature vanished. The See-er sat unmoving. Then a cloud swept across the scene, quickly evaporating to reveal a cave. It was glowing, blue icicles dangling from the rooftop identified it as being in the Ice Nation. The See-er was sitting over a small ice bench, a clay made bowl in front of him.

"A natural source from every Nation is now combined in this bowl, and will ensure unity," he murmured. "But when will it be required?"

He raised his head as if he was hoping to receive an answer from the spirits. All was silent.

"Then it shall wait here until it is time," he concluded. He turned to one of the ice walls and placed the bowl into a small shelf he had created. Then he sealed it with a tapping of his staff.

Azar gasped, gripping the bean bag tightly as he adjusted to where he was. He could feel sweat on the back of his neck. That had been the most surreal experience he had ever witnessed. He felt this remarkable energy pulsing through his veins.

"We have not finished," came the See-er's voice.

"I don't know what happened," Azar replied with a pant.

"You lost your focus. Now hold the bowl and retrain your thoughts."

Azar noticed the room was filled with a lot more mist than it had before. Taking a deep breath, he held the bowl in his fingers and closed his eyes once more.

1600: Ice Nation Cave

The See-er raced into the icy cave, his breathing long and raspy. Orven was searching for a way to break the Peacekeeper's portal restrictions and create an open, limitless path between their universe and the Supernatural one. Surely it was time. He removed the ice on the wall and brought out the clay bowl. The elements he had gathered years ago were liquified, but not frozen. He put it on the ice bench.

"Spirits, I have responded to your warnings. Give this universe a chance to challenge the impending evils," the See-er pleaded. A few minutes passed, nothing but the wind drifting through the cave's entrance disturbing the quiet. The See-er smashed his staff into the icy ground. "No!" he yelled. "I have done everything. I have united the Nations. What more is required?"

"Hello?" came a new voice, a young voice. Male. The See-er froze. How could anyone have found this location?

"Unless they were supposed to," he finished out loud. "Of course!"

A young boy emerged from the passageway into the freezing room. He looked no older than ten years of age. He had a large scar across his right cheek, his eyes were open wide.

"Of course," the See-er repeated. "To unify the Nations, it requires blood. Give me your hand, boy," he ordered, stretching his bony fingers towards the newcomer.

"I know not what events I have awoken to. One moment I was home with mother, now I am here," the boy said fearfully. The See-er tapped his staff and the boy suddenly lifted off the ground and gravitated towards the ice bench.

"Please," the boy begged.

"You are going to play a very important role in the course of history," the See-er explained. The boys' hand was forced out above the bowl, and a small cut appeared across the palm of his tender hand. A drop of blood fell into the bowl. Immediately a figure appeared across the other side of the cave. The same creature that had given the prophecy. For a moment the image blurred. Azar was briefly aware of himself for only a moment before the vision consumed his consciousness once more.

"You have unified the Nations," the female said. She made her way over to the bench, her fingernails brushing the side of the bowl. Suddenly a bolt of electricity shot from her fingers, a deep glow channelling through the bowl. Then it disappeared, and the spirit turned back to the See-er.

"To act as one, they must be consumed by one." She turned to the boy, who shook his head slowly. The See-er picked up the bowl and moved towards the frightened child.

Azar awoke to find himself on the floor, his shirt now drenched in sweat.

"No more," he gasped. His mind had returned to its familiar sense. The mist had vanished.

"The spirits called him an Oklem," the See-er said, finishing the story. "The only thing that could challenge the darkness. They made me forget the ingredients, for it was said that the Oklem would live for only as long as it was required."

"So you forced that boy to drink the potion and then you've forgotten its ingredients?" Azar asked.

"It was a necessary sacrifice," the See-er said, his bland voice lacking any sympathy.

"Sounds like something a Pirate would say," Azar replied coldly, sitting up and facing the ancient creature, unable to find even an outline of any features, his hood blocking all light.

"Do not allow your mind to be engulfed by wild emotions," the See-er warned.

Azar stood up, massaging his neck from where he had landed on it.

"That vision was from centuries ago. The spirit said that for these ingredients from every Nation to act as one, they must be consumed by one. How many others have there been before me, and where are they?" Azar asked.

"Three have lived before your time. Each arriving at a time when their blood was needed in one way or another. Each one unique. You have certainly not strayed from that factor. You have a doppelganger, which makes you part supernatural. Yet you carry the blood of an Oklem, a creature built off purity and unity. Maybe it is finally time that you will be the resolution nature has desired for so many years," the See-er concluded.

"I guess the challenge is finding out what that resolution is," Azar concluded.

"Each Oklem in the past has had a different reason to be here. You must remember that there will be a time when you are exactly what is needed."

Azar remembered the voice he had heard in the Fortune Caves:

The moment where you are so frightened is the moment when courage will lead the right people to the truth.

"I have one more question, but I don't know if you will answer it."

"There is only one way to find out," came a croaky response. Azar could feel the See-er was tired and weary, but he needed an answer before he stepped foot outside.

"Can the Peacekeepers be trusted? Should I tell them that Orven is alive?"

A long silence followed, almost to the point that Azar thought the See-er had fallen asleep. Eventually a long sigh led to a response.

"You are correct, I cannot answer that. The Peacekeepers of the Nations are very powerful beings. They are sworn to protect, facing the most painful and everlasting purgatory if they break their code against nature. But power and greed can so easily influence even the strongest of minds, so I have always asked myself that if they are as intelligent and pure as the people are told they are, why do they end up going to war against the same enemy once a century?" Azar stopped moving, taking in that strange yet surprisingly true statement. The Pirates always managed to spring a large attack. Why hadn't the Nations permanently removed the threat? He wasn't a fighter or a diplomat, but he was an Oklem, and he was going to start delving into the world where every time he neared an answer, he met a road block.

"Thank you, See-er. For everything. I need to go and prepare for a dinner," he said, turning towards the entrance.

"Then go my boy, and never reject your emotions, for they are what makes you a true Oklem." Azar bowed his head and made his way out of the hut, a new-found motivation keeping his mind focused. No more distractions.

Chapter 17

Emma knocked lightly on Peacekeeper Drand's door. She had quickly called Jake and informed him of the interrogation, and he was now on his way to join her, saying he had equally worrying news. Emma decided she would start things off, hoping Drand would come clean about what he knew of the Queen of the Pirates.

"Enter," came a woman's voice. Emma entered the private meeting room. She didn't hide her surprise to see Peacekeeper Serain sitting alone on the orange lounge, a twig engulfed in flames hovering slowly in place above the table. The Peacekeeper was in another one of her spectacular blazing dresses, and what looked like a vine was stretched out from her back, brushing her smoking hair. What was strange, Emma thought, was that for a brief moment, a similar expression of surprise flashed across the Peacekeeper's face.

"Peacekeeper Serain, I thought you had returned to the Fire Nation," Emma said.

"Tomorrow, my dear," Serain replied, avoiding eye contact. "With the chaos that has taken place today, I think it is a safer choice to wait for our security to clear any lingering threat. What brings you unsummoned to these private quarters?"

"I have just interrogated Robert Johnson about the attack on Mintor's bank. I have some very concerning news," Emma replied, still standing just within the doorway. She had entered this room many times, yet somehow she felt like she was violating Drand's privacy without him being present.

As if he heard her thoughts, Peacekeeper Drand emerged from his room, a clipboard in his hands and a very grim look on his face. He was wearing a black robe with a single diamond on his left shoulder, the symbol of the Mortal Nation on the right. Emma's stomach turned. This outfit was only worn on days where terror had taken the lives of innocent people. She certainly hadn't expected to see it so soon after the war. Two maids quickly made their way out, heads down, holding Drand's casual robes, presumably to wash.

"Emma Flare? I do not recall requesting you," Drand said, indicating for her to sit on any of the four lounges present. Emma cautiously made her way across the room, sitting on the blue lounge. "I know all attention is directed towards the bank attack, but I have learnt something in which I must seek your knowledge on," Emma said, though he looked as if he was about to leave. "Are you planning to make a public speech?"

"He cannot make an appearance until he has more facts," Serain answered. Emma could see she was unusually tense, like she had been caught off guard. Had she? Drand began pacing around the room.

"It's true," he said, "the people of Mintor will expect me to have a plan of action when I speak to them, so I have decided to wait until tomorrow, as we will have more information from the crime scene. I am wearing this out of respect to those we lost today."

"I wasn't aware of any civilian deaths. That's devastating," Emma said.

"You said you had concerning news?" Serain asked.

"Yes," Emma replied, although for a moment her mind flashed back to the references of betrayal she had heard from both the Pirate she engaged and Robert Johnson. She shook her head, realising she was talking to Peacekeepers. Proud leaders of their respective Nations.

"Johnson said he was brought into the scene as a delivery driver, but once his identity was exposed, he decided to leave a mark on our Nation," Emma explained. "Long story short, he worked with Jessani, and they have apparently released someone called the "Queen of the Pirates."

Immediately the Peacekeeper's looked at each other, making no attempt to hide their dismay. "I'm guessing this means that there is someone who holds this title," Emma observed.

"She was immobilised long ago, before Orven was sent away to the Supernatural Universe," Drand explained. "Her absence led us to believe that she had died. She has made no appearance in the last ten years since Orven returned."

Just then the door opened and a woman came in dressed in a suit.

"Jake Flare has arrived," she informed the room.

"Bring him in," Drand replied. The woman turned around and moments later Jake entered, quickly taking in the scene. He joined his sister on the blue lounge.

"Before you ask further questions, I think it best to leave this Pirate queen issue to Drand and I,' Serain commented, looking at the siblings.

"Do we have a name? A description? Johnson was pretty confident that she is here in Mintor. Maybe we can stop her from escaping," Emma suggested.

"Absolutely not! You would get yourself killed if you faced her," Serain warned rather aggressively. "As well as that, she would most certainly have left the moment she was free."

"I have to agree with Serain on this matter," Drand said, "we have to deal with this new information personally. As soon as I have a plan, I shall inform you."

Emma was not impressed. This secrecy was very strange coming from Drand. She did not like to be left in the dark. She turned to her brother.

"What news do you have? Is Azar alright?" she asked.

"Well. I don't know," Jake replied.

Emma raised an eyebrow at him. He continued.

"I went to see him, instead I got his doppelganger. I checked his work, he hasn't shown up. Azar is missing."

Emma dropped her head, and Peacekeeper Drand took a slow, deep breath.

"Where could he have gone?" Serain asked, clenching her fist and immediately extinguishing the flaming twig. It dropped harmlessly onto the table. Nobody could answer Serain's question.

"Did Lux know where he is?" Emma asked Jake.

"If he did he certainly didn't act like it. I don't understand. Azar wouldn't have run away," Jake said, failing to hide his concern from Emma.

"Unless he was offered something he couldn't refuse," Drand said slowly. Emma started to follow Drand's train of thought.

"His parents," Jake answered first.

"That could mean he is no longer here in the Mortal Nation," Serain pointed out.

"We need to confirm this. Emma and Jake, your top priority is to find Azar and make sure he is safe," Drand ordered. Emma was going to bring up the fact that she was personally targeted whilst she had been heading to the Bank, meaning someone had been following her. But gut instinct deterred her, so she rose with Jake and followed him out of Drand's quarters and into the hallways. They moved away from nearby security and staff, huddling together along a wall. "You were going to say something back there—why didn't you?" Jake asked.

"No I wasn't," Emma replied hastily.

"Emma, we're twins. You've figured out things about me, and I have about you. I know you withheld a detail. What are you hiding?" Jake pressed, leaning against the wall.

Emma took a moment to acknowledge what her brother had said. He was right. If she was starting to have doubts about who she could trust, Jake was the only person she could trust completely.

"I was targeted on the way to the bank," she said quietly. "I was attacked by a Pirate a fair way down the road from the bank, and there was no way he could have known me unless someone else was watching elsewhere and directed him to me. Then in the interrogation, Johnson admitted I was a threat and needed to be distracted. There is somebody working against us here Jake, but I have absolutely no idea who."

Jake pushed himself off the wall and placed his hands on his sister's shoulders.

"I will not let anyone harm you," he said, looking into her eyes, then he embraced her. Emma held him close, and for a moment they said nothing. Jake took a step back.

"I need to go and investigate the bank," Emma said. "If Jessani wanted to keep me away from there, I'm hoping I will find something of use. What are you going to do?" she asked her brother. "I am going to find Azar," Jake replied with a determined look in his eyes.

"Don't get yourself hurt," Emma warned. As Jake headed towards the main entrance of the palace, Emma went down a corridor which connected to the senate. She had never taken an interest in politics as her primary duty was to prevent any threat to the Peacekeeper, a threat which mostly came from the Pirates in Skull. She hardly knew who Azar's parents were before they became suspects. Just as she was about to reach the back courtyard where she had a personal parking spot for her bike, she heard a commotion before two large brass doors burst open. Journalists with cameras were racing backwards, all eyes on a woman who stepped through the doorway with tall black heels. She wore a purple dress which stretched out across the red carpets, and half her head was shaved, the other half a dark brown, curling down to her shoulder. On her right cheek was a large scar. Emma had never seen the woman before, so she pulled aside a passing security officer.

"Who is that?" she asked.

"That is Lisa Sparrow. She is mayor of a small town in the Fire Nation," he replied.

"What is she here for?" Emma asked. It was very strange that someone like this woman would be summoned to the Mortal Nation. The security officer raised his shoulders.

"All I know is she was summoned by the Peacekeepers, for what I have no idea."

The officer walked away as Emma took one last look at the newcomer. Drand had not mentioned this woman, either. Why was she suddenly being left out of the loop? What did the Peacekeeper's need with her? A sudden whim of doubt allowed a dark thought to creep into her mind. Yet she wondered if somehow that woman had a connection or even was the Queen of the Pirates, and the Peacekeepers were helping her. She shook her head in surprise. Where had that idea even come from? She needed to trust Peacekeeper Drand, and she needed to find the answers herself. Starting with the bank.

Chapter 18

Emma ducked under the rope taping off public access to the bank, placing her investigator's badge into the back pocket of her pants as she passed the officers. It had been a while since she had investigated an active crime scene as large as this. She pulled out her phone to take pictures. There was a lot of damage to the stairs, and a few areas were covered in dried stains of blood from the battle with the Pirates.

"Fast and unstructured can sometimes be effective," she observed out loud. "It can also leave clues."

She ascended the stairs and entered the bank. She needed to track where the Pirates were headed. Tellers, which would usually have a line of customers waiting to be served, were silent along one wall. A tall and open ceiling meant the air was much cooler, even out of the wind.

High columns were spaced out along the sides of the main path. To the right was a small cafe, where staff were repairing tables and chairs from the attack. A police officer emerged from a side room, a notepad in his hand.

"Can I help you?" he asked. Emma pulled out her badge once again, displaying the sign of the Mortal Nation. She had always thought it was very basic, simply a splash of water. Yet water was vital for the survival of mortals.

"Depends on how much you know. I'm Inspector Flare, private investigator for Peacekeeper Drand."

The officer seemed unimpressed.

"I'm Officer Short. Hopefully you are not as obnoxious as your partner."

"Partner?" Emma asked with a frown.

"He came in not more than five minutes ago. Do you have anything in particular you are looking for?" Short inquired.

"Motivations," Emma replied, although her mind began to wonder who else was in the building. Was it the one that was targeting her?

"Initially my officers assumed they were looking for the safe, which is down that corridor over there," Short said, pointing to the left.

"Assumed? Meaning they were incorrect?" Emma probed.

"We do not yet have confirmation. Whilst the safe is that way, the Pirates made their way to that corridor on the right. It's possible they were just lost, but given these thugs should be scrambling to the shadows of the universe since they lost the war, I think there was something here that they *needed*."

"For an initial report, that is a very thorough investigation which should be commended," Emma noted. She turned her head to the corridor on the right.

"What is in that direction?" she asked.

"Private safety boxes and vaults, managers offices, storage rooms. Not much wealth," Short answered.

"Thank you, Officer Short. If I have any more questions I will be sure to find you," Emma said. Short moved away as Emma headed down the right hand corridor, which narrowed as it went along. She passed countless offices until reaching two large doors with the sign *Personal Deposit boxes and Safes* written above it. The door was dented to the point of almost being snapped in half. It wasn't shut all the way either, as one of its hinges lay on the ground.

"There you are, partner," came an unfamiliar voice. Emma turned around and peered at the newcomer.

"Azar?" she asked softly, surprised.

"Guess again," the boy replied.

Emma's body tensed slightly as she acknowledged it was the first time she had seen Azar's doppelganger.

"Amazing," she whispered.

"I must say I am a little bit flustered that I can surprise the great Emma Flare," Lux said.

Emma regained her thoughts.

"Why have you come into the bank?" she asked suspiciously.

"The question is, why are you here? I'm sure a local crime scene is not something worth your time," Lux said, placing his hands on his hips. Emma's experience in dealing with difficult people, both criminals and witnesses, allowed her to take a different approach.

"Firstly, a Pirate attack is hardly a "local crime." I have just met you, but I don't feel threatened by you. So I shall change my train of thought. Like the Pirates, you wouldn't be here unless there was something in this place that could not be ignored. If you are not on the Pirates side, you shouldn't have a problem with me accompanying you to wherever you are headed," she concluded matter-of-factly, placing her hands on her hips as well.

"I like you," Lux said with a slight nod of his head. "Why else would I have waited for your arrival? I may be able to trick some officers into thinking I too am an investigator, but many have seen Azar's face. I'll let you do most of the talking."

"Or I could arrest you. Peacekeeper Drand would love to have a talk with the mysterious doppelganger," Emma said. She knew it was unlikely she'd actually be able to arrest Lux, if the stories about his strength and speed were true. But she wanted to assert her status between them.

"Peacekeeper Drand is so oblivious to what is going on, it would be a waste of all our time. Now can we please proceed?" Lux asked, pointing to the doors.

"Okay then," Emma said. It was true that she did not feel threatened by Lux, but she was highly cautious. What a bizarre turn of events. Keeping her guard up, she turned back to the door and opened it, revealing a square room lit by blueish white lights. A desk with a sign labelled *Security* sat in the left corner. Two more doors lined the wall opposite Emma, both needing a combination to enter.

A heavily armed officer stood up from the desk, looking at Emma as she approached.

"Officer Short said I should be expecting some investigators. What can I help you with?" he asked, his voice a very high pitch.

"We are trying to trace the steps the Pirates took when they attacked. Is this the room they entered?" Emma asked, indicating the room they were in with her hands.

"Yes, this is where those Pirates were arrested. Couldn't get past me. We've searched the room but found nothing, and neither the deposit nor the safe doors were damaged," he said. Emma frowned. Something didn't make sense, it sounded too simple.

"How did you fight them without sustaining any injuries?" Emma inquired.

The officer glanced down at his armour.

"Look at me. Tough as steel. Needless to say their confidence ran short once they barrelled through the door."

Emma was not convinced. Out of the corner of her eye, she saw Lux make his way to the *Safes* door. He ran his fingers along the border, and then pushed on it with a finger. It opened slightly. No alarm sounded.

"These doors weren't damaged," Lux said slowly, "because you let someone in."

Emma spun around as she saw the officer pull out a canon pistol. Her golden whip uncurled off her wrist, then she flung it at the officer's hand. The pistol was shattered in an electrifying display. Emma was astonished. The pistol was a weapon made only for the Mortal Nation's military and nobody else.

An equally surprised expression flashed across the officer's face. That was all he managed to do before Lux had darted across the room as fast as lightning, grabbed him and smashed his head against the wall. Emma gaped at the crumbled body lying at the doppelganger's feet.

"He's not dead, relax," Lux said. "He wasn't a Pirate, just a corrupt officer. Love the whip by the way," he added. He then strutted his way through the *safes* doorway, a bewildered Emma close behind. The unusual duo travelled through what felt like a maze, some corridors and pathways ending with blank stone walls. Upon their forth dead end, Emma gave an exasperated sigh.

"Do you know what you are looking for?" she asked, starting to think even Lux had not anticipated this scenario. Lux looked up, his eyes unfocused. He was in deep thought, Emma saw. Lux turned from the blank wall, going back to the corridor. Looking to his right, he gave a small triumphant cheer.

Emma followed him to a door labelled *Miring Seethe*.

"What am I missing, Lux?" Emma asked irritably.

"You wouldn't believe me if I told you. This is the safe the Pirates were after," Lux said.

What was he not telling Emma?

"Are any Pirates still in there?" she inquired. It was possible that the traitorous officer had been delaying Emma to allow whoever he had let inside more time to find what they were looking for. The doppelganger cocked his head slightly, listening. He shook his head.

"I cannot hear anything. But be cautious. I'd hate for our first adventure together to be our last." He took a step back then thrust himself at the door, sending it crashing to the ground. The noise echoed heavily off the stone walls, startling Emma, who then looked at Lux with a raised eyebrow.

"Oh I'm sorry, did you have a key?" he asked.

Emma shoved past Lux, making sure she entered first in order to hide the slightest smile creeping up the corner of her mouth. Lights immediately flickered on.

"This is huge," Emma whispered. Cupboards, desks, wardrobes and many more bits of furniture lined the stone pathway, stacked on top of each other. It was more like a storage facility than a safe.

"Why would anybody use such a large safe to dump furniture in?" she asked nobody in particular.

"To ensure anyone nosey enough to find this place would ask that very question and leave, uninterested," Lux replied.

They went deeper into the safe. It looked like years and years of possessions had been collected. But why? And by whom? They eventually reached the end of the safe. The light barely reached them as a large shipping container sat there, stretching across most of the room.

"What on earth is this doing here?" Emma asked. Nothing was making sense, which in a bizarre way did make sense. There must be something hidden in here, she thought.

Emma pulled out her phone, turning the torch on. Her eyes were drawn to a bunch of scribbled notes lying under an old wooden chair on the ground. Upon reading the first page, she saw it was dated back to the late nineteenth century. The second page had a title: *Freedom.* She grabbed the papers and stood up. In her amazement and intrigue, her foot accidentally kicked something else on the ground. She paused, looking down. It was a large black ring with a grey centre.

"Um, Lux?" she asked, looking for the doppelganger. She tucked the papers into her pocket as Lux appeared.

"A used portal," he said, crouching down to look at it.

"What do you mean "used"? Portals vanish after use, otherwise the Nations would be littered with these," Emma replied, pointing to it.

"Portals made today are temporary and disappear. But everything has an origin," Lux explained, outlining the shape of the portal with his fingers. "This is from the very early twentieth century at the latest."

Emma began to understand what Lux was saying.

"I have read many stories about portals," she said, "none of which have mentioned the term "used portals". I have read in some books that there once was something called a one-way portal. An entrance or exit-only one." Lux stood up, turning to her.

"Well, you were reading facts. This is an exit portal. Because of their physical structure, they don't vanish. It simply waits for its one use then is laid to rest as it is now. Now to our problem. Somebody portalled out of here."

Emma put a hand to her head and started walking back and forth.

"Why was it left here for so long? What was it put here for?"

"Or for whom?" Lux added.

"Nobody in that attack could have known it was here and trusted they could access it as an escape route unless…she stopped, turning to the large container. It was far too big to have been brought into the safe.

"Unless they came here to get somebody. Somebody that has been here for a while. A long while," she finished.

"Very impressive," Lux commented. Emma approached the container.

"This container could only have gotten here through a portal. This building was built centuries ago, meaning before or during its construction, anyone could have snuck in and portalled it here," Emma continued, sizing up the container with her hands. She wouldn't admit it out loud, but this was her favourite part about being an investigator. The part where you put together a theory and then prove it.

"I have two theories, one far more realistic than the other," she said. "Either a Pirate took something from the bank and used this portal to escape the attack. Or they came here to free somebody who has been in this safe from at least the late nineteenth century." Lux made his way over to the crate.

"It's actually a bit of both those theories. A Pirate used the portal to escape, but it wasn't something they took with them, rather *someone*."

Emma came up next to him. Lux ran his hands along the steel container. His fingers stopped at what appeared to be a random point of the crate. He pushed in, and a white handle pushed out. "Ladies first," he said, stepping back.

Emma grabbed the handle and pulled. The crate door opened outwards, creaking as it went. A long wooden box sat within. On its side was the symbol of Skull. It was a red skull with a black circle around it. Not much effort was put into it, but Pirates weren't exactly the smartest ones around, Emma thought.

"It looks like a coffin," she said.

"It does but it isn't," Lux replied. "It's a perpetuate container. If used with the correct ingredients, it can preserve one's body. They only make them in the Earth Nation."

"I guess that would mean somebody was in here. A Pirate," Emma said, looking at the Skull emblem again.

"Shall we open it?" Lux asked.

"I think I'd have nightmares wondering what was in it if we didn't," Emma replied.

Together they grabbed the lid and lifted it slowly. They peered in. It was empty. Emma glanced across at Lux, and saw a look of dismay but not surprise on his face.

"This is the real reason why you came to the bank, isn't it," she said. "You came to see if whoever was in here was free. And if I'm not mistaken, Robert Johnson informed me that he had assisted in the return of an apparent 'Queen of the Pirates'. Is that who was in this container?" Lux bowed his head. He has had some past history with this Queen, Emma concluded. He turned to her.

"Her name is Lara Sokolov. I'd make it a mission to avoid contact with her at all costs. One small problem with that is I think it is possible that Azar is with her," he said, shutting the perpetual container lid.

"How?" Emma demanded, following suit and shutting the shipping container door. She couldn't think of any reason linking this Queen and Azar together. Lux put his hands behind his back and began pacing.

"Every year, followers and leaders of the Pirates have gathered at a mansion in the wilderness of the Trail of Tales. Orven would generally host a meeting, where he would bark out his new orders. Now keep in mind this started centuries ago when Orven was first trying to open the Supernatural portal. When he returned ten years ago, he still managed to host this event until he died," the doppelganger explained.

"And the Peacekeepers have no idea about this?" Emma asked in disbelief.

"Oh they do," Lux replied. Emma's skin crawled.

Another betrayal. She began to feel numb in the pit of her stomach. The belief was that Peacekeepers were bound by nature to serve their respective Nations, they could not be traitors. Yet she was beginning to lose confidence in that belief.

"You think Azar is at this dinner?" she asked. It would explain his absence.

"King Orven might be dead, but his Queen will most certainly want to meet the mortal doppelganger," Lux said. Suddenly his presence shifted, his body losing the confidence he so easily expressed.

"Lux maybe you can clarify something for me," Emma said. "I get that Azar is an Oklem, and they have been important in the past. But the war is over. Why does Peacekeeper Drand consider it to be so pivotal to keep Azar safe?"

Lux paused, his eyes looking at the ceiling, as if he was carefully choosing his next words.

"I would be asking that very question had I not been there when Orven created his own portal to return from the Supernatural Universe ten years ago," he said. "The thing is, Orven could not have returned without the help of someone. Someone whose allegiances are unknown."

"Who was it?" Emma asked.

"I cannot answer that. All I can say is that their involvement with Azar has Drand worried. But as we've discussed, the Peacekeeper's have their own secrets. I've been around for centuries and still don't know who to trust."

Emma thought over what Lux was saying, trying to figure out who was putting Azar's life in danger.

"I suppose," Lux went on, "we need to remember that nature chose Azar to be an Oklem, so there must be a reason why. Only he can figure it out, we just need to keep him alive."

"You mean there is an unknown threat and the only person who can figure it out is not only missing, but a boy who's so against the whole war and supernatural elements of our world?" Emma summarised.

"Correct," Lux said. Emma was slightly surprised at how much care Lux appeared to have for Azar's safety. Was it just because of a possible threat from the Pirates?

"I don't mean to engage in personal affairs," Lux said, breaking Emma's train of thought, "but I want to take your brother with me to the Trail of Tales. We both know they have an interest in each other, Jake's more than Azar's, but I think Azar might need to see someone he naturally trusts."

Was Lux asking permission? The doppelganger who has been alive for centuries doing whatever he wanted, was asking for something?

"I'm not in charge of my brother," Emma answered, "if he agrees to go, then take him. I have a lot to deal with here."

Lux nodded his head in understanding. Then his body snapped up straight, his head inclined to the left.

"Our officer friend is waking up," he said. He zipped away with incredible speed.

Emma looked around the room. It was almost incomprehensible that she was trusting Lux, yet she did. She pushed the containers handle back into the steel wall and was about to continue exploring when she smelt something. Oil. Suddenly flames shot out from unnoticed nozzles on the back wall.

"Dammit!" she exclaimed.

The flames began spreading, revealing a coating of oil along the stone. The place ignited rapidly. Devastation swept over Emma. So much evidence was about to be destroyed, perhaps crucial answers, but the flames were moving too quickly for her to do anything. She realised the oil covered the walls all the way to the door, obviously to cut off anyone escaping. Furniture began to set alight as Emma took off.

She didn't get far before she was tackled. She turned over as she fell and stared straight into the face of a creature with flaming orange eyes. It was twice her size with a fur coat. The impact from landing had temporarily winded her, she could also feel a pain in her left wrist, but the weight of the creature pinned her down. It had a blazing red iron in its hand, and with a blood curdling screech, brought it down towards her. Using her entire body, Emma rolled herself to the right, sending her attacker toppling to the ground, the iron missing her face by centimetres. She leapt up, her whip snaking out. The flames on the wall were now past her, meaning she had little time to engage in combat. She slashed the creature as it stood back up, halving it. Then she saw another one leaping from cupboard to cupboard above. She sprinted for the door, desperate to make it out.

She saw a small wooden chair ahead, and a quick glance over her shoulder showed the creature was almost upon her. As she raced past, she grabbed the chair, spun on her heel and swung hard. It collided with the creature, who had lunged at her, sending it spiralling into the flames. Emma cleared the door and slammed it shut, just as the fire surged forward.

Taking a few deep breaths, she began to feel her body ache from the hard landing, but a particularly stinging pain on her left wrist brought reflex tears to her eyes. She lifted her sleeve away and saw a small gash bleeding. It must have been from the iron. Emma then remembered the papers she had put in her pocket. Reaching back, she sighed with relief. They were still there. Her head was spinning as she slowly made her way back through the maze of corridors. There was so much to worry about. How had those Supernatural creatures gotten into the safe? Did Lux know about them? Who else had been trapped inside? She began to feel dizzy. Her wrist was now feeling like it was burning, and her vision began to blur. As she got to the security room, she saw two officers handcuffing the crooked bank guard. Lux was nowhere to be seen.

"Ah Investigator Flare, there you are," Officer Short said, entering the room. He paused. "You're hurt?"

Emma heard no more. Everything went black.

Chapter 19

The past three days had been paradise. Azar was left alone to explore Lisarow, visiting the busy marketplace. He'd also gone for a swim at the beach, from where the heat of the sun combined crystal-clear waters with blazing white sand. He had just visited the Mortal Nation complex, where he bought a black formal suit from a tailor for the dinner his mother had told him to attend. He opened the door to his inn and placed the bags on his mattress. Suddenly he saw movement in the doorway to the small bathroom, and he looked up to see Brett, who was standing in nothing but a towel.

Tension immediately flared between them. Azar had enjoyed being alone.

"You've been busy," Brett observed, his usually messy hair brushed back. He was still wet, meaning he had just emerged from the shower.

"I've been happy. I'm guessing you've spent the last few days plotting the events of tonight's dinner with my mother," Azar said.

"My possessions are still here," Brett said, neither confirming nor denying Azar's allegation. "Can we have a mature conversation please?"

"I need to get ready so what do you have to say?" Azar replied, taking his suit out of the bag. He could feel a slight hesitation to his stubbornness from within his heart, but he pushed away the uncertainty. Brett walked over to his bed, which had been untouched for days, sitting on its edge. "Do you not understand that everything I have done in my life was to protect you? That even when your parents left, I was there every day. I was hoping we'd be in a much more romantic location than we are now, but I need to tell you that I love you, Azar."

Azar felt gooseflesh ripple across his body, but this time there was no emotional attachment to it. He let out a long sigh before turning to Brett.

"I have moved on. It took a while, but it's done. You know it too. Maybe you're just afraid because you can no longer have a hold on me. There was passion between us but no *love*. You're five years older than me, we just didn't have that connection. I know who I am now, so you don't need to be in my life anymore."

Azar saw genuine hurt flash across Brett's face, yet he didn't care. What Brett had done was unforgivable, something that couldn't be undone. There was only one thing left that Azar wanted to know. The ultimate answer that is behind everything that has happened.

"How did you do it? How did you make me an Oklem and then manage to extract the blood and send it to Orven?"

Brett sat in silence for a long while. Eventually Azar gave up, grabbed his suit and went into the bathroom. Once changed, he emerged to see Brett still on his bed. The Oklem made his way over to a large mirror on the wall, adjusting his bow tie. Then Brett's voice broke the silence.

"I slipped Oklem blood into your milkshake when we went out for my birthday three weeks ago," he answered. Azar thought back to that night. He could not recall anything unusual happening.

"If you already had Oklem blood with you, you could have just sent that to Orven. You didn't have to make me one," Azar said.

"Nature needed a new Oklem," Brett said. "Your parents wanted you to become one, but even if they didn't, you were always destined to become one. There are no accidents when it comes to being an Oklem. When we returned home after we had our milkshakes, and after we had a pretty sensational session in bed, I cut your right arm "accidentally." It bled pretty quickly. I used my hand to cup the blood as we went into the bathroom to wash and cover it. When you were washing it, I went to my kitchen and let the little pool of blood drip into a sealable test tube. That was all I needed. A small drop is all anyone needs to create a personalised portal."

Azar stood in astonishment at what he was hearing. His blood had been used to create the portal that Orven escaped through. He was in part responsible for keeping Orven alive. He was speechless, looking through the mirror as tears began to slide down Brett's face.

"I'm so sorry, Azar," Brett said quietly, "you never have to forgive me, but I am sorry. You are a beautiful person. Don't shut your love out because of me, let that love be your defining trait." Azar had a slight suspicion that Brett was not just talking about relationships, but he didn't think about it too much. Never had such a genuine sentence left that boy's mouth. Azar simply did not know what to say next. All his emotions were trying to tear through his numb body. Fortunately, he didn't have to speak.

"What a lovely sentiment," came an all-too-familiar voice as someone suddenly barged through the front door. Azar turned around in bewilderment, staring at his doppelganger.

"Lux?"

"Aren't we looking delicious," Lux replied, looking at Azar in his suit. Lux had such a fierce attitude and confidence that Azar was admittedly curious about. He could never imagine himself to behave like his doppelganger, but sometimes he felt like he could manage things better if he had the same wit and sass. Lux looked around the room, his eyes resting on Brett, who was still in a towel.

"Oh I'm sorry, did we interrupt a private show?" he asked in amusement.

"We?" Azar asked. Nobody else had come in the door.

"He'll be here shortly. I'm glad you're dressed and ready to go, we have a dinner to attend," Lux said, clasping his hands.

Azar noticed Brett looking cautiously at Lux, as if he was anticipating to get hurt. Did they know each other? A slight frown came across Lux's face.

"Did I accidentally step on the pause button? We need to go," Lux said, pointing to the door, then he went back outside. Brett stood up, went to the small wooden wardrobe to get his suit, and stepped into the bathroom. All of Azar's thoughts about being an Oklem temporarily left his mind as he latched onto the distraction that was the upcoming dinner. He followed Lux outside, where the sun had set and the stars were out.

"What do you know about this dinner?" he asked his doppelganger.

"Only that it's not your usual turn up, eat, have a few lame speeches, go home type of event," Lux replied. Then he moved closer to Azar and lowered his voice. "Remember that this event has always been hosted by Orven. He may not be here anymore, but everyone you see despises the Nations and Peacekeepers. Lisarow is a safe city, but outside it's golden walls, anything can happen."

"Where will you be?" Azar asked.

"I'll be staying out of the spotlight," Lux said, turning to go.

"Wait. I want the truth. Why are you really protecting me? How else could you have known I was here? If I'm in so much danger why not just get me back home to the Mortal Nation?" Azar said, crossing his arms stubbornly. Lux spread his arms.

"I'd love nothing more than to do that, but it's too late to leave. From what I've managed to find out, the Pirates would most definitely be making sure you attend. Now your escort is approaching. For your sake I'd try and talk to him, at least. I'll see you later on," Lux said. Once again Lux knew far more than he was letting on. Who was Azar's escort? The Oklem turned around and watched as somebody rounded the corner from a hut across the pathway, and Azar's heart skipped a beat. Jake was wearing a dark blue suit, his hair combed back, his face clean shaven. He stopped at the base of the staircase. Azar hadn't seen Jake since the Brinx Club. He had learnt so much since then, but realised he still didn't know who exactly Jake was. After a long silence, Jake was the first to speak.

"The last time we saw each other, you had almost died because I lied to you. I am hoping to clear the air between us and start again," he said, looking at the ground.

Azar was reminded of the first time he had seen Jake, on the hill, arriving at just the right time when things were starting to fall apart. There was something about him that made Azar feel like he needed Jake's company.

"Well, if we survive tonight, I'd like that too," he replied slowly, pushing himself to raise his eyes and meet Jake's quick glance.

Just then Brett came out of the inn, closing the door behind him. An awkward silence followed. "Let's go," Brett eventually said, stepping down onto the cobblestone path. As Brett passed Azar, the Oklem got a whiff of his cologne, one that had on many occasions sent butterflies through his stomach. But for the first time, Azar was not aroused. He felt nothing but fear for what the night held. *The moment where you are so frightened is the moment when courage will lead you to the truth.* The words of the See-er came back to him now, and as he walked alongside Jake, it gave him strength.

Chapter 20

1627: The Grand Hall, Trail of Tales

Jessani entered the grand foyer, handing her broad-brimmed hat with plumes to an awaiting servant. Candles hung from the walls, and a large fireplace burned, keeping the air warm for the guests. She was wearing an open high-necked chemise, red sleeves tied on with ribbon points, her dark, curly hair falling past her shoulders. As she adjusted her white gloves, she peered into the dining hall through large open brass doors. Dozens of round tables were positioned around the room. Another waiter came over to her, younger, carrying a tray.

"Champagne, my lady?" he asked in a deep tone.

"Sparkling wine?" Jessani commented in a pleasant surprise, looking at the glasses on offer. "Very new, and very delicious," the waiter said with a wink.

"I do hope you are not being impertinent and are talking about the wine," Jessani warned, though she followed it with a wink of her own.

"Of course," he replied.

"Well, here's to new discoveries," Jessani said, taking a glass and holding it up. The waiter bowed his head and moved on. Jessani sighed, watching the boy make his way through the new arrivals. Not looking where she was going, Jessani turned to enter the dining room when she bumped into someone.

"Oh my, I'm so sorry!" she exclaimed, holding a hand to her mouth.

"The fault is mine," the boy replied. He had thick brown hair which looked like it had been very roughly combed back. His piercing blue eyes lit up his face and ignited a sense of desire within Jessani. She cleared her throat.

"Are you here for the ceremony?" she asked, blinking rapidly. It was an unfortunate habit when she was humiliated.

"Is there any other reason?" he asked slyly.

"I would certainly hope not," she giggled. "My name is Jessani Sway."

"Marvin," he replied, kissing Jessani's outstretched hand.

As she was about to ask for his last name, a ringing bell cut through the chatter, and Jessani realised the ceremony was about to begin.

"I look forward to continuing our conversation later," she said to the mysterious boy, rushing into the dining hall. She made her way to the tables, sitting in front of the podium. Once everyone was seated, a tall man made his way to the front of the podium. Cheers and applause erupted. He was wearing a dark cloak. His grey hair was slicked back, and his face was scarred. It was Orven, leader of the Pirates. He raised his arms to silence the room, before grinning.

"Welcome, ladies, gentlemen, supernatural beings, to a night that will be remembered for a very long time. Tonight we shall bring forth the Tychun, dark creatures that will ensure the end of the Peacekeepers rule, and the start of a new era shall arise!"

Applause broke out again from the audience. Orven had long demanded a change to the leadership of the Nations, believing the Peacekeepers had always put themselves first, and paid very little attention to Skull. There were many guests from all four Nations, plus Pirates from Skull. A few members from the Supernatural Universe were in attendance also, though they presented themselves as mortals for the occasion. As this was the most important night, Orven had demanded that everyone travel the same way as a Mortal would, in order to erase any suspicions. Supernatural beings could portal to Skull before changing their appearance, one slight advantage of the Peacekeepers lacking intervention with the Pirates homeland. However the Tychun were specifically bound by the Peacekeeper's magic as they were deemed too dangerous, meaning no portal could let them in. But tonight, Orven believed he had found a way. As silence fell across the room once more, Orven continued.

"We now welcome our three other very special guests, who will be making this historical change possible, to come forward. Lara Sokolov, long serving member of our cause, dedicated Pirate and enemy of the Peacekeepers."

Lara walked on stage to a loud ring of applause. She was a masculine woman who had purple hair which stretched down to her knees. She smiled warmly, embraced Orven and sat at one of the seats provided on stage.

"Richard Balkins, one of the supernatural leaders who will sacrifice his life to open the path," Orven announced. An even louder round of applause erupted as Richard appeared. He had just one eye in the centre of his head, and green skin. Jessani wasn't familiar with what he was, the closest link she could make was some sort of cyclops. Just then she saw movement to her left. Turning, she spotted Marvin standing in a doorway. He was looking directly at her, signalling with his head for her to join him. The crowd were on their feet as Richard shook hands with Orven. Using this as a distraction, Jessani quickly weaved her way through the tables and crowd and out the door as Orven announced the third and final helper.

Chapter 21

Azar, Brett, and Jake shared a horse-drawn carriage in silence as they wound their way through the hills away from Lisarow. The distinctive lack of automobiles allowed the chirping of the birds and the whistles of the wind to vibrate through the trees and over the grassy hills. The moon was so bright it made the Trail of Tales look like a dream land. It felt magical, which in turn made Azar feel like he was in some way disconnected from the "real world." But at the same time it allowed him to feel independent and reflective, experiences that reminded him of being on the hill outside of Mintor. Despite never imagining himself to live in Lisarow, he could understand how others would choose a life of simplicity and peace. His mind was relaxed. It was now that he realised he could hear something, whispers. He could feel an energy pulling him within, the same energy he felt in the Fortune Caves, and with the See-er. For a moment he was caught in between reality and a blur, and saw a faint outline of the same ice caves.

He was so deep in thought he hadn't noticed the carriage stop. Brett snapped his fingers across Azar's face, bringing him back to reality, immediately extinguishing the subconscious feeling. "Feel free to open the door," Brett said, pointing to the handle. Azar shook himself from his daze, grabbed the handle and pushed outwards. A wide red carpet stretched up a long driveway, surrounded by pebbles. Two black iron fences bordered the sea of red, with soft golden lights running along the top of them. In the distance Azar could see a white mansion.

Guests flooded the pathway, the women in dazzling woven dresses with various patterns and diamonds, the men in suits. The other boys followed Azar out of the carriage. A gentle breeze was all that prevented the walk up the carpet from becoming a muggy trek. As they approached the main courtyard, Azar realised that many guests looked different to the Mortal Nation citizens. Some glowed a fierce red, others a cold blue, some a lush green.

"You will find that there are far more visitors from the other Nations than you see in Mintor, and that here in the Trail of Tales they are more connected to their original Nation, hence their glowing skins," Brett explained, reading Azar's expression. Azar said nothing, although he did find the concept fascinating. He was pleased that Jake was there, and Azar really wanted to talk to him, but having Brett with them made any real discussion awkward.

Just then a person stepped out from behind a group of women talking, halting Azar.

"I'm so glad you could make it," Jordan said, dusting his suit down with his hands, his orange hair messy.

Azar straightened his back.

"I couldn't miss this opportunity," he said. "I'd have hated for you to have gone to so much trouble getting me here just to have me not show up."

Azar pushed past and made his way up a large staircase on his own. People were turning their heads, murmuring to each other as he passed by. He slowly stepped through the doorway and into the grand foyer. The golden theme continued with a large chandelier hanging from the ceiling. A fireplace on the left-hand side was the only object on the polished marble floor, which led into a vast rectangular room. Azar entered and saw tables covering almost every inch of the room. Many of the guests had taken their seats, champagne filled glasses in their hands. Azar noticed a large podium at the end of the hall, where four chairs sat with cushions. He walked along the border of the room, hoping not to gain too much attention.

"Oh how long it has been since I have seen that face," came a soft voice. Azar turned to see a middle aged woman standing near a large, blue window, a half filled glass of wine in her hand. Her thick brown hair was tied in a neat bun.

"Of course you're the newest doppelganger," she added hastily. Immediately Azar raised his guard.

"How do you know my doppelganger?" he asked casually. He was doing his best not to sound too surprised, knowing it would reveal he knew very little about what was taking place.

"I remember when I first met him, in this very room. Saturday the twentieth of March, sixteen twenty-seven," came the reply

"The seventeenth century?" he asked in disbelief. The woman nodded.

"Yes, the night when the universe should have been ruled by Orven and the supernatural creatures," she said, her face darkening. Azar gaped at her as she took another sip.

"Right," he eventually stammered, cursing himself for the lack of conviction.

"It would have been perfect if your doppelganger hadn't ruined everything. But I suppose that is for another time. I must run along."

"I didn't catch your name," Azar said.

"Nor I, yours. It's not important dear," she said dismissively, disappearing out a door on the other side of the room.

Frowning, Azar went back to the foyer in search of Jake. A woman made her way through the entrance doors, her long black dress snaking across the floor, her silky hair blowing gently behind her. She was holding a small handbag in front of her, and soon spotted Azar standing alone by a wall.

"I'm surprised you had the balls to come here, Lux," Jessani said as she approached him. Azar tensed. Now that he knew who Jessani was, he suddenly felt a little more exposed. He noticed a slight flicker of sadness in her eyes as she spoke. He had to make it look like he knew what he was doing.

"Sorry to disappoint you again but I'm the boring doppelganger," he replied with a shrug.

"What a shame," she said, peering around the room.

"I've learnt a little bit more about you since we first met at the Brinx Club," Azar stated.

"You know only what others want you to know," Jessani replied, not hiding her disinterest in the conversation.

"I know you have a history with Lux," Azar said.

A passing waiter stopped as Jessani took a glass of red wine. She didn't reply to Azar's statement, so he continued.

"I suppose I should ask how Orven is?"

Jessani cocked her head slightly, and for a second Azar saw not so much surprise but curiosity flash across her face.

"Probably burning in hell," she replied, taking a sip. Azar's eyes narrowed. Was she lying? Surely she had to know Orven was alive. He decided he would not find anything more about the Pirates leader from Jessani, so he reverted back to his first topic.

"How did you first meet Lux?" he asked.

"I met him in this very foyer in sixteen-twenty seven. Only briefly, for Orven was introducing some very special guests," Jessani said, her gaze distant as she remembered the night.

A tap on Azar's shoulder made him jump. A Pirate stood there, his silver armour and sword an obvious give away.

"Your mother wishes to see you," he said in a gruff voice before walking away into the dining hall. It was time to see why his mum wanted her son to be here tonight, Azar thought. Jessani cleared her throat.

"Sending messengers? She must be busy, you don't want to keep her waiting," she said.

Azar stepped in front of Jessani as she made her way around him. With incredible strength and using only her left arm, she grabbed Azar's throat and pushed him up against the wall.

Azar immediately grasped her hand, trying to free himself, but his efforts were in vain.

"Do not ever challenge me again," she hissed. She released her grip.

"How have you survived for so many centuries? You aren't a supernatural creature," Azar stammered, coughing straight afterwards.

"The same way Orven did, the same way Lux has. You need to embrace the Supernatural Universe. There is endless magic over there."

"So you can cheat death?" he asked.

"Of course you can't,' Jessani snapped, running her hands down her dress, removing any creases. "Firstly you can never be immortal, part of life is death. Life however, is not limited to the span of a mortal being from one of the Nations. You can delay it, but as with everything, there is not a risk without a consequence."

"And what was your consequence?" Azar probed.

"Go and see your mother," Jessani said, striding into the dining hall. Azar looked for Jake or Brett, but couldn't see them anywhere. He turned to see the Pirate was waiting for him near a small door to his left. He was going alone. He hoped his mother wouldn't see how his hands were shaking.

Chapter 22

Azar followed the Pirate down a flight of stairs and through a cold, stone corridor. Candles set at uneven intervals created large shadows which danced across the walls. Azar could not hear any sounds from the event above. The clanking of the Pirates sword and a foul body odour was all he got. They eventually stopped outside a steel door. The Pirate opened it and signalled for Azar to go in. He did so, and was secretly relieved to be unaccompanied when the door was closed after him. More candles lit up the small room. Maree Geminus was standing by a chest of drawers in a purple dress. There was a coldness to her face as she looked at her son.

"Thank you for attending," she started, "it is sure to be a night to remember." Azar immediately got the feeling that he had walked into some form of ritual.

"I have no desire to be here in this room with you, mother. So please put me out of my misery and get things over with," Azar said, not moving from the doorway.

"I have accepted that our relationship has been tarnished, but that will be temporary, and I shall not allow it to disrupt our intentions for you."

"Speaking on behalf of dad again? I haven't even seen him yet," Azar pointed out, crossing his arms.

"You will see him tonight," Maree said, though Azar picked up the slightest hint of sorrow. "I am going to explain what is happening this evening. In Orven's absence, a new leader must be elected. Your father was initially going to run for the position, however there has been a change of plans. A true leader has made a return to our universe, and tonight, the Queen of the Pirates shall reclaim her throne." Queen of the Pirates? To Azar it sounded more like the storyline of a video game. Despite what his mother said, Azar wasn't surprised to hear his father had run for Orven's position. His parents' loyalty had well and truly been established. Maree made her way around the drawers. Azar decided to step further into the room, and as he did, he saw a black bowl was sitting on top of them.

"It doesn't matter who becomes your leader," he said. "The Peacekeepers will come here with vengeance. The big question is, why do you need me here for whatever this ceremony is?" Maree went to a small shelf protruding from one of the walls. She picked up a knife. Azar immediately tensed.

"The Peacekeepers are corrupt," Maree said, twirling the knife in her hand, inspecting it. "I want you here tonight because I do not want this queen to be crowned. I do not want the Pirates to be victorious. The other night on the beach, when I found out you are a doppelganger, I found a way to speed up my plans. You are mortal born with two supernatural counterparts, the doppelganger part, and now the Oklem part. An Oklem's blood can open any portal to anywhere, it cannot be restricted by the Peacekeepers or nature. It opens and closes at the command of the Oklem only."

"So you want my blood to open a portal?" Azar asked, trying to put all the pieces of this mystery together.

"A very special portal," Maree said. "The Supernatural Universe has been blocked for centuries, yet nobody ever seemed to put together that Orven returned ten years ago from there. Nobody realised that an Oklem is the reason why Orven and everyone else that was banished came back.

The Peacekeepers are ignorant. They have lost their touch with their Nations. The Pirates are senseless murderers. So that leaves one option for leadership. Supernatural leadership." Maree moved to the drawers and picked up the bowl in her other hand. Then she looked at Azar. "Mum, stop this is crazy," Azar commanded, raising his hands. What could he do? He couldn't fight, and despite what she had done, he could not hurt his own mother.

A sudden commotion from the other side of the door drew their attention. Azar hoped like hell it was Lux. He had been left pretty defenceless so far.

"No!" Maree cried out angrily. She hurried towards Azar, a psychotic look of panic on her face, her dress appearing to be floating behind her, the knife pointed towards her son.

There was a loud thud from outside. Azar turned to race back to the door. A second later, his mother's knife flew inches past his head, thrown with such force it impaled itself into the steel door. Azar froze in horror. As he turned back to his mother, he saw she was grasping another knife, smaller, but the steel door burst open, and somebody raced past Azar at the speed of light, knocking Maree off her feet. She fell back, hitting her head. Lux stood over her. He grabbed the knife she had dropped and prepared to drive it down into Maree's chest.

"No Lux, don't kill her!" Azar shouted. He raced forward and grabbed Lux's arm.

Suddenly, as if his entire consciousness had vanished, Azar's mind exploded, and a series of distorted visions consumed his mind. Just as what had happened with the See-er, he was no longer a physical presence, powerless to do anything but witness a scene unfolding.

"Mama! No!" came a cry of heartbreak and terror. The visions were so distorted, that for a moment Azar was back in his body and he fell to the ground, gripping his head with both hands.

"Arabella! Papa!"

Images of bodies strewn across a dusty kitchen floor flashed through Azar's mind. Then they vanished, and Azar was left gasping on the floor. He looked up to see Lux gaping in sheer astonishment. He dropped the knife.

"Lux was that…?" Azar couldn't finish. What had he witnessed? It was as if he had just seen visions of Lux's past.

"You need to leave, Azar. Now. Get Jake and go back to Mintor," Lux ordered. There was no opportunity for discussion in Lux's tone. He staggered towards the door, this time using none of his super speed abilities. "Your mother is alive, which is more than what she deserves. Leave her."

Azar looked at his mother's body. He hated everything she had done, but he could not let her die. Despite Lux's stern warning, he wasn't going home yet. After everything that had happened since the end of the war, he was going to attend the dinner. The Pirate who had escorted him down was dead, his body resting against the wall. Azar slowly dragged the body into the room, the armour adding more weight and making the move almost impossible. The steel door had an internal lock. Azar turned the lock and shut the door, disabling access from outside. He hoped his mother would stay passed out just long enough for him to see what was happening upstairs. Lux was nowhere to be seen as Azar made his way back up to the foyer.

Azar walked into the dining hall, scanning the room for Jake. A red curtain now hung behind the podium. Food platters lined the tables, and there was an energetic buzz of anticipation in the atmosphere. He saw Jake sitting towards the back left corner of the room, Brett and Jordan with him. He weaved through the tables, turning heads and sparking murmurs from the guests, sitting next to Jake.

"Where did you go?" Jake asked. It was now Azar caught a scent wafting from Jake's body. His cologne was not something Azar had smelt before, but the rich scent made the hairs stand on the back of his neck.

"My mother wanted to see me," Azar replied quietly.

"Your mother's here?" Jake said in surprise. How much did Jake know about the night?

A silence fell over the room as all eyes turned expectantly to the podium, waiting for the host to step out on the stage.

"I'll explain later," Azar said, sitting up.

Peering to his right, Azar could see Jessani sitting a few tables away with a blank expression on her face as she stared at the ground, moving her glass of champagne in slow circles. He thought about how many times she had been to this hall, how many times she had seen Orven address the audience. After centuries, with Orven presumably not present, was it possible that she was in fact nervous about who would be hosting the dinner?

The curtain behind the stage suddenly stirred, and then a figure stepped out from behind it. Azar froze.

"Good evening ladies and gentlemen,' the host announced. "As you are all aware, tonight marks the first night in which our grand leader Orven, King of the pirates, is not attending. I am Steve Geminus, and tonight I will be the host for this very special dinner."

Azar felt numb, heavy, as if he was glued to his chair. He could do nothing but watch. His mother had torn his heart, and now his father stood in place of the biggest enemy Azar had known to live. His father was a tall man with short dark hair and a rough beard. He continued. "As is protocol, tonight's dinner shall be a celebration of Orven's work, but it is also a night to establish the new leader of the Pirates. And I must say, we could not be in safer hands." Azar looked around for a sign of the new leader his father was talking about, but everyone was seated, and doing the same thing as him.

"They will make their entrance shortly, but first, let us toast to our King, and make sure we honour his death by ensuring his goals are achieved," Steve said.

"To King Orven," came a collected response, glasses tapping together. Azar stole a quick glance at Brett, and saw his eyes were closed. What was he doing? Jordan and Jake began eating, and Azar's suspicions grew stronger.

"I have no idea how this event has been able to survive for so long, but the food is great," Jake said lightly, a little too relaxed.

"Jake, why are you here?" Azar asked.

"As in why did I come with Lux? Because I had to find you," Jake said, keeping his gaze on his food.

"No, why did you come to this dinner? We barely know each other. You knowingly travel to a dangerous event with my doppelganger. You've just found out my missing mother is here, yet you haven't even tried to advise me to leave. Lux even took that precaution. I thought maybe you had no idea what was going on, but you know more than I. Now tell me," Azar demanded, doing his best to keep his voice down.

Jake continued to chew his food, a tactic that soon paid off. Brett suddenly shuddered and let out a small gasp, opening his eyes. Before Azar could say anything, his father spoke.

"My friends, it is now time to introduce our new leader. To welcome her on stage with me, I would like to invite up a special man who served a major role in her revival. He organised his loyal men who dwell within the shadows of Mintor to attack the Bank, allowing us to free an ancient leader through a portal. Please welcome, Brett Ullandra!"

Azar's head snapped back to stare at Brett in complete astonishment. Brett could not hold the Oklem's gaze, directing his sorrowful eyes to the floor as he stood up. Azar's mind exploded with a million more questions. What attack? Who did Brett help revive? Brett made his way up towards the stage to a round of applause.

"Is he expecting me to congratulate him?" Azar asked in rising anger. Jordan turned to him.

"I honestly cannot see what Brett saw in you Azar," he said. "You're so quick to jump to conclusions, you refuse to let others explain themselves. In all your anger at his actions, did you ever stop to think how Brett has felt?"

Azar did not have an immediate reply. He was slightly taken off guard by Jordan's response. "Why should he?" Jake intervened. "Cheating is unforgivable."

"Ah yes, the knight in shining armour," Jordan said, turning his gaze to Jake. "What Brett is about to do is far more noble than what either of you will ever come close to doing." Then he sat back and turned to the podium as the hall began to quieten.

What did Jordan mean? Azar began to feel a sense of worry inside of him as he watched Brett shake hands with Steve. "Ladies and gentlemen, please welcome our new leader. A legend amongst the tales, the Queen of the Pirates, Lara Sokolov!" Steve cried out.

Instead of applause, gasps and stunned expressions swept across the room, making Azar's heart rate increase even more. His mother had mentioned this Queen. The clicking of heels on the marble floors grew louder, the echo like a warning siren of danger approaching. All heads turned towards the main brass doors as a woman walked in. The first noticeable feature was her thick, purple ponytail which stretched down to the back of her knees. She wore a black singlet which revealed her large biceps, and brown pants running to her ankles. A belt hung off her waist with what looked like two pistols in it. She looked dangerous, and suddenly Azar felt like he should have listened to Lux and left when he had the chance. Lara's eyes scanned the room as she ascended the stairs to the podium. She stopped in the centre, arms by her sides, hands clenched in fists.

"Tonight we feast. Tomorrow, we plot. Then, we finish what our great King Orven has started." This time the audience burst into a combination of cheers, applause and toasting of glasses. Lara had a deep, harsh, and bold accent, and her presence was so captivating, so demanding of attention, Azar thought she gave Lux a good run for his money. He looked behind her at Brett, who was staring straight ahead, his face blank. But there was something in his eyes that Azar had learnt to identify over the years. Fear, dread. But why? Lara made her way behind Brett and Steve, placing her hands behind her back.

"These men have shown their unwavering loyalty to our cause," she said slowly, stopping in between the two of them. Brett slowly raised his head and locked eyes with Azar.

"However," Lara continued, "there must be assurance that my position is not threatened by those who are corrupted by a mere drop of power and control. So whilst they still retain their honour, they must now sacrifice their lives."

Azar's stomach dropped.

"NO!" he shouted, springing up off his chair, sending it toppling into a woman sitting behind him. In a second Lara whipped out her pistols and pulled the triggers. Brett and Steve, who had offered no resistance, crumbled to the floor with a blood-spattered thud.

"Azar," Jake hissed, grabbing Azar's right arm. "This is beyond our control. Do not draw her attention, because I am pretty sure her next bullets will be at us."

For some reason, Jake's voice temporarily cut through Azar's shock, but it was too little too late. Rage consumed Azar as he stormed towards the stage. Why had Brett allowed himself to die? Why had his father? Why didn't Azar do something sooner? Lara was not looking directly at Azar as the crowd watched on in silence.

"Well well, how long it has been, Marvin," came Lara's amused voice. Azar got to the top of the stairs and stopped. Lara towered over him, but it didn't stop him swinging an arm at her. She easily manoeuvred out of the way, then grabbed his outstretched arm and swung him across the stage, through the curtain.

As he landed, he immediately felt the pain ripple through his body.

"Remove the bodies and begin the feast," he heard Lara command. Music and chatter began. Did nobody care what had just happened? Lara emerged from the curtain, her strides slow, her ponytail swaying behind her. They were in a small rectangular room with a staircase leading to a door at the end.

"You are not Marvin," Lara said, "he would not be so foolish."

Breathing heavily, Azar looked up at the Queen. She cocked her head in fascination. "A doppelganger. You are supernatural. Should we not be on the same side?" she inquired.

"I will never join the Pirates, no matter what my parents tell you," Azar said through gritted teeth.

"You certainly know your way with words, for you just gave yourself a bargaining tool to spare your life," Lara replied. She stepped closer.

"You wouldn't kill me," Azar said, "Orven wouldn't allow you to."

"Orven is no longer in charge. I have no reason to bring forth the Tychun from the Supernatural Universe. And I most certainly have no desire for an Oklem. Getting rid of you prevents Orven's plan from happening. When I said you have a bargaining tool, I was referring to your parents. I assume based off your sudden outburst, you are the Geminus son. From what I've learnt since I got out of the safe, they loved to boast about you. The hero of a new law and order. Steve Geminus was a strong leader, but he is mortal, and we know corruption is a very common trait of the Mortal Nation. Maree is focused on herself and how others perceive her. Perhaps if they were from the Ice Nation and full of nobility, things could have turned out differently," she added. There was no sympathy to her icy words.

The rage was beginning to subside, not because he wanted it to, but because Azar knew he could not fight this opponent. He held onto it, however, as it otherwise meant he would move on to the next stage of the mourning process. Just then the curtain stirred and Jessani entered the room, her dress swirling around her feet.

"Well, thank you for making the night a little more interesting," she said to Azar.

"Jessani, escort our doppelganger to a safe room. I shall speak with him once the night is complete," Lara ordered, going back to the curtains.

"Why are you against opening a supernatural portal?" Azar asked, sitting up. "The Pirates cannot rule the Nation's themselves."

The queen stopped, putting her hands behind her back again.

"This universe lacks leadership, not numbers. I intend to change that. A strong leader who can expose the Peacekeepers will already have the support of everyone living in the Nations. I certainly do not need Supernatural assistance."

She pushed through the curtains.

"Get up Azar, you're hardly scratched," Jessani said, making her way past the Oklem.

"I don't understand," Azar said, standing up slowly. "Her goal is different to Orven's. How can she be the Queen of the Pirates if she does not believe in their cause?"

"These are very uncertain times. Nobody seems to know what happens after a war," Jessani said.

"That doesn't answer my question," Azar said, not moving.

Jessani reached over her back and pulled out a small knife, somehow tucked into her dress. Azar took the message, following Jessani as she descended the stairs and opened the door. They went through a large corridor, where the walls looked like they had been painted by a rainbow. Azar felt like he could probe some answers out of Jessani. He was unsure if she knew Orven was alive, but the one connection that everybody seemed to have in common was Lux.

"At what stage did Marvin become Lux?" he asked.

They rounded a corner and Jessani's hand suddenly shot out in front of Azar.

"About the same time I abandoned this young woman," Lux said, shaking his head as he stood in the middle of the hallway. He had obviously used his hearing abilities to find where Azar was. Lux allowed a pause to extend for several seconds longer than normal, then he cocked his head. "Good evening, Jessani. It's been a while."

Jessani stood frozen, completely caught off guard. Relief flooded through Azar, an act which caught his doppelganger's eye.

"Azar when I tell you to leave, I mean leave," Lux said with his usual level of sass and command. He displayed no sign of the distraught Azar had last seen him with. Jessani regained some composure.

"You only took ten years to come out of the shadows, Marvin," Jessani replied darkly. "Our promise to find a way to live forever was broken by you—"

"Even now you use a name that only existed when we were together. It is staggering that after quite literally centuries, you still have not accepted the fact that we were never meant to be," Lux cut her off.

Azar could begin to feel his repressed emotions coming forward. He needed to leave, so he started to take a step down the corridor when Jessani grabbed him. Lux shot forward, fast as ever, and grabbed Jessani, who let go of Azar as she was slammed up against the wall. The force of it released a small vibration through the hall. Azar saw both of them were breathing heavily as they looked each other in the eyes. The tension was so incredibly intense, Azar felt like moving a muscle would slice through it.

"You. Are. Nothing to me," Lux said icily. Even Azar was taken aback at how ruthless Lux had said that. He released Jessani, turned to Azar and grabbed his arm. In unimaginable speed, Azar was suddenly whisked away and found himself standing near the horse carriages down the end of the driveway. Dizziness disorientated him, and he collapsed against the cold steel of the carriage. How could Lux move so quickly? How could he say that to Jessani? What was their history? Then his mind began to remember they were missing someone.

"Jake," he suddenly said, trying to straighten himself.

"I will get him," Lux said, "he will meet you at your inn. Listen. Lisarow is a safe place. Nobody supernatural can get in. But you go first thing in the morning. Back to Mintor. You will be long gone from here by the time the Pirates notice you are missing. Do you understand me?" Azar wanted to probe further, but he could no longer hold off his emotions. He nodded his head, clambered into the carriage and moments later burst into tears. Everything was ruined. His life was over. He had tried to be tough, but now he had lost two of the closest people he had grown up with. His parents! His mother's betrayal cut him to the core. He hadn't even had a chance to tell his father goodbye. And what had Brett done to get himself killed? Overwhelmed by grief, he let himself fall across the seat, allowing the rhythm of the hooves and the bouncing of the carriage to whisk his limp body away.

Chapter 23

A machine beeped. Emma slowly opened her eyes, taking in her environment. The undeniable scent of a hospital ward filled her nostrils. A raging pain swamped her entire left arm. She was in a white gown with no sleeves, and her eyes widened in alarm as she saw her left arm was completely black. She tried to remember what had happened. She was attacked in the safe. But the creatures that attacked her were not Tychun, so she couldn't have been infected with Tychun blood. What had happened? Her whip was curled up on the bedside tablet. The door opened and a nurse entered. She saw that Emma was awake and came over.

"How are you feeling?" she said.

"What's wrong with my arm?" Emma asked, her voice very hoarse and weak. Her throat was dry. The nurse's eyes looked to the ground for a moment, making Emma's heart rate increase. A tube was attached from her waist, connecting to a machine.

"You were bitten by a Supernatural creature. Unfortunately it was not a common bite mark we can treat like from a goblin or vampire. The creature that bit you had Tychun blood," the nurse said softly.

Emma's eyes widened and she tried to sit up, but couldn't. She felt herself plunge into fear. It wasn't possible. Tychun blood could not possibly be in their universe.

"Where's my brother?" she asked.

"Peacekeeper Drand has tried to contact him, but so far there has been no response." The nurse put a glass of water to Emma's lips, who eagerly welcomed the cool liquid.

"I will let the Peacekeeper know you have awoken. But for now, please, get some rest. Staying calm makes the venom take longer to spread."

The pain began increasing throughout Emma's entire body.

"Can I have more for the pain?" she asked.

The nurse left with a nod and Emma put her head back. How had the creatures gotten into the safe? Surely Lux would have known they were there. Soon enough the pain became too much, and Emma fell back into a deep sleep.

****

The carriage pulled up just inside the golden walls of Lisarow. Azar didn't move. His tears had dried on his face. However his body was still numb. He didn't know what time it was, but the stars continued to sparkle in the clear night sky. He was torn. Both Brett and his father died because of their choices, but Azar still had a grounding love for them that could never be broken. He removed his blazer, its cuffs drenched from the constant wiping of his eyes. What was he going to do? What did Mintor have for him anymore?

In the silence he heard the sound of approaching footsteps on the cobblestone. If he remained still, he hoped they would simply walk past. But whoever it was stopped right outside the carriage.

"I could be wrong, but I do believe a bed is much more comfortable than a carriage," came Jake's voice. Azar sat up, turning his head to see Jake standing outside, resting his arms on the top of the door and peering in. Despite how he felt, Azar's heart skipped a beat.

"I think I'd rather be in a coffin underground," he replied, rubbing his neck.

"There was nothing you could do," Jake said. Azar suddenly felt a pit of anger swelling in his stomach.

"You knew Brett was going to die," Azar said.

"Only when you had walked off into the hall on your own," Jake replied. "Both Brett and Jordan told me it was inevitable, he had to sacrifice himself."

"Why?"

"I don't know," Jake sighed, "Brett said that one day you will find out. Trust me, I wish they had told me what was going on."

"It's not so fun when it's you left in the dark, is it?" Azar said coldly. Immediately he regretted what he said.

"Look can we please talk about that at least?" Jake asked, keeping his voice controlled.

Azar shook his head, desperately trying to hold back tears.

"I can't do this anymore, Jake," he said slowly. "Everything I have believed in growing up is false. Apart from unexplainable visions and weird whispers in my head, I haven't experienced any feelings of empowerment since being told I am an Oklem. Maybe I should just give up my miserable life."

Azar moved towards the door as Jake opened it for him. He stepped out and saw a third figure standing at the back of the carriage. After a mini heart attack, Azar realised it was the See-er, his black staff clasped in his hand.

"Woah!" Jake exclaimed, grabbing Azar's arm defensively.

"It's okay Jake, this is the See-er," Azar said, although he waited for Jake to remove his grip, rather than shake him off.

"The time has come to make contact with the Oklem who have all passed from their life in this universe," the spiritual being said, his voice hoarse.

Azar didn't reply. He was not really sure he cared about being an Oklem anymore.

"What do you mean make contact?" Jake asked, stepping in line with Azar.

"Those whispers you speak of are the calls from previous Oklem. The spirits of the Mortal Nation have sent me to you. The decision, however, lies with the living Oklem," the See-er said, turning his head to Azar. Then he tapped his staff on the ground and with not even a plume of smoke, vanished. Jake turned to Azar.

"I've never seen a See-er before. Emma will be jealous. Anyway, what is he talking about?" he asked.

"I don't think I care anymore. I need to sleep on it," Azar answered, holding back more tears, putting his blazer over his shoulder. Jake reached inside his own blazer and pulled out two small bits of paper.

"Lux gave me two tickets to fly out of here tomorrow morning, the legal way," he added, reminding Azar of the style in which he had arrived at the Trail of Tales.

Azar nodded his head and the two boys began walking along the cobblestone pathways. Azar recognised where they were from his earlier explorations, so he directed Jake as they went. "What do you think I should do?" Azar suddenly asked his…*friend?* What was Jake?

"Obviously I don't know what visions you have experienced, but I think you should come back to Mintor and speak with Peacekeeper Drand. Emma has told me of her growing suspicions of the Peacekeepers, but I trust Drand," Jake said.

"Surprisingly, the honesty of the Peacekeepers has come up in discussion here, too," Azar replied. But he has known Drand all his life, and without any evidence to accuse him, Azar needed some guidance from somebody who knew about the supernatural side of the Nations. Somebody not immediately involved like Lux was.

Thinking of his doppelganger raised another curiosity.

"What do you think of Lux?"

Azar was trying to distract himself more than anything. Jake spread his arms.

"He's a bizarre character. Apart from his incredible ability to move as fast as he likes from a crawl to the speed of light, he is determined to achieve a goal. He's also fought to keep you alive, so I'm not going to judge him just yet. Although some more light on what his actual intentions are would be helpful," Jake said, hinting for Azar to find out with a wink.

Azar smiled, and a shudder went through him. He was never planning on being even remotely happy ever again when he was in the carriage. Yet here he was smiling, and some of the dense levels of sadness deteriorated. Just a bit.

They were a block away from the inn when a boy rounded the corner, his wet sandals squishing into the ground with each step. He passed a fire beacon, and Azar could see he was not wearing a shirt, just board shorts and a towel wrapped across his shoulders. His hair was tied in a small bun. Azar's eyes locked with his as they passed each other. Not a word was exchanged, but Azar knew from his experience of meeting other gay boys in the past that there was a keen interest in those eyes. But Azar couldn't do anything, he was…free. The moment had passed, but Azar suddenly realised that he was no longer in a relationship. The acknowledgement felt weird, and he was so distracted thinking about this that he almost missed Jake's sly comment.

"Damn he was hot," Jake murmured, running a hand through his dark hair, his blonde tips reflecting off the light from the beacons.

Surprised, and caught off guard, Azar turned and saw Jake's face was filled with terror. A fear that Azar could immediately identify and resonate with so easily.

"Hey it's alright—" Azar started.

"How did I just say that? I've never said anything like that before" Jake said in a mixture of bewilderment and fear, taking a step backwards.

"Jake it's alright, I know that is a massive step to take," Azar said, trying to keep his voice steady.

"No Azar…I-I-I can't," he stammered, and he suddenly walked off at a fast pace, holding a hand to his head. Azar stopped. As if the night hadn't been enough of a roller coaster yet, the mood had deteriorated in seconds. Some of

Azar's toughest memories began to flash through his mind. How he first realised he liked boys instead of girls. The fear that it brought if anyone ever found out. Growing up pretending to like girls but experimenting with boys. The angst of getting caught. The dread of realising he was different almost too overwhelming before Brett showed up. Jake had just done something that terrified Azar to even think about. Jake had not only just experienced the first moment he realised he was gay, but he told someone about it. And Azar concluded that just as Brett was there for him, he now needed to be there for Jake.

He raced after Jake, who had only gone to the steps leading up to the front of Azar's inn and was sitting on them with his head in his hands. To Azar's slight relief, this event had meant he could stop thinking about his personal horrors of the night for a short while. He sat down next to Jake, and after a few moments of silence, began.

"You know I have never really "come out" as such. I met Brett on an app. I was seventeen, he was twenty-two. I had met with a few guys before that, but Brett was different. We were both seeking a relationship. He was mysterious, a bit of a bad boy. I was curious, mostly because being with him took me out of my comfort zone. He was a risk taker. When I found out he was a part of the underworld, I was scared. But I was more afraid of going back to the lonely boy who never socialised, never explored, so I stayed with him."

Jake removed his hands from his face, tears smeared across his flustered cheeks.

"I'm not new to this part of me," he said, snuffling. "I've been with guys too, but I just don't like talking about it. I don't like acknowledging it as a part of me and I don't know why."

"Because we are different," Azar replied, "and being different is still pointed out, making us feel more insecure and exposed than what we really are. The one thing Brett taught me that I will cherish forever was that when you are with someone that will love and fight for you every single day, you can never be hurt."

"What happens when they break your heart?" Jake asked. Azar expected the question, but it still brought a sick feeling to the pit of his stomach. He thought about it for a long while.

"The pain is worse than anything else you could possibly expect. It made me so mad, and I shut Brett out completely. Now I will never get to talk to him again, and despite what he did, I still wanted us to find some closure."

They sat in silence for a short while. Azar was exhausted. Eventually he stood up.

"What you did was incredibly brave, no matter how accidental it was. The reason I told you about my past is because Brett was always there for me. So I am going to be here for you."

Jake gave one final wipe across his face before standing up as well.

"It's ironic," he said.

"What is?" Azar asked.

"I thought tonight would be all about me comforting you. I guess the night had other plans. Thank you, though," Jake said.

The Oklem gave a nod of his head.

"I think I'll take up your suggestion of a bed over a carriage or coffin," Azar replied, going up the stairs and to his door.

"So, uh, are we friends, then?" Jake asked. Azar turned back to him.

"Friends," he replied. Despite the tragedy that had taken place, a small part of him was glad that the night had ended with a little sliver of light.

Chapter 24

The alarm blasted through the room, startling Azar. He opened his eyes, rolled over and looked over to the other bed at Jake, who had reached across to his phone sitting on the bedside table.

"Sorry, I didn't want to miss the flight," Jake said wearily. The sun was radiating around the border of the curtain covering the only window in their room, next to the door. Azar usually slept without a shirt, but decided to wear one with Jake present. He felt it may have made Jake feel a little awkward, especially after his ordeal the previous night.

"Anything from Emma?" Azar asked. Jake had spent a bit of time the night before trying to contact Emma.

"No. I left a message with the palace's reception for her to call me as soon as she gets it. It's unusual for her to be off the grid," Jake explained.

Azar clambered out of his bed, grabbed a fresh set of clothes and went into the bathroom. He immersed himself in the hot water of the shower, hoping each drop would wash away the memories. Everything. The war. Brett cheating, his parents leaving Mintor, them being guilty of treason. Death. Despite this, he had decided to do as Jake suggested and return to Mintor. It was half because he wanted to see the Peacekeeper, but it was also because he wanted to make sure Jake returned home safely. He had risked a lot to come and find Azar who had left without a word of warning.

Although it was warm in Lisarow, Azar knew the Mortal Nation's weather would not be so inviting, so he put on a pair of blue jeans and a white shirt. He emerged from the bathroom and let Jake go in to freshen up. He stood in front of the mirror on the far side of the room, and for a moment remembered looking through it and seeing Brett standing behind him. Brett's few possessions still sat in the corner near his bed. Azar wished he could have been able to bury his ex and father, but there was not a chance of that happening now. Even if he could find their bodies, he would certainly be captured by the Pirates. He also assumed that Lara would be most upset about his escape, and Lux was not going to bail him out. He determined that he didn't need to take home many of the new clothes that had been bought. There were multiple places in Lisarow that would happily take in the items at no cost. As he picked up the white denim shorts he had worn to the beach a few nights back, he felt something tingle. Reaching into the back pocket, he pulled out the necklaces from the market. He recalled the beautiful child, and her grandmother.

He'd forgotten about those. He put them into a small carry-on bag Brett had bought when he got all the clothes. It avoided the airport baggage hassle. Azar could hear the shower was on, and was about to sit down on the bed when there was a knock at the door. Curious, he went over and grabbed the handle, pulling the door open. He froze.

"Knock, knock," Jessani said, striding through the doorway and grabbing Azar around the collar. Then with incredible strength she threw him onto Brett's bed, slamming the door shut.

"We were not finished last night," she said icily. Azar recovered quickly and rolled to the side of the bed, standing up.

"Actually," he replied, "we were. Not even you could forget the ultimate shut down from Lux." Jessani laughed.

"You're going to use a bad relationship as a weapon against me? You of all people cannot talk of that," she said. Azar clenched his hands into fists. Jessani continued.

"I am here for a reason which partially includes your little spy friend, so sit while we wait for him," she ordered, pointing to the bed.

Azar reluctantly did so, crossing his arms. Jessani was wearing black thigh high boots and a purple skirt. Her silky jet black hair was in a neat bun. She still had a lot of makeup on, a sign Azar was beginning to think represented her insecurities, some he was going to try and expose. "Why have you stuck by Orven's side for so long?" he asked.

"Why do you support the Peacekeepers? Because you believe that what they believe in is true," she replied.

"And what does Orven believe in?" Azar queried.

"Eternal life," Jessani answered, slowly pacing around the room. "He believes politics simply divides a community into the poor and the wealthy. He'd much prefer a Nation where everyone is equal: well housed, well fed, all contributing to their society, and a strong leadership that ensures no issues arise.

Unfortunately it is something one cannot achieve in a mortal life time, so he found a way to stop aging."

Jessani paused in front of the mirror, looking herself up and down.

"Orven is alive," Azar stated, and saw Jessani's face turn cold in the reflection. "It's not new information to me, just getting confirmation," he added in response.

"You don't seem particularly rushed to spread the word on this," she said, turning around and facing the Oklem. After a moment, her eyes narrowed. "Hmmm, interesting. You're unsure of who you can trust."

"Is there a way to reverse the age prevention?" Azar asked. She turned back to the mirror. "No," she said softly.

Just then the bathroom door opened and Jake came out, wearing black jeans and a red long sleeve shirt, his hair damp. He looked at Azar briefly before halting in the doorway, turning his attention to Jessani who was looking at him through the mirror.

"I hope you're feeling refreshed," she said with fake enthusiasm.

"What do you want?" he demanded.

"Just filling in some details," the villain said, facing the two boys. Azar stood up again.

"When I spoke with you at the dinner, you said you cannot cheat death. But Orven made a potion where he cannot die from age. Why did nature allow that potion to exist? What's the loophole against it?" he asked.

"Ironically, mortality is the answer. Those who consume the potion gain incredible strength, however we can still be killed. We can gain no further supernatural attributes like speed or fangs. If we get ill, we must take mortal medicines. Our travel is limited, not physically, but in terms of survival. If we travel to the Supernatural Universe, the slightest cut or illness cannot be cured, and it's game over," Jessani replied.

"That sounds more like torture than anything," Jake said, leaning against the doorway.

"Looking at it now I agree, but at the time I took it, I was blinded by love. Before I went to the Supernatural Universe, I was having a secret relationship with Lux. At the time he was known by his birth name, Marvin. He was already a doppelganger, and as we know, a core trait of being one is that they cannot age from the moment they become one."

"Does that mean Azar won't age once he gets to the same stage of life Lux was at?" Jake asked.

Azar was listening to every word. He was half surprised that he was getting this information from Jessani of all people, but he'd rather learn as much as he could now. Jessani lifted her shoulders.

"That I don't know. Azar is also an Oklem, so perhaps it changes the rules that Lux has followed. You don't have any wine or something here, do you?" she added, looking at Azar.

"No, but seeing as you're an open book, why are you telling us all of this information?" he replied.

"She wants something," Jake said, standing up straight and stepping into the room. Jessani cocked her head.

"As a matter of fact, yes. Lara Sokolov has been revived after centuries of waiting in preservation."

"Well, she is the Queen of the Pirates. Shouldn't you be happy she is here?" Azar said, raising an eyebrow.

"You helped free her in Mintor," Jake said. "My sister's life was put at risk."

"Where did you get that theory from?" Jessani asked. Azar's stomach began to turn. Before going to sleep the night before, Jake had informed Azar about the recent events in Mintor and what Lux and Emma had discovered in the safe. Azar had been surprised to hear that Lux so willingly told Jake about the bank visit.

"Your hit man, Robert Johnson. Spilled the beans pretty quickly after Emma caught him," Jake said.

Jessani shook her head.

"Oh dear, not just Jake, but Emma Flare being fooled too? I did not release Lara Sokolov. She is a direct enemy of Orven's. Why would I bring her back?" she asked. Much to Azar's disappointment, and confusion, he believed she was telling the truth.

"You're lying," Jake said, raising a finger. "This is what you Pirates do. Maybe you're just jealous that Lara took the crown and not yourself."

Jessani suddenly stormed across the room, but instead of going to Jake, she pulled a long knife from out of her right boot, grabbed a surprised Azar and held it to his throat. Jake immediately tensed.

"I will not be challenged nor accused of being a Pirate," she hissed. Azar did not struggle. He knew her strength.

"Why do you try so hard to distance yourself from the Pirates when you openly admit to working with them?" he asked, trying to keep his voice calm.

"Because I am not a follower of Orven's," Jessani said slowly. "I am his daughter."

Azar could do nothing but look at Jake, who mirrored his expression of astonishment. The coldness of the blade began to press deeper into Azar's skin, just stopping short of piercing it. Jake raised his hands.

"If Orven is the king, and Lara is the queen, is she your—"

"No she is not my mother," Jessani interrupted. "She once was in love with my father, but that was a very long time ago, when they were nothing but mortals. So Jake, you are going to find out who spearheaded the operation to bring her back."

"What makes you think I'll help you? If there is a war within the Pirates ranks, that helps the Nations," Jake said.

"If you let me finish my love story, perhaps you will find some more incentive to help," she said, tapping the knife on Azar's throat. "Sit."

She moved the knife and indicated with it for Azar to sit on the bed again. He did so, though hinted at his dissatisfaction with an exaggerated sigh. He wasn't sure where this conversation was heading, but he knew that the longer they were in Lisarow, the higher the risk of getting caught by the Pirates. It was possible that Jessani was buying time for the Pirates, but with what she was saying, Azar believed she genuinely was against Lara Sokolov.

"Lux and I spent a very long time together," Jessani began. "I ensured I went with him to the Supernatural Universe, but the longer we were there, things started to change. I wanted to become what he was. I wanted to find all the ingredients that had been used in making the potion that led to Lux becoming a doppelganger. My prime issue was that most of the ingredients were from our universe, meaning I could not find them over there and recreate the potion. My father refused to allow me to become immortal, so whilst he planned with the supernatural leaders about opening a portal back to our universe, I searched over there for a resolution. The Supernatural Universe is not so easy to travel across. There are many creatures lurking in every bush, there is no sun, just dark red moons. But I charmed my way into people's hearts, some their beds, and finally had all the ingredients for a supernatural potion to stop aging all together."

"What were the ingredients?" Jake asked.

"That's where it gets tricky," Jessani said. "When I became immortal, my memory was wiped of the ingredients. Almost as if Nature itself cursed me for finding a way to stop the natural course of life, ensuring I could not share it with others."

Azar remembered that the same thing had happened to the See-er when he created the original recipe for the Oklem.

"Before taking it, I told Lux about what I had done. To my absolute devastation, he disapproved. We began to see cracks within our relationship. I told him that it was because we could not yet ensure our love would last for all eternity, but he was not convinced. So despite his warnings, I took the potion. As I mentioned last night, trying to change the natural path has consequences. Lux suddenly stopped loving me all together. He seemingly vanished. I was set for eternal suffering, eternal loneliness. I thought he was seeing another woman, but soon rumours spread about a doppelganger who could not love. Upon hearing this, Orven revealed to me that it was true, however it was not Lux's fault. It was yours," she said, turning to Azar, pointing the knife at him.

Immediately Azar felt a warning shiver race down his spine.

"Mine?" he repeated cautiously.

Jake had taken a few steps closer to the bed.

"You were born," Jessani continued. "As the Mortal Nation's doppelganger, you got the best part about Lux, and he lost it."

Azar was speechless. How was it possible to lose the ability to love?

"But you spent well over a century with him, every couple would love to have that," Jake said.

"We wanted to be in love *forever*. Both immortal, don't you understand," Jessani said through gritted teeth.

"You can't blame Azar for being born," Jake retorted.

Azar could feel the tension rising, and was concerned it would soon boil over into a violent outbreak.

"Since Azar's birth, I spent the first ten years of his life in the Supernatural Universe heartbroken, with my father, planning our return. Then, ten years ago, the path reopened. We came back with vengeance. We built our armies and attacked the Peacekeepers. Orven had his own agenda, total domination of the Nations, and I had mine. I was hoping to find Azar during it, whilst you were much younger and more vulnerable. But you were well protected," Jessani added icily.

Azar's heart rate was increasing. His parents had been working with Orven for some time, and had wanted Azar to be chosen as the next Oklem. So it was most likely that it was Jessani's own father that aided them in keeping Azar safe. He was almost twenty years of age, meaning Jessani's story did mathematically match up with his birth date.

"How is it possible that my birth removed Lux's ability to love? If that was a normal thing to occur for a doppelganger, it would have been expected," Azar stated. "What if it wasn't me? I know Lux became a doppelganger in our universe, so maybe if you tell me how he became one, I can see if there are any clues."

Jessani scoffed.

"Lux's story is certainly one to be told around a tissue box. Jake should keep that in mind when he asks Lux about it. Now I certainly did not appreciate Lux's parting words last night, but I must face reality. He no longer loves me. All these years I had been hoping we could restart the flame of our relationship. Now I have a new goal. I intend to make sure that whatever he came back to the Nation's for is removed for good. Unfortunately, that appears to include you," she said, moving towards Azar.

Jake leapt onto the bed. Azar backed up along the mattress, his back hitting the head of the bed. Using his height, Jake aimed a kick at Jessani's chest. She manoeuvred around it, grabbing his leg and pulling him off the mattress. He tumbled onto the ground as Jessani lunged at Azar, holding the knife above her right shoulder. She brought it down at the Oklem, who grabbed a pillow and held it in front of him with as much force as he could muster sitting down. Jake leapt up as the knife cut through the pillow and pierced the other side, but Azar's opposing strength temporarily stopped Jessani's attack. He soon began to weaken, however, and the knife inched closer towards his face. Jake came around the side of the bed, forcing Jessani to relieve the pressure on her attack and face her opponent. She swung her right heel at Jake, who grabbed it and pulled, causing her to hop away from Azar on her left leg, and she let go of the knife. Azar immediately threw the pillow sideways, away from everyone, sending the impaled weapon with it.

Jessani used her momentum from being pulled away and lunged at Jake, shoving him onto the opposing bed. Azar leapt up and grabbed Jessani from behind. She immediately thrust an elbow back, colliding with his chin. Unlike Jake, Azar was not used to engaging in combat, and the immediate pain saw him reflexively let go of Jessani. Before she could turn, Jake aimed a kick at the centre of her stomach, causing her to double over. He sat up and grabbed her around the throat, locking in his arms. Her resilience began to weaken as she gasped for air.

"Don't kill her," Azar suddenly said, holding a hand up to reinforce the plea. Jake looked at Azar in surprise. Jessani's gaze turned to Azar, her eyes wide and unsure, but her struggles became less aggressive. Azar realised Jake was knocking her out. Soon her eyes closed and her body went limp. Jake let her fall onto Azar's bed.

"She just tried to kill you," he said.

"She is heartbroken, Jake. I understand why she did that, because it was what I wanted to do to Lara when Brett died. But did she really want to kill me? Yes she had incentive, but if I am that important to Orven, she would never seriously attempt to take my life. She's lost, now that Lux is a lost cause for her, she has no driving motivation anymore. This is the one chance I am giving her. If she tries to attack me or you or anyone we know again, I'll give you the knife to kill her with. Now let's tie her up and go home," Azar said.

Jake reached up and pulled the curtain off the window. Using the cord attached, he tied Jessani's hands behind her back, and then tied her feet together.

They left the inn. Azar followed Jake as he had travelled through the airport when he arrived, which was located at the farthest end of Lisarow, still within the golden walls. When they pulled their tickets out, Azar noticed something written on his. The letter 'L' was followed by a series of numbers. Azar realised it must be Lux's phone number. How random, he thought. Jake tried to contact Emma, unsuccessful once again. The skies were clear as the plane took off. Whilst Azar gazed out the window, he remembered the necklaces in his bag. He looked across at Jake, who was sitting next to him and had fallen asleep. Azar could no longer deny the fact that he was somewhat attracted to Jake, but is a relationship really what he wanted? He still did not know Jake that well. Brett's involvement in the underworld had come as a surprise, so not wanting to go through that again, he decided he would wait a while to see who Jake is as a mortal being before acting on his emotions. Soon after he too fell asleep, allowing his mind and body to be free from his consciousness.

Chapter 25

Azar was right behind Jake as they emerged from the elevator on the fifth floor of the hospital.

Jake sprinted to the receptionist desk. It had taken approximately eight hours to travel from the Trail of Tales to the Mortal Nation. It was late afternoon when they had arrived at the Whistle to the news about Emma's injury.

"Where is my sister? Where is Emma Flare?" Jake asked the nurse desperately.

"Three doors down on the left, Peacekeeper Drand is there," she replied.

Azar's body tingled at the sickly scent the hospital brought to his senses. He hadn't had much experience being in one, and was quietly relieved about that as he entered Emma's room. It was small, with a window opposite the entrance. Peacekeeper Drand was standing at the foot of Emma's bed, in an official white robe with diamonds on the shoulders. Jake didn't even acknowledge him as he went to Emma's side. As Azar joined the Peacekeeper, he could not hide the expression of horror from his face at what he was looking at.

Emma's left arm looked as if it had been plunged into a barrel full of black paint. Red blisters sizzled across the skin. Her face was flushed in a deep shade of red, and if it wasn't for the heart monitor beeping slowly next to her, he could very well have been looking at a corpse.

"Tychun venom works very quickly," Drand murmured, holding a hand on his chin. "She is fighting hard. Usually one would not last more than a day from being bitten. In saying that, I do not believe she can resist much longer."

"How long?" Azar asked, watching as Jake sat silently on Emma's right, holding her right hand with tears streaming down his face.

The Peacekeeper turned his head to the Oklem, a look of sorrow in his eyes.

"She will be gone by morning."

"How did she get Tychun venom in her system?" Jake asked with a choked voice.

"She was attacked in the bank's safe by two supernatural creatures. They themselves were not Tychun, but they had been injected with their venom," Drand replied. "A very clever tactic from the Supernatural universe."

"Where are the creatures? Maybe we can gain some knowledge from analysing them," Azar said. Drand shook his head.

"Unfortunately the creatures perished in the flames. Once a supernatural being is killed in our universe, they are forever bound to their own universe, body and soul."

A feeling of despair hung in the room. Was that it? Was Emma just going to die? There had to be something Azar could do.

"Azar I must speak with you in private," Drand said. "I know the circumstances are not ideal, but I do believe we need to discuss whatever happened these last few days in Lisarow."

"I want to talk as well, but I cannot do that until I have tried to help Emma," Azar replied.

"Can we hold a discussion off until tomorrow?"

"Of course," Drand said, the briefest look of irritation flashing across his face. "Do whatever it is you need to do. I will make sure Jake is not left alone."

Time was of the essence. Azar's heart broke at the sight of Jake's suffering. There was only one person he could think of that he hoped could give him some form of positive news. The one person who had told him so much yet managed to remain so vague about his role in everything. It was time to find out who his doppelganger really was.

"Jake, can I borrow your phone?" Azar asked. Brett had taken Azar's when he was kidnapped, and now it seemed Azar would never know where it was. He pulled out his plane ticket and put in the number Lux had written.

He hoped it was Lux's number. As it began to ring, he left the hospital, heading for the hill where it all began.

****

1627: The Grand Hall, Trail of Tales

Marvin signalled for Jessani to leave the hall. Orven announced the second guest, Richard.

Balkins, and during the applause, she made her way out.

"This does go against my father's wishes," Jessani said cheekily. Marvin beamed.

"I suppose that makes me a "dangerous boy" and one you should stay away from?" he asked slyly.

Jessani giggled. Orven's voice echoed throughout the building. "Please welcome our third guest, our strongest weapon, Peacekeeper Serain!" he cried out. Marvin and Jessani peered around the doorway, ensuring they weren't seen. Serain made her way onto the stage in an orange dress, her body glowing a fierce red, her eyes brushing over every face in the hall.

"Isn't it wonderful? Tonight could finally be the night that we can coexist with the supernatural's," Jessani exclaimed, clasping her hands.

"Doubtful," Marvin replied casually, watching as the three guests sat down on the podium. Jessani turned to him.

"What do you mean?"

"They're missing one key ingredient."

He whispered something in her ear.

"How would you know such things?" Jessani asked, frowning at the boy. Her father had always told her that the existence of the Oklem was their little secret, so how could Marvin know? Marvin spread his arms out.

"I'm full of surprises," he said. There was a lot of mystery surrounding this boy, yet Jessani could not refute a growing attraction towards him. She wondered whether there was a future between them. If so, she hoped it could last forever.

Chapter 26

The stables were a thirty minute drive from the Whistle, a little less from the hospital. The taxi pulled up at the drive way. Azar handed over a few notes he had in his wallet, then got out. The country air brought a sense of freedom and life with it. Dogs were barking nearby, cattle grazed the fields. The stables were property of the Peacekeeper, a place where those who lived in the Whistle were allowed to keep their horses under the care of paid staff. Starc immediately raised his head as Azar entered one of the barns. Starc was a brown Thoroughbred, and loved to run free in the paddocks. Azar quickly saddled him up and without hesitation, Starc galloped across the field to the trail leading up the mountain. The hill was not steep, allowing Azar to ensure his horse ascended at a steady pace. Would Lux show up?

Azar wasn't even sure if his doppelganger would know anything about Tychun venom, but he had to try something.

Azar stopped at the lake opposite the pathway leading to the park. There was a certain silence in the trees. Dismounting, Azar wound his way through the bushes, the pathway having become more overgrown since he was there last. He came out at the opening and saw the old, rusted swing set. A figure sat on the edge of the cliff, dressed in black, legs tucked underneath him. Azar slowly approached Lux. The sun was setting in a magnificent sea of orange. Silence consumed the hill, no wind, no birds. It was as if everything was holding its breath for this moment. "Coming back to the place where it all began," Lux observed. Azar stopped just behind his doppelganger.

"I consider it to be more of a restart to everything bar the riddles and half answer responses," Azar said.

"Perhaps you should stop asking the wrong questions," Lux said.

Azar went and sat next to Lux. He looked across the city. For the first time he was not looking at it with joy. It was fast becoming a reminder of his losses.

He decided to ease into his pending interrogation for answers, starting with a reflection of himself.

"The day the war finished I raced to Brett's to tell him the news. Things suddenly looked much brighter. I knew he'd be home so I didn't bother knocking or even texting, I was just going to surprise him. I ran into his room and saw him wrapped in the arms of this boy with orange hair. Having to see the two of them since then has been hard. But now that Brett is gone, I don't know if I should remember him as a cheater, or as my boyfriend," Azar reflected.

"You need to ask yourself if he was really someone who you thought you could love forever. Can you honestly say Brett was the one?" Lux asked.

"I think I am just scared to admit it, because it would also be admitting to failing in my goal to find real love," Azar said. Lux looked at him.

"You have been incredibly open with me, I mean with your sexuality, considering I am essentially a stranger."

Azar shrugged.

"For some unexplained reason, I trust you. Maybe it's because we're doppelgangers. Or maybe I've just been stupidly revealing all this information to a double-crossing Pirate," he said.

"However I doubt that, considering I called you saying it was an emergency and you showed up."

"Ah yes, calling. Texting, social media. Phones are so time consuming," Lux said, his gaze drifting. Azar could feel there was something else his doppelganger wanted to say, but was struggling to.

"Is Jessani really Orven's daughter?"

Lux nodded his head.

"That's not where all the shocking truths end, though."

"Lux, what was that vision we both shared at the mansion? How come merely touching you allowed us to see events taking place that I certainly wasn't at?"

Azar needed to know who Lux really was. He knew he was being pushy, but Emma's life being on the line sat at the back of his mind with every moment. Lux stared down the hill for a long while, causing Azar to feel like he was about to be told something very personal, and terrible. "That was my family,' Lux eventually answered. "Dead. I found them like that on what had already been the worst night of my life. The night I became a doppelganger."

"But how did I see that?" Azar asked.

"Because you are an Oklem. The mind is your weapon."

Azar remembered his ability to view an event from centuries ago with the See-er. Was it possible that he could do so with anyone?

"Can I do this with anybody? Can I even touch someone without delving into their minds?"

"I don't know much about Oklem, Azar. I assume like everything, you just need to learn to control your ability."

"Were you thinking about the night your family died when I came into contact with you?" Azar queried.

"How could I not? That mansion is where I became immortal," Lux said.

Azar raised his eyebrows in surprise. Jessani had said Lux's story was sad, but Azar didn't realise how dark a story it was.

"How did you become a doppelganger?" he asked Lux.

"Azar—"

"I need to know, Lux," Azar said, sounding a little more aggressive than he intended.

"Why?" Lux demanded.

A brewing frustration, built up by the recent revelations and deaths, suddenly exploded within Azar.

"Because I need to *believe* that I can trust you," he snapped. "I have lost everyone I love. Jessani told me of the night she met you. I keep hearing that you're nothing but a troublemaker and an enemy. Why does everyone say you're the bad guy? What did you do?"

"I did what I had to do!" Lux shot back, leaping to his feet. "I made the mistake of allowing my heart to determine my actions and I lost my family because of that."

Azar was not backing down, knowing he needed to fire Lux up in order to extract information.

"What did you *do*?" he asked again.

"You really want me to relive that nightmare?" Lux said heatedly.

"If that is what it will take for you to prove to me you are not my enemy," Azar answered.

"The night I met Jessani in Sixteen Twenty-Seven, I fell in love with her. It was the night when Orven would first attempt to open the portal and bring forth the Tychun. But he was missing an ingredient. I told Jessani what that was, oblivious to the fact that she was Orven's daughter," Lux explained, though his tone was aggressive.

"Okay and? What does that have to do with you becoming a doppelganger?" Azar asked.

"The ingredient was Oklem blood," Lux replied.

Azar shook his head in confusion.

"How could you have known about Oklem blood all those years ago?"

"I knew the first Oklem. And I led him to his death."

Azar could hear Lux's voice start to choke. He was stunned at Lux's vulnerability. Talking to Lux was like talking to a brick wall, there was never any displays of emotion from him. Until now.

"I can't retell the story," Lux said. "I can't. You want to know what happened. Come here."

He held his arm out.

"Just like in the mansion. Make physical contact and enter the vision."

Azar paused, his heart thumping. He was nervous about this ability, and unsure as to what he would see. But he needed to know. He stood up and slowly made his way to Lux. Then, taking a deep breath, he closed his eyes, relaxed his mind, and grabbed his doppelganger's hand:

1628: The Grand Hall, Trail of Tales

"Ladies and gentlemen, welcome to the second year of celebration and success!" Orven cried out, waving to a full dining room. "Tonight, we shall open the gates to the darkest depths of the Supernatural Universe. The Tychun will walk amongst us!"

Cheers erupted around the room. Marvin was kneeling behind the curtain on stage, hands bound. Next to him was Peter, the first ever Oklem to exist. He was in his mid-thirties. Peter had been a family friend, closest to Marvin's father. Orven had spent the last year scavenging the Nations in search of him. He had been caught in the Ice Nation. His blood was the final ingredient. Oklem blood. Marvin regretted telling Jessani. How could he have suspected such a beautiful woman to be the product of such evil?

"We finally have all that is required. Please welcome Oklem Peter, who will be sacrificing his life for a greater good!" came Orven's travelling voice.

Two Pirates emerged from the red curtains and carried Peter onto the stage to a round of applause. Marvin fiddled with his restraints, managing to loosen them slightly. He was terrified. Right now his family was being held hostage by

Lara Sokolov, known as the Queen of the Pirates. If he didn't die tonight, his family would. His parents had told him to let them die. But how could he?

Just then he heard the unsheathing of a sword, and soon after a dreadful cry of anguish followed by a sickening thud. A collective "ooooh" sounded from the crowd. Marvin's entire body shook as he realised that Peter had been killed.

"Our final guest, with our final ingredient, is a very special boy. We had to dispose of our blood samples from last year, but we found out that this guest has a very special blood type. Please welcome, Marvin Stokhold!"

Marvin was dragged out to the stage. The room was fuller than the previous year. A large cauldron sat in the centre, steam drifting out from it. He knew that many ingredients had been added, with Peter's body slung over the edge of it, blood seeping in.

"For maximum efficiency, we will add the entirety of the Oklem's blood into the potion. This will ensure the portal has an unwavering strength and cannot be easily broken by weapons from the Nation's nor the Supernatural Universe. We also won't be needing an Oklem again, after all." Laughter broke out around the room as Orven made his way towards Marvin, standing him up. "Fortunately for yourself, my daughter is very fond of you," he said quietly, "and your life does not need to be taken for this to work. So your freedom shall be returned after providing a significant dose of your blood."

"What about my family?" Marvin asked.

"If you comply, I shall not harm them," Orven replied. He pulled a small knife from his coat. He sliced Marvin's bounds off and escorted him to the cauldron. Marvin glanced to the other side of the stage, where his eyes met Peacekeeper Serain's. He did not understand her involvement with all this. She was supposed to prevent these evil acts. Then he glanced to the front row of the crowd.

Orven cut Marvin's hand, a deep wound opening. He flinched as his blood started seeping into the cauldron. His eyes locked with Jessani's, which were staring widely at him. He knew she had fought to keep him alive. But she was also the reason his family was taken hostage.

As his blood continued to drip into the cauldron, Marvin saw someone enter the grand hall. The unmistakable ponytail, which was purple and stretched to her ankles, made Marvin's stomach turn. Lara Sokolov was supposed to be with his family, holding them hostage. Perhaps she had left them, knowing he would comply with Orven's terms. As she made eye contact with Marvin, she pulled a small dagger from her belt and made a slicing motion across her throat. Dread immediately swamped over Marvin.

"No," he said, looking at Orven. "You promised they'd be safe."

Orven turned to him, his face inches from Marvin's.

"I told you that you would live, and that I would not harm your family. Ms Sokolov can do what she likes," he said, an evil gleam in his eyes. His crooked, yellow teeth sent a shiver down Lux's spine.

Everything was over. There was nobody left to fight for.

A burning rage began to creep through Marvin's body. He had to act. Jessani looked at him with a similar expression of shock, but shook her head slightly, urging him to say nothing and comply. But Marvin could not do as she said. He could not be with her. Jessani was a beautiful woman, she would find love again. So he gave her one last look before pulling his arm out of Orven's loose grip. Immediately he swung it back at the Pirate, but Orven let out a growl of frustration and grabbed Marvin's head, dunking it into the cauldron. For a moment Marvin held his breath, but soon his mouth opened in a natural attempt to grasp some air. The potion raced down his throat. The taste was dreadful, making Marvin imagine he was consuming burnt faeces. But soon after he felt a sensation come over him.

An energy ran through his veins. Suddenly he felt incredibly strong. Orven's grip was no opposition as he stood up, taking a large breath. With excessive force, he knocked the cauldron over, the contents spilling across the stage. Screams and gasps echoed off the walls as he faced Orven. Just then a dagger slammed into his left shoulder. It hurt, but not as much as it should.

Marvin pulled it out, and to his astonishment, the wound began to heal itself instantly. He took one glance at Peacekeeper Serain, who had thrown it, before making a beeline for the end of the stage. He was there in a second. He was dumbfounded as to how he could move so fast. His vision was excellent. He felt phenomenal! Before anybody could take more than two steps to catch him, Marvin had already left the building, escape the only thought on his mind.

Chapter 27

Azar gasped as he opened his eyes, letting go of Lux's hand. The pain. The emotion. The feeling of empowerment. He had felt it all. He was breathless, sitting down on the edge of the hill. "There are benefits to being a doppelganger," Lux said, standing still and looking at the ground. "The speed, power, strength. But there is also an emptiness, an isolation, and most of the time that is not worth it."

Azar wrapped his arms around himself.

"I'm so sorry for what happened to your family. It's horrible," he said.

"It's life, you play with the big players you are bound to be hurt," Lux replied.

"There's one thing I don't understand. In the See-er's vision, I saw Peter become an Oklem in 1600. In 1627, Orven failed with his portal because he lacked Oklem blood. I get that you told Jessani which is what led to the vision we just saw, but why did it take so long for Orven to even attempt the portal?"

"Orven had not yet found a place to activate his portal. The Peacekeepers had too strong a hold on the Nations and Skull to allow such a portal to operate. So he had to find a place they could not interfere with,' Lux said.

"That's the Trail of Tales," Azar said, gaining a nod from his doppelganger.

"He also needed to have all the ingredients, and that took time," Lux explained. "He was only just starting to experiment with Supernatural herbs and serums. It was especially difficult because he was running not just from the Peacekeepers, but from an ex-lover."

"Lara Sokolov. Jessani told me they were together for a while when they were mortal," Azar said.

"Correct," Lux replied, sitting next to Azar. "The reason Orven has not had another attempt at bringing forth the Tychun, after I ruined his potion and became a doppelganger, is because he has never had another Oklem. He had killed Peter, and nobody knew of any other Oklem. Then the year of 1840 came and we were sent to the Supernatural Universe. You know the rest after that." Azar was confused. The See-er had said there were three Oklem before him. He wondered who they were, but decided that Lux had told him all he knew. He moved the conversation along.

"Jessani believes that my birth somehow removed your ability to love, thus ending your relationship with her. Is that even possible?" Azar asked.

"Not at all," Lux said, raising his eyes to Azar. "I cannot love, but it is because I took something in the Supernatural Universe to break it completely. When I learnt of Orven's plans, and that Jessani supported them, I knew I could not stay. We would not be able to keep our relationship a secret. Besides, she had already broken my trust once and gotten my family killed. But our love was intense, and I couldn't do it alone."

"Wow," Azar said, a little stunned at what he was hearing. The sun was now spreading its final rays of the day across the sky.

"Do you trust me yet?" Lux asked.

"Yes. I do," Azar said. "And I want to help you."

"With what?" Lux said, standing up again.

"When I went into your memory, I could feel what you felt. That emptiness, you have to deal with that every day. I want to help you get your love back," Azar replied. Lux clicked his tongue.

"What makes you think I want that?"

"Let's call it doppelganger intuition," Azar said with the slightest smile creeping onto the edge of his mouth.

"Please tell me there is a genuine emergency you wanted to talk to me about," Lux said, neither agreeing nor denying with what Azar said. Suddenly Azar remembered Emma. How had Azar forgotten? He leapt to his feet.

"Emma is dying. Peacekeeper Drand does not think she can make it through the night," Azar explained quickly. Lux tensed.

"How is she dying?"

"She was bitten by a supernatural creature with Tychun venom at the bank," Azar said.

"What? I was at the bank. There was no threat when I left," Lux said, sincere concern on his face.

"I don't know why you seem to care about her, but it does mean that if you know any way to counter the venom, you'll tell me, right?" Azar asked.

"Azar, we are talking about Tychun venom. It is fatal to both mortals and supernatural creatures," Lux replied, exasperated.

"No," Azar snapped, "there has to be a way. Jake needs her."

For the first time, Azar saw Lux look at him with pity in his eyes.

"By morning, Jake will need you," Lux said.

Azar's breathing started to sharpen. He could not, would not, accept that. He was struggling enough without having to try and manage Jake's suffering from Emma's death. He racked his brains, trying to think of anything that could help. Then it came to him. Lux noticed the slight change in his doppelganger, looking at Azar expectantly.

"In Lisarow, I learnt about the origin of the Oklem. The Oklem was created to counter the Tychun. The See-er told me that every Oklem has had a different purpose. Yet they all exist on the basis that they oppose this supernatural evil."

"But..." Lux began, stopping suddenly as his eyes widened. Azar continued.

"We know that Oklem blood can open portals, but what if it can counter the Tychun's venom as well? What if my blood can save Emma's life?"

"Of course," Lux replied. "In the supernatural realm, creatures can both kill and heal venomous bites with their blood. Vampires are well known for that ability. It would certainly make sense."

"And that is all I have got," Azar said, running past his doppelganger.

"Azar, it'll take you forever to ride back to Mintor," Lux said. "I'll take you there."

"What about Starc?" Azar asked.

"I'll come back for him. I look just like you—he won't notice," Lux said.

Azar was sceptical, but knew Lux was right. He had been left dizzy from the short trip between the mansion and the horse carriages in Lisarow. How would he feel after travelling at Lux's speed across a much longer distance?

It didn't matter, a life was on the line.

"Let's hope I don't throw up," Azar said, grabbing Lux's arm.

"Just aim it away from my shoes," Lux added.

Then, as if he was on a rollercoaster, only faster, Azar was moving. But he could only see distorted shapes and lights around him. His heart was pounding and his head began to ache. Suddenly he stopped, losing his balance as one would standing on a bus when it brakes hard without warning. He was right outside the hospital. He took a few moments to recover on the pavement before standing up.

"I don't know if it will work," Lux said, leaning against the wall, "but we're here now."

"Are you going to come in?" Azar asked.

Lux shook his head.

"Thank you," Azar said.

"For what?" came the sassy reply.

"For showing me that I can trust you."

Lux looked away. "You look for the good in people, Azar. You just have to find that good in yourself as well. Now go," he said, tossing his head towards the doors.

Azar hurried into the hospital.

Chapter 28

Azar took the hospital's elevator and once again found himself running out of it before the doors had completely opened. He raced down the ward and into Emma's room. Jake was now sitting on the bed with Emma, his arms wrapped around her. Her entire body was now covered in a charred black. Peacekeeper Drand was seated on a chair near the window. Both of them looked up as the Oklem entered.

"I need a syringe," Azar said, taking his jacket off.

"Why?" Jake asked, his face wet with tears.

"I have no idea if it will work, but I think my blood can save Emma," Azar replied. A moment passed as Jake's eyes widened and Drand stood up.

"The Oklem was created to counter the Tychun," Drand said, one hand on his chin in thought. "I see your logic."

Drand went to the monitor next to Emma, which displayed her heart rate that was now beating very slowly, and grabbed a syringe from a small steel tray.

"Shouldn't we get a nurse?" Azar asked. Drand looked up.

"I am a Peacekeeper, Azar. I have done far more than a simple blood transfusion."

Azar paused, the thoughts of doubt surrounding the Peacekeeper's trust whirling through his mind. Just then the heart monitor began beeping, a warning sound.

"Hurry!" Jake pleaded.

Azar looked at Jake's expression of despair, and he forgot about his suspicions. He held his right arm out, and Drand pushed the syringe in, extracting his blood. Azar still felt a little numb from the travel with Lux, so he barely felt anything.

Drand held the syringe up.

"Does she drink it?" Azar inquired.

"It is a counter to the Tychun. It goes directly onto the initial wound," Drand answered. He went around the bed as two nurses burst into the room. Emma's life was on the verge of being taken away.

"What are you doing?" one of the nurses demanded. Azar turned to them.

"The Peacekeeper is trying to save her life," he said. "Please let him."

Drand placed the syringe over Emma's left wrist, where the initial bite mark was. Then, grimacing, he put the syringe into the wound. He pushed down, Azar's blood seeping into the infected skin. For a moment nothing happened, the machine continued blaring. Then suddenly it slowed and with a heavy gasp of air Emma's eyes burst open and she sat up. She looked around the room, her eyes resting on her brother. Very slowly, Azar could see the blisters starting to fade. The entire room appeared to release a sigh of relief.

"Jake?" she asked, looking disoriented.

Jake embraced her tightly.

"It's a miracle," the nurse whispered, holding a hand to her mouth.

Azar was relieved as much as he was astonished. It had worked. Jake explained to a confused Emma as to what had happened, how she was bitten, and Drand turned to the nurses.

"I sent Azar to find what I hoped would be an antidote in my palace," he lied.

"Remarkable work, Peacekeeper Drand. She has completely healed," the nurse said, observing the monitors.

"I advise we give the siblings a moment. I shall sign whatever papers are needed to let our patient leave," Drand said. After checking the equipment and Emma's vital signs, the nurses left the room. Emma's pale skin colour began to return.

"I think it is best that we don't make it common knowledge for everyone to know what you are, for your safety," Drand said quietly to Azar.

"I completely agree, I have enough attention as it is," Azar replied, still wide eyed and surprised. Drand left the room as Azar turned back to the siblings.

"Thank you, Azar," Emma said with a smile.

"I can't really explain it, but you're welcome," Azar responded.

"I am not going to stop until I find out who let those creatures in," Jake said through gritted teeth.

"Why don't you let me handle the investigations, Jake," Emma replied, stretching her arms. "When I am out of here, I want to hear all about the Trail of Tales. Did you meet the Queen of the Pirates?" she asked.

"More than that, Azar got a private showing behind closed curtains," Jake replied, hopping off the bed and trying to suppress a grin. Azar avoided eye contact, something in which Emma picked up on.

"Why don't you two go back to the Whistle. I feel exhausted, so I might stay here for the night. I'll call you when I talk to the nurses," she added, looking at her brother.

Azar and Jake agreed and after a farewell embrace, they left the hospital. The sun had well and truly set by now, leaving the air cool.

"How did you discover that your blood was the cure?" Jake asked as they walked along the rather quiet city streets.

"I went to see Lux. I learnt some things about him and suddenly the idea came to me. I was not confident that it would work at all," Azar replied.

"I thought she was going to die too," Jake said softly, looking up at the stars, suppressing tears.

"There have already been too many deaths this last week. I want to try and stop talking about it, and I have just the topic to do that," Azar said.

Jake stopped walking, looking at Azar with intrigue. The golden streaks through his hair lit up under the lamp post, making Azar's stomach turn.

"Peacekeeper Serain is working with the Pirates," he said.

"What?" Jake asked in surprise. "How do you know?"

"Lux showed me."

"Showed?" Jake inquired.

"Long story short, I seem to have the ability to witness events that have happened in the past. The See-er first showed me in Lisarow. Tonight I saw the moment Lux became a doppelganger. Peacekeeper Serain was present, introduced as the Pirates "biggest weapon",' Azar explained.

"What? Have you told Peacekeeper Drand?" Jake asked, his face tense.

Azar was a little bit surprised at how Jake was responding. Not the fact that Jake was shocked, but that he appeared to be almost devastated, veins exposing themselves on his forehead.

"I have not been sure I can trust any of the Peacekeepers," Azar said quietly, hoping there was nobody around.

"Before I came to Lisarow, Emma mentioned her doubts of the Nation's leaders as well," Jake said. "But I cannot see how Peacekeeper Drand especially is against our cause. He just saved Emma's life. You have been told a lot, but remember who you have heard the information from. Your parents, your doppelganger, people who have either broken your trust or are still yet to earn it."

Jake had a point, and Azar needed to talk to someone who had substantial authority. They continued to walk towards the Whistle, approaching an intersection.

"I'll go and see him tomorrow," Azar said, "I need someone who can give me a sense of direction. I think I might have to go to the Ice Nation though."

"Why?"

"It's where the Oklem started. When I was in the Fortune Caves, I saw an outline of some tall, snowy mountain peaks. Maybe there is something there I can use to help figure out how to use my mind effectively. Do you know much about the Ice Nation?"

Jake shrugged.

"I know it's cold. I also know that aside from designated hologram and telephone points, you cannot contact anyone there from outside the Nation."

Jake began to cross the road, Azar behind him. They didn't speak until they approached the Whistle. They went through the first room of security before travelling through the tinted revolving doors, stopping in the foyer. It was mostly deserted, with two officers sitting at another security desk along the wall.

"I think I'll be okay to get to my room from here," Azar said. "You didn't have to come all this way."

"You're a popular target at the moment," Jake replied with a shrug, "and I may need your blood again if Emma keeps snooping."

Azar laughed. Suddenly Jake's body language shifted. He put his hands in his front jeans pockets and kicked the ground.

"I haven't really known how to bring up *the* topic again," he said quietly, avoiding eye contact.

"I know how you feel," Azar said. "I'm exactly the same. It is so scary thinking what would happen if random people found out. I'm more okay with them knowing I'm an Oklem doppelganger than gay. I think we just hate the thought of being seen as different."

"Yeah," was all Jake said.

A phone started beeping, and Azar realised it was Jake's.

"Emma has messaged," he said. A moment passed as Jake read the text before he cleared his throat.

"Looks like she is going to stay at the hospital just for the night."

"May as well stay on the side of caution," Azar replied. "It's pretty late, do you want to stay here in the Whistle? You can sleep in my bed and I can use my parents' room."

Azar wanted to kick himself. Just as he had done when he first met Jake, there was some unexplained internal desire to stay around Jake, and as a result it had made him say something bizarre.

"Honestly, that'd be great. Only if you're okay with that. I know your parents…" Jake trailed off. He didn't seem to indicate any noticeable change from Azar.

"I'll be fine," Azar said, "besides, maybe it'll be better with some company."

Azar led the way to the elevators. The doors opened at one of them and two men in suits walked out, followed by a woman. Azar immediately noticed the scar on her right cheek. Half her head was shaved, and she had a dark purple nail polish. She stopped for a moment as she locked eyes with Azar, before allowing a smile to spread across her face.

"Forgive me, you just looked like someone I once knew. Hi. My name is Lisa Sparrow. I'm a newly appointed mayor of a town in the Fire Nation," she said.

"I'm Azar, this is Jake. Welcome to Mintor," Azar said hesitantly. A brief pause followed before Lisa clasped her hands.

"Sorry to hold you up, it is rather late. Peacekeeper business never sleeps, I'm learning," Lisa said. She then followed her security as the boys entered the elevator.

"Well, that was weird," Jake said.

"What Peacekeeper business does she have? I thought Drand was still at the hospital. I'll need to talk to him tomorrow," Azar said.

The elevator reached level fifty-eight and Azar walked along the corridor to his room. Since returning to Mintor, he had only been there to change before racing to the hospital with Jake. The door required a fingerprint to access it. This was only a requirement for the levels housing senators and special guests. Azar's parents were also given access to his room, as he was underage when he was first moved from sharing with them.

"That explains how Lux got in," Jake murmured.

"When was Lux here?" Azar asked as the door opened.

"The night you left for Lisarow," Jake conceded. "Obviously you've got the same DNA prints." Azar turned on the lights as he went through the narrow entrance corridor and into his room. The bed was neatly made, the curtains drawn, and a blue dressing gown sat in a heap on the floor. Azar had received it as a gift last year, but had never personally worn it.

"Gross," he said, more to himself than anything. Jake went and looked behind the curtain, gazing down at the city lights.

"I wish my view was like this," he commented.

"I love it," Azar replied, "I just wish I had someone to share it with. Brett could never stay the night, I was too afraid my parents would catch us. Ironic hey."

Jake stepped away from the window, facing Azar. The Oklem immediately felt a nervous shudder ripple through him. He opened his mouth to say something, but his throat locked up.

"I know you miss Brett," Jake said slowly, fiddling with his fingers in front of him. "I know you feel like you haven't let go. I can't say that accepting who I am is easy, but I also cannot deny my feelings. There is something between us, Azar. We both know it. However I will never accept that we can be together if I feel like you haven't let go. So tomorrow, after you see Drand, I am going to take you back to that hill where we first met, and we will create a memorial for both Brett and your father. After that, when I know you have had some closure, we will see what happens."

Azar stood still for a long while.

"Wow," he eventually said, "I think that's exactly what I need. Thank you."

Jake nodded his head in acknowledgement. Azar picked out a few of his clothes, preparing to go to his parents' room.

"Bathroom is in there," he said, pointing to a door on his left as he made his way for the exit. As he got to the door, he stopped. His mind was racing at a million miles an hour. What was holding him back? Brett was dead. His parents would never come back to the Whistle. He was about to embark on a journey to a Nation he had never been to before, where anything could happen. How much longer was he going to wait for an apparent moment where he would know he was ready to move on?

"No," he said, turning around and dropping his things. Jake was back near the bed, looking at him with a slight frown.

"Emma is just the latest example reminding me that life is unpredictable, and that we could die at any moment. I want to have lived taking risks, doing things that will make my heart race," Azar stated.

Jake's face immediately softened as he realised where Azar was going. Before he could think about what he was doing any further, Azar marched forward and kissed Jake. For the first time since Azar had walked in on Brett and Jordan, he felt a sensation blitz through him. A passion. Jake's lips were warm, and his hands moved slowly along Azar's back.

They parted, Azar's heart pounding.

"I guess we'll both stay here," he said with a sly smile that slowly widened. Whatever the future held for Azar, he was glad that he had this moment. A moment where the love and hope he thought was lost was suddenly in his arms.

Chapter 29

Azar could barely contain his excitement as he put the coffees onto the customers table. The entire cafe was vibrating with excitement. Wendy came out from the kitchen and placed a small radio on the counter.

"Peacekeeper Drand has just released a statement confirming that Orven has been killed, and the Pirates attack has failed, meaning the war is over," a newsreader was saying.

A cheer erupted around the cafe, many people on their phones reading the reports or calling loved ones. The war was over. Ten long years of a threat so evil the thought of it succeeding brought a shudder to every citizen's shoulders. Azar would finally be able to see his parents again. The clock ticked over to midday, signalling the end of Azar's shift. He raced into the back room where Wendy was opening another bag of coffee beans.

"What a remarkable day," she exclaimed.

"Indeed it is," Azar replied, taking his apron off. "I need to go and celebrate."

"Don't get too carried away. You are always just so wild," Wendy said sarcastically. Azar gave her a brief kiss on the cheek and headed back out. As he went through the door, he almost ran into Sophie, who was carrying a tray of dirty plates.

"Sorry," he said, steadying the tray. Sophie's eyes widened.

"It's fine. Are you finished for the day?" she asked.

"Yes."

Sophie's facial expression dropped.

"Oh, well have a good afternoon," she replied, walking past Azar. He paused for a moment at Sophie's strange response, but quickly forgot about it as he headed towards Brett's apartment. The sun was shining on a crystal-clear winter's day. Azar refrained from texting Brett of his arrival, wanting to surprise his boyfriend. He opened the apartment complex's gate with his own key and entered the building. The elevator was out of service as usual, so he scaled the four levels of stairs. He opened Brett's door and went in. The kitchen was empty, as was the small dining area. Azar's eyes diverted to the floor, where a pair of white sneakers sat under a green t-shirt. He'd never seen those before. Azar put the keys on the table as he went to Brett's bedroom. How was he still asleep? He barged through the door, flicking the light on as he did so.

"Alright, time to get up and celebrate with me!" Azar announced, looking at the bed. Immediately he froze. Brett sat up in the bed, naked. Beside him was another person, his orange curly hair visible above the sheets. More clothes were spread out across the floor. Azar's knees nearly buckled as the weight of the situation came crashing down onto him.

"Azar, wait," Brett said, holding a hand up.

"Oh my god," Azar murmured. In a split second his world had shattered. Then his vision slightly blurred. He must be crying. He needed to leave.

"Azar," Brett called out. "You need to go."

What was he talking about? Azar raced back to the front door, wrenching it open. Brett was standing on the other side.

"The ice caves. Go," he ordered.

****

Azar's head was spinning. He opened his eyes and jumped, startled. He was in his bed at the Whistle. Daylight was trying to break through the curtains, signalling the following morning had arrived. It had been a bad dream. Or had it? Looking to his right, Jake was beside him, rolled over with his back to the Oklem. Azar slowly got out of bed, going to the bathroom. He washed his face, the cold water waking him up. His mind seemed to have a mission of its own. He needed to speak to Peacekeeper Drand. He went back into the room. Jake had woken, rubbing his eyes as he sat up, looking at Azar.

"Morning," he said with a cheeky grin. The events of the night before came back into Azar's mind, reminding him that he had now physically taken the step to move on.

"Morning," Azar replied. Jake cocked his head, noticing Azar's lack of enthusiasm.

"Are you okay?" he asked.

"Yeah, I just had a bad dream."

Azar went to his wardrobe, deciding on what he would wear to meet the Nation's leader. He hadn't noticed Jake come up from behind, wrapping his arms around his waist and kissing Azar's neck. It felt good.

"Whilst you see Drand, I'll go check up with Emma," Jake said. "I'll tell her all that happened in Lisarow, from the dinner to Jessani."

"What about Peacekeeper Serain's betrayal?" Azar asked, turning around.

"I will mention what you've been told. Even if it is true, the take down of a Peacekeeper is no easy task. We'll meet at the stables later and talk about it all. Then you need to go to the Ice Nation," Jake replied.

Azar showered and once Jake was ready, they left the Whistle. Before meeting Drand, Azar wanted to visit Wendy at the cafe. His dream reminded him that he never told her he was leaving. Not that it was his choice, but he still felt bad. Jake headed for his own apartment, leaving Azar to reflect on the night before. He felt a lot better, as if he had finally offloaded the growing weight of regret and sadness. He pushed through the glass door to the cafe, the scent of coffee and toast making his stomach rumble. The cafe was at its usual busy levels with those grabbing their morning dose of caffeine.

"Azar?" came a soft voice. Sophie was standing nearby, wiping a table down. Suddenly Azar remembered the invitation he had received to her party. He had well and truly missed it.

"I am so sorry, I didn't plan to be away," he said.

Azar could see the hurt on her face, far worse than what he could have anticipated.

"No, it's okay," Sophie replied. She turned away and went back behind the counter. Azar waited a moment before following, passing her and pushing through the doors to the kitchen. Wendy was standing near one of the sinks, her head resting in her hands.

"Wendy?" Azar said.

She immediately stood up straight, looking at the visitor.

"Oh Azar," she said, moving forwards and embracing him. "I'm so sorry for your loss."

Azar was bewildered. "How did you know?" he asked. Wendy took his hand and led him out a back door, stopping next to a dumpster in the alleyway. She glanced around, ensuring they were alone.

"Peacekeeper Drand came to me this morning, just before I opened the cafe," she said. "What did he say?" Azar inquired.

"He knows of the events that took place at the Trail of Tales."

Azar looked at her, his question written on his expression. Wendy couldn't refrain a slight smile from clipping the corner of her mouth.

"He said you'd have such a lack of faith in him," she said. "Drand has people everywhere, watching, reporting. I am one of them, though very low on the chart. I simply observe those that enter the cafe, looking for any sign of trouble. He told me of your losses, and sends his apologies in advance."

"For what?" Azar asked. Thinking over it, he was not all that surprised to find out Wendy was working for Drand. She often had strange guests meeting with her in the same area they were in now, and sometimes envelopes directed for her instead of the business.

"He has left Mintor for a while, his destination was not revealed to me," Wendy answered.

Azar took a step back. Why had Drand not told him? Azar remembered Drand had wanted to talk to him at the hospital. Maybe it was far more urgent than Azar had realised. Wendy saw Azar start to panic, his breathing quickening. She gripped both his shoulders with her hands.

"He told me that you have been unbelievably brave, Azar. I was not surprised to hear it, your life has been far from easy, but every day you have turned up to work here, to make sure other people's days are better than yours. Now it is time that the next adventure is for you. It is somewhere you must travel to alone."

"But I need to talk to someone who knows more about it than I," Azar replied.

"You have already gotten everyone you need, sweetheart," Wendy said.

She reached into her white apron and pulled out an envelope and small package. She gave Azar the package first. He opened it to find a new phone. Azar looked at Wendy. What else did she know?

"All the answers you seek are in here," Wendy said, handing him the envelope.

"Please be safe, Azar. When you're ready to come back to work, you know where to find me." She gave Azar one final embrace before going back into the cafe, leaving Azar alone. Why had Peacekeeper Drand left without warning? Where had he gone?

Sighing, he opened the envelope, pulling out a small rectangular piece of paper. It was a plane ticket to the Ice Nation's airport. The flight was leaving Mintor at nine o'clock that night. "Great," Azar murmured. No time to rest. He was about to throw the envelope into the skip bin behind him when he saw another folded piece of paper inside. He pulled it out and read it:

Azar,

I am sorry we did not have time to talk about the events that took place in Lisarow. The recent attack on Emma has forced me to meet with the other Peacekeepers to ensure there are no more victims. I know there is so much you want to ask from me. Truth be told, the Oklem have always been private people, meaning information about them has been scarce, even for Peacekeepers.

Therefore, I know you will benefit more from going to the Frowl in the Ice Nation. There is a cave there where only Oklem can enter. If, after that, you still have questions, I will most certainly discuss those with you. I have a guide who will travel with you upon your arrival. You cannot be in better hands.

Regards,

Peacekeeper Drand

Azar was a little more comforted by the letter. At least Drand had told him where to go. He was starting to feel like he could genuinely trust the Peacekeeper. Maybe Serain had somehow managed to keep her betrayal a secret. Using his new gift, Azar messaged Jake, telling him he was going to head towards the stables. Then he tucked the letter and ticket into his jacket and left the alleyway.

Chapter 30

Emma left the hospital first thing in the morning. After resting up, her body seemed to have completely healed, the blisters and dizziness gone. She returned to her apartment to have a shower and get into a new pair of clothes. She noticed Jake wasn't there, his bed was still made as she had left it days ago. Did he come home? As she tied her hair up, she ran through her plan for the day. It was fairly straight forward. A briefing with Peacekeeper Drand, then she was going to find out who was working against the Nations. Who had followed her during the attack on the bank? Who had let creatures laced with Tychun venom into Mintor? To her, everyone was a suspect. She could not rule out foul play from anyone.

Emma hurried through the foyer of the senate, following the maze-like structure before getting to the palace's interior entrance. She came through a tall, open doorway which was opposite the elevator used to travel underground between the palace and Whistle.

A woman with very short black hair and wearing a grey suit looked up from a small desk, eyeing Emma over the top of her glasses.

"Can I help you?" she asked sharply. Emma had seen the woman almost every week when she visited Drand for briefings, but it appeared no amount of time or familiarity could break through her shell.

"I am here to see Peacekeeper Drand," Emma announced, placing a hand on her hip to enforce her dominant status as Drand's private investigator.

"He is currently away," the woman said.

"What do you mean?" Emma inquired.

"He isn't here, Flare. Can I take a message?" the assistant asked, closing her notepad and standing up with a frustrated look in her eyes.

"You can tell me where he is," Emma said, placing her badge on the desk. The woman gazed at it for a moment before tossing her head back in frustration.

"He went to the Earth Nation for an emergency meeting with the Peacekeepers. I do not know where exactly, nor what the topic of interest was."

Emma believed her, slowly sliding the badge along the desk until it reached the edge, then picked it up. The Peacekeeper had never left without informing Emma of where he was going. Something didn't add up.

"I'm just going to have a brief check in the meeting room. I am rather concerned he did not inform me of his travels," she said, walking to the door.

Emma's job granted her access to every room in every building if necessary, apart from a Peacekeeper's personal quarters. She made her way through the small waiting area and into the room. The four coloured lounges sat in the centre, the table bare. No tea or wine on the table was a sure sign that Drand was absent, Emma had come to learn.

Nothing seemed out of the ordinary.

She was about to turn around when she heard the faintest of sounds. A beeping noise, coming from the far corner of the room, near a table located next to the huge glass window pane. As she approached, she realised it was a holographic video messenger table. It was designed for when Peacekeeper Drand could not talk with the caller at the time, so recorded messages were stored and displayed when he was next available. A yellow light was flashing above the label *new message*. Should she press it? On the one hand it would be a severe breach of the Peacekeeper's privacy. On the other, Drand had left without a word. Why? Trust and who to place it in had quickly become a question without a clear answer, maybe this would reveal something for Emma to work with. She pressed the button.

A hologram sprung to life. A man was standing alone, hands held behind his back, his face hidden under the shadow of a cap.

"I have some startling news to report, Drand," he said. Emma could tell his voice was altered, making it sound mechanical in order to keep his identity a mystery. Most likely to remain anonymous to those like Emma, who was snooping. He continued.

"I did some digging into Jessani's past, and I can now confirm your suspicions that she is in fact Orven's daughter. I decided it was of interest for me to see who the mother is. I found something, not a name, but perhaps a hint. Jessani went to a jewel maker here in Lisarow after her run-in against the Oklem. She handed over a bracelet. I faked a story to the jeweller and discovered that the bracelet was a gift from her mother, with the initials LS on it. I will continue to research more. I hope this information has helped you."

The hologram vanished. Emma stood still for a while, thinking things over. If Drand was searching for information about Jessani's family, it was clear to Emma that he was not faking his loyalty to the Nations. Ignorant, for a Peacekeeper, but not an enemy. She turned around slowly, looking at the lounges. There had been a lot of suspicion thrown onto the Peacekeepers, none more so than Peacekeeper Serain. The front door opened and the assistant came in.

"I think we've had enough time snooping, wouldn't you say?" she said, crossing her arms.

"How does it feel, being you?" Emma asked, taking a few steps towards the door. "Working for the Peacekeeper of the Mortal Nation, yet always being left on the wrong side of the door. Is that why you despise me?"

"I think it's time for you to leave, Investigator Flare," the assistant replied coldly, also turning to go out. Emma unleashed her whip and flung it past the woman, wrapping it around the door handle and pulling, slamming it shut.

"As Drand's assistant, you would have heard a great deal of things over the last few years, some rumours, others facts," Emma said slowly.

"And what are you after? A rumour or a fact?" the assistant asked. Emma walked right up to the woman, her boots clicking on the marble floors.

"A name. Specifically, Peacekeeper Serain's first name," she said.

"What's in it for me?"

"Your job," Emma snapped. Her tone was much deeper, more threatening. This assistant suffered from a big ego, and Emma had no issue reminding her of who is higher on the chain.

"Fine. Louvinia Serain," the answer came reluctantly.

"Wonderful," Emma replied, striding out the door and back towards the foyer of the senate. Louvinia Serain. LS. Knowing that Jessani's father was the leader of the Pirates was bad enough, finding out that her mother was the Peacekeeper of the Fire Nation was far worse. She had no idea what schemes Serain had been implementing, or how far along they had come. Emma needed to contact Drand immediately. But how could she? He had vanished. She suddenly wondered if Serain had something to do with it. She went outside to her pink motorcycle, completely unsure of where to go next. She felt a huge responsibility had landed itself squarely on her shoulders, and time was of the essence. She decided she would call her brother. Maybe he knew something that he didn't realise was important to this revelation. As she reached for her phone, she felt the crackle of paper in her back pocket. She forgot she had stashed there the papers she had found in the safe. *Freedom,* was the title. There had to be a link between Serain and the Queen of Pirates, whom Emma assumed had written the document in the first place. She called Jake, hoping he would pick up.

Chapter 31

Azar and Jake rounded the final corner on the trail before arriving at their destination. The lake was a murky green after the recent days of rain had washed the dust, leaves and stones into it. Starc had been most satisfied with another long journey up the mountain, neighing at the sight of Azar holding a saddle at the stables. When Azar dismounted at the lake, Starc put his head over the Oklem's right shoulder, receiving a gentle pat along his mane. Azar told Jake about his encounter with Wendy, and how Drand had gone to the Earth Nation. Jake agreed that Azar had to go to the Ice Nation that night. He needed to discover who he really was. Azar was about to go through the scrub covered path to the park and hill when he paused.

"What's wrong?" Jake asked, leaving his horse with Starc.

"I don't want to make the park a graveyard for them," Azar said. "It's my place. They don't deserve to be there. I want to do it here, by the lake."

"Be my guest," Jake said, spreading his arms out. Azar walked around the trees, through the bush, searching for the right place to create a memorial. There was a little clearing where a small dirt mound had built up over a rock. This was it. Azar had brought an item representing each man he had lost. On the left, Azar put a photograph that had been taken of him with his father two years ago, laughing with burgers in their hands. Jake picked a piece of bark off the ground, shaped like a scoop. He knelt down and dug a small hole in the moist dirt. Azar gave him the photo, which was placed in the hole and covered. Azar clasped his hands in front of him. "Dad, you were a man who always fought for what you believed was right, even if it was an unpopular choice. You represented the people of Mintor, and were a friend to many. Somewhere along the way, you got lost. I don't know how a man who was so resilient could be manipulated into liking yourself to the Pirates in Skull. The consequence of your choice brought you to the end of your life. Today I am remembering you as the father I have known you to be. Loving, protective, and honourable. Rest in peace, Steve Geminus."

A gentle breeze was all that disturbed the silence. Azar tried not to think too much about the isolation he felt, abandoned by his family. He concentrated his thoughts on the memories, the times he remembered feeling happy and safe.

A few minutes passed before Jake rose and went to the other side of the rock, making another small hole in the ground. Azar's heart started beating faster as he reached into his coat pocket and pulled out a small snow globe. It was a confined version of the city of Mintor. Azar shook it one last time, watching as the "snow" rotated in the sphere, slowly covering the city in a white blanket. Brett had given it to him on his eighteenth birthday, as a reminder of what they called home. He gave it to Jake's outstretched hand, who placed it into the earth and buried it.

"What can I say, Brett," Azar began. "You were my rock, you made life worth living. When I first met you, I was intrigued at the boy with messy blonde hair and a nose ring. You were mysterious, handsome, a bit of a bad boy. Finding out the truth these last few weeks has been hard, and I know I gave you a cold shoulder. Despite the fact that it was planned for us to meet, I know that what we shared was real. You know everything about me, and showed me that I am exactly who I am meant to be. Most importantly, you made me not only realise but accept that it is okay to be gay. That is something I will carry with me every day, and pass on to others who need that reassurance. We may not be lovers anymore, but we are friends. That will never change. Rest in peace, Brett Ullandra."

This time Jake stood up and stood next to Azar, putting his head on the Oklem's shoulder and wrapping his arm around Azar's back. Azar didn't cry, he had already done that. Instead he felt closure. Eventually they parted.

Then Azar remembered he had one more thing in his coat. He pulled out the necklaces the little girl Fayre had given him in Lisarow. He had been told to give one to whoever he felt safe with. He held the purple and yellow necklace out to Jake.

"Take this," he said softly. He explained what they represented, and how the necklaces could not be separated. Jake traced the colours with his fingers.

"I've never really been a jewellery guy," he said, unhooking it and giving it back to Azar. "I suppose this is an exception. Could you put it on?" he asked.

Azar did so, then turned around for Jake to put the aqua necklace around his neck. Jake's fingers were warm as they brushed Azar's skin. As soon as he was done, Azar turned around and noticed the necklaces were glowing. Jake noticed too, his eyes going wide. Then Azar stepped forward and kissed him, their bodies pressed together. They stayed like this for a long while. It felt surreal, kissing a boy again. Azar had forgotten what it felt like to kiss someone he actually had feelings for. Jake's phone suddenly buzzed in his front pocket, the vibration rippling up Azar's leg. Jake pulled it out.

"Hey Emma, I—"

Jake stopped, his eyes widening as he listened to his sister.

"I'm with Azar," he eventually said. "Will do."

He hung up, looking out at Mintor.

"What's wrong? What did she say?" Azar asked, starting to get worried.

"I can't tell you yet," Jake said. "I need to look into this first."

Azar felt a little prang in the pit of his stomach.

"Secrets are what started our problem before," he said.

Jake turned back to Azar.

"Look, Azar. There's still a lot about each other that we don't know. My work involves a lot of privacy. I hear things, investigate them, and if they're true, I respond."

"So what did you hear?" Azar asked, folding his arms.

"I need to see if it's true first. Otherwise we'll jump to the wrong conclusions. Now I need to get you to the airport," Jake said, turning to go.

Azar paused. He understood what Jake was saying, and he didn't know Jake's work, but he didn't want to remain outside the circle of trust.

"Well, whatever it is, just don't get yourself hurt. I can get to the airport myself."

Azar turned and began to walk back around the lake. Jake followed.

"I know you can get there yourself, but that's not what I am going to let happen," Jake said as Azar reached Starc. Azar was half relieved to hear those words leave Jake, but half concerned that he was seen as being unable to look after himself. He wanted to be Jake's partner, not his work. Again he thought about everything he had been through in Lisarow, his abilities, his losses.

"Hey—" Jake said, reaching for Azar's hand after getting no response. As their skin touched, Azar suddenly felt himself whisked away, as if he was a mind with no body. It was exactly what had happened when he had touched Lux in the

Trail of Tales. A scene unfolded before him. Jake was standing in a dark room, a table in front of him. On the other side stood Peacekeeper Drand, who was placing something down.

"There is too much mystery surrounding the doppelganger's," Drand was saying, "Marvin has been lurking in the shadows for ten years."

"But there is no reason to assume Azar is aware of anything. I mean you didn't even know what Marvin looked like until very recently," Jake said.

"I believe Marvin may be fooling us all. Azar has been unusually absent since his parents went to the Trail of Tales. Knowing the tactics of the Pirates, and the doppelganger's abilities, I think Azar may be in trouble," Drand replied, pushing an item across the table to Jake. Jake picked up the knife, running a finger along the curved blade. He looked at the Peacekeeper with narrowed eyes.

"You think Marvin is impersonating Azar?" he asked.

"Or Azar is part of some scheme. Regardless, Azar is a risk to us all. Should Orven know he is an Oklem, he could very well be successful. You must put a stop to the threat."

"You want me to kill Azar?" Jake said with an obvious expression of shock.

"This blade is designed to kill both mortal and supernatural creatures. If my assumption is correct, it will be the evil doppelganger that you kill. Start your research and find out everything about Azar. Then make your move. And keep this task a secret. Not even your sister can know until it is done," Drand warned. The scene blurred then changed, and now Azar was looking at a moment he very much remembered. It was the first time he had met Jake at the top of the hill. Azar was standing up from the stone bench.

"My horse's name is Starc. I'm Azar," Azar said, extending an arm to Jake. In the pause that followed, Azar was inside Jake's thoughts, and could feel him twisting the blade around in his brown coat pocket. Does he strike this boy down? He didn't appear to be a threat, surely this was not Marvin. Looking into the boy's sparkling blue eyes, Jake decided to give it some more time. "Jake," he said, extending his right hand.

Azar gasped and woke to see he had fallen to the ground near Starc. Jake was looking at him in astonishment. Betrayal shot through Azar's veins, and fear. Was Jake going to kill him now the secret was out?

"Azar," was all Jake could say. Azar leapt up and shoved Jake backwards towards the lake.

"Stay the hell away from me," Azar said icily. He mounted Starc and took off back towards the hill, uncontrolled tears racing down his cheeks. He could feel he was barrelling towards a break down as he realised he was going back to square one. He couldn't trust anybody. How Jake could have kept that secret so long, especially after sleeping together, Azar didn't know. As Starc galloped along the trail, Azar had only one focus on his mind. He needed to learn what being an Oklem was so that he could stop being controlled by everyone else. He was going to the Ice Nation. He could feel his phone buzzing in his pocket. He looked at the screen and saw it was Jake. He declined the call, then turned his phone off.

Chapter 32

Emma drummed her fingers in thought as she sat at the table in her apartment. She was anxious as to what was going to happen next. Jake was going to meet her after he got Azar to the airport, what he didn't know was that Emma had invited a third person to the meeting. Whilst waiting, she decided to look through the papers she had retrieved from the bank before the safe went up in flames. She started with the page labelled *Freedom*. What did it mean? She was intrigued as to who wrote the papers, as Lara Sokolov was immobilised in the perpetuate container. She scanned the few lines on the page:

Today I am free from his debt.
My dream of a family will become a reality
I just have to find a way to get out of this room

Somebody else was trapped in the safe? How did they get out? When? Emma had so many pressing questions in which she hoped the following pages would hold answers to, but just then there was a knock at the door. Leaving the papers on the table, she walked through the small dining room and opened the door.

"I thought you usually barged into rooms," Emma said to Lux as he stepped into the room.

"Key word, usually," Lux replied, immediately giving himself a tour of the apartment, his hands brushing along the furniture. Emma closed the door and crossed her arms.

"Aren't you curious as to why I asked you to come here?" she asked the doppelganger. Lux stopped at the table, looking at the documents Emma had just been reading.

"I'm less interested in what it is you want to discuss, more so why you'd want to see me since you almost died last time we met," he said, his voice flat.

"Don't pretend like you don't care, Lux. Jake told me you got Azar back to the hospital in time to save my life. I don't blame you for what happened in the safe. But did you know there was somebody else locked in there, not just the Queen of the Pirates?" Emma asked, joining Lux at the table. The doppelganger shrugged.

"Whoever it was, they mustn't have been that important. Many people owed Orven over the years. He'd help them in exchange for their loyalty. It was most likely someone very ordinary in there," he said.

Lux's entire charisma was different. There was no sass, no attitude. Emma felt like there was something genuinely bothering him.

"I know it's the question everyone is asking, and I know you won't answer it until you're ready. But you came back ten years ago and didn't make an appearance that entire time. You're here for something I feel is much more personal."

Lux looked at her.

"Is this why you called me? A therapy session?" he asked.

"No," Emma replied. "I am saying that whatever your purpose, it isn't related to the Nation's or the Pirates. That means I feel I can trust you with something."

Lux cocked his head.

"We have company," he said, looking towards the door. Sure enough another knock came from it. It was probably Jake, Emma thought, but he had keys. She opened it and saw a boy who looked roughly the same age as Jake. Immediately she got a whiff of his cologne, and her stomach turned. It was the same herbal scent she had smelt on her brother the other week. He had short blonde hair and pale skin.

"Uh, hi," he said shyly, his cheeks flustering a deep red. "I'm guessing you're Emma. Is Jake here? He hasn't responded to my messages for a few days. I just want to make sure he's okay."

"Who are you?" Emma asked.

"Daniel. I've been seeing your brother," Daniel said, avoiding eye contact. Emma was unsure of what to do. What had Jake been up to?

"Well, that's interesting, because I've been seeing your brother too," Lux said, appearing suddenly behind Emma. Daniel's eyes widened in surprise at Lux. Emma turned and gave a quick, hard stare at the doppelganger. Then she sighed.

"We will sort this out. Here, come in and have a drink of water, you're incredibly red," she said, allowing Daniel to cautiously step in. Emma closed the door then sent a quick message to her brother telling him to get home as soon as possible.

"My name is Azar," Lux said, offering a hand to the nervous boy. Emma went to a cupboard in the kitchen and pulled out a glass. She filled it at the sink and handed it to Daniel, who sat at the table. Emma noticed the papers had gone. Where did Lux put them?

"This is weird," Daniel said.

"Yeah," Lux said, adding to the awkwardness. Emma knew Lux was enjoying the drama. She was annoyed because she wanted to discuss Peacekeeper Serain's betrayal but couldn't with Daniel present. Daniel finished his glass of water.

"I'm not sure how long my brother will be," Emma started, hoping the boy would leave. "I will tell him to call you as soon as—"

She got no further as she heard keys unlock the door. It opened and Jake walked in, tears smudged across his face. He stopped as he looked at Lux, then his eyes widened more at seeing Daniel.

"I'm so not dealing with any of this right now," Jake snapped, waving his arms carelessly.

"Well, I'd like an explanation," Lux said. He imitated the innocence of Azar perfectly, Emma thought.

"Jake, you practically bolted one night and then ghosted me. Is it because of Azar?" Daniel asked, standing up.

"We had a one night fling, Daniel. Get over it," Jake said, his breathing starting to get heavier. Something was seriously wrong.

"Okay, this is what we are going to do," Emma said, taking control. "I am going to talk to my brother, and then I will make sure he talks to both of you. Daniel, it's probably best if you leave first."

Daniel shook his head as he went to the doorway. He stopped in front of Jake.

"Don't bother," he said, then stormed out and down the corridor. Jake slammed the door shut.

"Jake what happened?" Emma asked, walking over to her brother.

"Leave me alone," Jake said, then he looked at Lux. "Don't you have a life, doppelganger? Get out."

Lux pulled out the papers he had tucked into the back of his pants and threw them onto the table. "Sorry you're having an emotional meltdown, but we have a serious problem," Lux replied.

"Yes we do. Peacekeeper Serain is Jessani's mother," Emma stated. Lux turned to her with a look of surprise.

"Where on earth did you get that assumption from?" he asked her.

"A spy from Peacekeeper Drand said he was trying to find the true identity of Jessani's mother. He said the initials were LS. Louvinia Serain. The Fire Nation's Peacekeeper is a Pirate," Emma explained.

"What?" Jake asked.

"Okay that is wrong," Lux said.

"How would you know anything?" Jake demanded. Emma was astonished at the hostility radiating from her brother. Jake started towards his room before stopping as Lux began to speak. "Because I dated Jessani for centuries. I know who her parents are. Serain had a relationship with Orven, but she was a Peacekeeper when they met, she cannot have children. Now coming back to my important point, I also know how we can find out who wrote this *Freedom* document in the Bank's safe," Lux said, holding up the papers.

"Tell us how," Emma said, her heart rate starting to rise. There was so much happening she could barely keep up. Lux pulled out one of the sheets and read from it.

"The container is still sealed. Orven has returned. It will not be long before the King and Queen reign once again'. Whoever wrote this wasn't trapped in the safe, they owned it. They visited it and made sure Orven's secret was kept hidden," Lux said.

"Do you know who owns the safe Lara was kept in?" Jake asked Emma. She shook her head.

"No but I can find out. Lux you haven't told us who Jessani's mother is," Emma added. Lux's eyes squinted and he clicked his tongue.

"Leave it with me," he said eventually.

"Useless," Jake said, marching into his room and slamming the door shut. Lux placed the papers back onto the table and also turned to leave.

"Wait, Lux," Emma said, raising a hand. "If Peacekeeper Serain is a traitor, how can I take her down? Why hasn't nature taken her out? I don't know what I should do, can I even trust the other Peacekeeper's?"

Emma was suddenly feeling lost. In the few years she had been on the job, she had never had so few people she could trust.

"I don't trust anybody," Lux replied simply, "it works better that way. I believe Azar is the key to removing this underlying threat. His Oklem blood is far more powerful because he is a doppelganger. It's like his abilities can be doubled. Whilst he finds out who he is, you should focus on what you can do now. Track down the owner of this safe. And snap your brother out of his misery."

After a brief pause, Lux opened the door and walked out. Emma's head began to ache. If the Peacekeeper's deceit wasn't enough, she had to find the owner of this safe, deal with Jake's unexpected breakdown, figure out why Lux was suddenly aiding them so willingly, because if he was not on sides, who else was he talking to? Lastly, and most importantly, she had to sit on the biggest question she could only ask Peacekeeper Drand. Her life had been saved by Azar's blood. Did that mean she was now an Oklem? She wasn't sure how she felt about that. It was at this moment that she suddenly wished she had somebody to talk to. Since being abandoned by her parents, Emma Flare had always dealt with life on her own. As much as she hated it, it appeared that this time was no exception. She gripped her whip which was latched around her right wrist, drawing comfort in the slight vibration it had as it waited for its next opportunity to strike.

Chapter 33

Azar exited the aircraft, wrapping a long coat around him. He had arrived at the Ice Nation, the origin of the Oklem existence. The airport compared to Mintor was very small, with only four plane terminals and two emergency ones. It was an outdoor terminal built at the base of a mountain, but, to Azar's awe, it also doubled as being at the snowy peak of another hill. Only the check in section was shielded within a room lined with glass window panes. The air was cold, the landscape was white. The journey had again allowed him to think about everything that had happened. His heart had broken over Jake's secret. But it had actually encouraged Azar to leave the Mortal Nation. He was done with the lies dwelling within his home city. Travelling alone meant he only needed to worry about himself, and right now that was finding out how to be an Oklem. He crossed the small runway and followed the signs directing the passengers to the lobby, which was just a large square with a steel roof, open sides offering no warmth. It was incredible how just days ago he had been sweating in Lisarow's heat, but was now considering putting a fourth jumper on under his coat. He carried with him a small suitcase he had quickly packed at the Whistle before leaving. Shivering, he moved further into the covered section, his feet sinking slightly into the soft and snow-covered ground.

He soon realised he was not too sure of where he was going, so he trudged over to the side, stopping next to a railing which overlooked what appeared to be a train terminal. At least there was something he was familiar with. He opened his bag to get his beanie out, feeling like his ears would freeze and snap off.

"I'm guessing you're Azar," came a new voice. He turned to see a woman standing there. She looked to be slightly older than Azar, perhaps in her early or mid-twenties, with dark skin and long black and blue hair.

"How did you know?" he replied, pulling the wool cotton over his head.

"Your doppelganger told me what you'd look like," she said. Azar stopped. The woman broke out into a soft laugh.

"I'm kidding, Peacekeeper Drand informed me of who you are. He is the one that advised you to come here, right? I never imagined I'd be the one to introduce an Oklem to the Frowl, it is rather exciting. My name is Reena, your travel guide."

"Great to meet you," Azar said, silently relieved he wasn't going to be completely alone in the snowy wilderness. "You said Drand informed you about me?"

Reena nodded.

"He was extra driven to tell me how imperative your safety is whilst you are here. I can assure you there is no current danger I am aware of. I am a scout for this Nation, I know its entire layout, what mountain peaks to avoid due to avalanches and so on."

"I don't suppose you can control the weather," Azar replied. "Is it always this cold here?"

"You get used to it after a while," Reena replied, her eyes appearing to glow blue.

"Please tell me we're going to a nice warm hotel or something," Azar said, preparing to move with his suitcase.

"None of that here," Reena said, turning to the station. "The train terminal is the closest thing to a building you'll see here. This Nation is very different from the others. As you know, our core trait is our nobility. We always keep a promise. I have been told not to waste time, so we are going to go straight to the Frowl."

"Lead the way," Azar said.

Azar followed Reena into the busy and elegant railway station, where blue bullet trains came and went at a rate faster than Azar had thought was possible. The platforms were flooded with an endless stream of passengers.

"This is the Central Rail Station of the Ice Nation. From here, the lines go direct to their destinations," Reena explained.

"So everyone has to get a train here to go on another line? Doesn't that cause massive time delays?"

Just then another train sped into the station and stopped. Reena turned to him, tightening her scarf.

"As I've said, we are very different from the other Nations. There are only villages and towns here. No cities. No suburbs in between. Transport goes to one stop, and it's free. This is faster, trust me," she said with a wink.

Free transport? Reena led a stunned Azar to platform seventeen, where a sign on it read *The Frowl Rail Line*.

A train pulled into the platform. A few people got out. Azar and his guide boarded, and the Oklem looked around. It was a wide, single level carriage, with two rows of seating split down the centre by the aisle. The trains were heated, and the seats were very soft and for a moment Azar wondered if he'd be able to get off them.

"Don't get too comfortable, it isn't a very long ride," Reena warned.

The train took off. Azar peered out the window, but all he could see was a sheet of white snow. It was only a couple of minutes before the train began to slow down. The snow suddenly cleared just enough for Azar to get a view of some mountains. But these weren't just random ones. It was the exact view he had seen in his visions. This was the place. He had arrived. The train pulled into a station, which was just a raised, snowy ledge.

"We're here," Reena said, getting up. Azar grabbed his luggage and followed her off the train. The doors shut and the train took off.

"This is it," Azar murmured to himself. On the other side of the rail line was a sea of white. He could just see the outline of mountains spread around, and realised they were very high up. Behind them loomed more mountains.

Just then he felt a sensation come over him. This time he knew what it was. A calling. A pulling within his mind. Reena grabbed his arm.

"Hey are you okay?" she asked worriedly. Azar took a few deep breaths.

"I'm not entirely sure what that is, but it's related to being an Oklem. Let's just get to where we need to be."

"This way," she said, walking down a snowy pathway. Azar had to carry his suitcase as the snow didn't allow for its wheels to be of much use. They approached an ice cave and started a descent. They passed a family making their way to the station. As they passed, the family smiled warmly and greeted them. Reena replied enthusiastically, whilst Azar, caught off guard, greeted them hesitantly, awkwardly.

"They are a friendly bunch here,' Reena added as they continued into the mountain. They rounded a corner of the tunnel and Azar stopped. They were on the edge of a precipice, looking down into a brightly lit town within the caves. "Welcome to the Frowl."

"It's incredible," Azar said in awe. The roof of the cave shimmered a very light green, and reflected the lights from the igloos below. They made their way down the hill. The igloos were much larger than he had thought they were, and as they approached, Azar realised the lights were candles sitting in sealed jars. Reena seemed to know exactly where they were headed.

They made their way past the igloos, going further into this enchanting ice town. Reena stopped at a fenced area, where a wooden sign labelled *Inns* stood, dug into the ground at the front. "You'll be glad to know we each get our own igloo to stay in," Reena said cheerfully. She ducked into an igloo labelled *Reception*, emerging a short time later. She led the way into the igloo campgrounds.

"This is yours, mine is right next to you. Say fifteen minutes before we go to the Oklem area?" Reena said.

"We're going now?" Azar asked.

"I don't think we have time for a vacation, Azar," Reena said. "Drand wants you to discover who you are, and the sooner, the better."

She disappeared into her igloo. Azar went over to his, where in between each block of ice stuck together, a blue glow shimmered. To his surprise, his igloo had stairs leading down to a wooden door. He walked in and looked around. A small fire burned in the centre of the room. At the back was a bed, and to the right a small open doorway which turned out to lead into a bathroom. The interior too glowed a very light blue. He was blown away. Mintor seemed to get more boring by the minute. He dropped his suitcase to the side in relief and sat by the fire. It was the perfect temperature inside. He wished he could call Jake, but the reception in this Nation was limited to its own borders.

"Ready to go?" came Reena's voice from outside. She wasn't kidding, Azar realised. Sighing, he wrapped himself up again and left his igloo.

"Do we have a key to lock it?" he asked, already feeling the cold air on his flustered cheeks.

"This is the Ice Nation, Azar. We are not entirely without crime, but I can assure you nobody will be breaking into your igloo," Reena replied. To his astonishment, Reena was no longer wearing a coat, just a black shirt. The skin on her arms rippled with blue streaks shooting through her veins. She was incredibly attractive, Azar observed. Was it weird to think that? Reena had made her way back out to the main pathway. Azar followed her along the icy ground for a few minutes before she ascended a hill on the left and stopped at a cave archway.

"This is as far as I go," Reena said, turning to the Oklem.

"Why?" Azar asked cautiously.

"Only Oklem can go any further. As I said earlier I don't know much about you, nor does anyone here, but nobody has been able to enter this cave apart from the three previous Oklem. I'll be in the restaurant back in the middle of the igloo town. Come and find me when you're done. Good luck," she said brightly, leaving Azar alone at the hill. He glanced inside, looking for a sign of what to expect, but the pathway didn't go far before turning a corner. This was it. Where the Peacekeepers, the See-er, his visions, had been telling him to go. Taking one final deep breath, Azar stepped in.

As soon as he cleared the mouth of the cave, a blue forcefield-like shield covered the entrance. Blue was a common colour in the Ice Nation, he observed. He rounded the corner slowly, and could hear whispers. The cave opened into a large, cold, stone room. Azar recognised it straight away. This was the same cave the See-er had created the Oklem all those years ago. This was Azar's supernatural place of origin. The walls had a light greenish glow within them, but other than that, there was nothing else in the cave. He felt the familiar pulling within, but this time he was not feeling like he would be knocked out from it. Instead a buzzing sound grew louder, then the walls lit up a brighter green. Azar closed his eyes. The whispers grew louder, faster, almost chanting the word "Oklem". A sudden breeze swept through the room, and Azar opened his eyes. He was still in the cave, but it was now covered in a green haze. As he looked around, the haze also revealed a person standing in front of him, covered in a white cloak.

"At long last you have entered your subconscious, Oklem," the figure said. Azar's heart rate began to increase. The stranger removed his cloak revealing his face. He had messy brown hair, and was older looking with a short stubble around his face. Azar had seen it before, briefly, but couldn't pinpoint it yet.

"If it was this easy all the time I'd have done it a while ago," Azar replied, trying to keep his voice steady. His heart was now thumping.

"It will be from now on," the stranger said, "now that a physical connection has been made. I am Peter, the first Oklem."

Now Azar remembered. Peter, the little boy in the cave he had seen through the See-er's vision. The same man that had died the night Lux became a doppelganger.

"Your life was cut short when Orven—"

When Orven almost unleashed devastation, were it not for your doppelganger," Peter finished, a tone of gratitude in his voice. That was the first time Azar had heard anyone praise Lux.

"Why am I here? What is it about this cave that allows me to see you?" he asked.

Peter spread his arms.

"This is the birthplace of our kind. Nature's weapons against the supernatural realm. Even after all these years, I do not know why we exist, for Orven remains a threat to this day. We have failed."

"We haven't failed," Azar said. "Your life was lost on the night Orven's plan was ruined. But you still stopped the Tychun from coming through. You knew Lux's family, resulting in him doing something to honour your death. If you had never met him, you could very well have been alone on that podium, and then it would have been a failure."

A silence passed over them for a few moments.

"Your positive outlook on situations is refreshing," Peter commented.

"I've been told there were three Oklem that lived before me. If you're the first, who are the others? What did they do in the fight against evil?" Azar asked.

"Their stories are theirs to tell," Peter said. "They are confronting. We have all lived difficult lives. You have a unique gift. A mortal Oklem mixed with the mysteries of a doppelganger. One can only imagine what lies ahead for you."

Just then another cloaked figure appeared to emerge through the wall, startling Azar. Peter cleared his throat.

"Unfortunately one of the Oklem is held up with a family event. She will be here shortly."

Before talking to the Oklem that had just arrived, Azar wanted to get a timeline in his head.

"When was she alive?" he asked.

"At a time when Orven was locked away in the Supernatural Universe. Her struggles were against those trying to reopen the portal, but they were no match against the combined strength of the Oklem and Peacekeeper's powers," Peter answered.

Azar looked at the third Oklem, who had still not yet spoken or revealed their identity.

"I'm confused," he said, frowning. "If Peter was the first Oklem, turned by the See-er when Orven was starting to work towards domination with supernatural aid, and this other Oklem was alive during the time Orven was not around, when did you exist? Before Orven was sent away, or after?" he asked the newcomer.

"Both times, but that's not what the worst part is," came the brisk reply. Very familiar.

Azar froze, goosebumps rippling across his entire body, watching in complete astonishment as the mystery Oklem lifted his hood and revealed his face.

"Hello, Azar," Brett said.

Chapter 34

Azar was unable to hold himself upright, dropping to his knees. An intense weight was suddenly bearing down on him, making him feel as though gravity was pulling him into the ground. "You're dead," Azar eventually managed to say. Brett nodded.

"Yes I am dead. So is Peter. But we are Oklem, so we live on here in this cave, and through the Oklem that are alive," he said.

Azar sat in silence for a long while, and the Oklem appeared to wait for him. Azar began to bring his thoughts together. Brett was an Oklem. That...didn't make any sense.

"You've been working with Orven, Brett, how can you be an Oklem?" he asked.

"I have never been working with Orven," Brett said defensively. "In saying that, I have not necessarily been on side with the Peacekeepers. Azar you need to realise that being an Oklem does not mean being with the Nations. It means preventing the Tychun from ever crossing into our universe. Sometimes, everything must be put on the line, and allies may become foes." There was something off about Brett, Azar thought. There was an unfamiliar coldness coming from him, as though he were a stranger. Although it seemed fitting, considering he was dead. Peter stepped forwards, drawing Azar's attention and snapping him out of the sudden darkness his mind had plunged into.

"Our goal is to find what nature has called you forth to achieve," Peter said. "We are in very uncertain times, and there is no telling when or how the Tychun plan to cross into our universe."

"So that's it? Our world will forever be threatened by the Tychun in a never ending cycle," Azar said. Brett then walked over to Azar, offering a hand to help Azar stand back up. Azar paused. "You can touch me?" he asked cautiously.

"Only whilst in the cave," Brett said, waiting for Azar to accept his offer. Azar didn't. He couldn't.

"I admit I did consider the possibility that we were in a never ending cycle," Brett said, rolling his eyes at Azar's rejection as his ex stood back up. "But as you've been told, you have more than just Oklem blood running through your veins. You're a doppelganger, and I believe that by having a unique tie to the supernatural universe, you can potentially stop travel between the universe's permanently."

Azar was tired of hearing about his "potential". He was still uncertain of the world he had been dragged into.

"I keep being told I can create portals, that Orven used my blood to escape his death at the end of the war. Where did he go? My mother said his plan couldn't work because I am a doppelganger. If you've been able to watch me, you must know where he is."

"No," Peter said, "we can only watch other Oklem. And that can only happen when you allow us in."

Azar remembered the multiple times in which he had felt dazed or as if his mind was trying to explode out of his head. It made sense that it was the Oklem trying to make contact with him. He looked at Brett.

"You just said being an Oklem doesn't always mean being with the Nations. Is there a different reason as to why you gave my blood to Orven?" he asked.

"Yes," Brett said abruptly. Azar began to form an idea.

"Because it's more powerful," he said. Peter and Brett both nodded, but Azar could tell there was something else he was missing out on.

"What we're about to tell you is big," Peter said. He walked over to one of the cave's walls, and brushed his hand against the ice. Immediately the wall was covered in drawings. Azar did not know what all the symbols meant, but could see it was telling a story of sorts.

"Your Oklem blood is mixed with doppelganger blood," Peter continued. "It allows you to create a portal to anywhere, including the Supernatural Universe. Orven wanted your blood to be able to do this."

Azar remembered the vision he had seen in the Fortune Caves. Orven had escaped capture by going through a portal. Looking at the images on the wall, a mortal figure was seen jumping into a circle, presumably representing a portal. The next image shows the figure standing in a pit of spikes with deformed creatures surrounding him. Brett confirmed Azar's next question before he could ask it.

"Orven successfully escaped capture and went to the Supernatural Universe. He's still there, somewhere."

A little shiver rippled through Azar's body. His blood had let Orven escape death and hide in the Supernatural Universe.

"We think we can stop him coming back forever if we can seal the path permanently," Peter said. "Well, considering I have no idea how to do anything with portals, there might be a small problem," Azar replied.

"We will teach you how to use portals, and how to use your mind ability," Peter continued. "In fact, you are going to do it again, right now."

Azar turned away from the wall, looking at Peter.

"What do you mean?" he asked.

"I am going to show you some of my past memories of being an Oklem," Brett said. "I am hoping that afterwards, you will know what we know, and then leave here with a mission." As much as Azar didn't want to go into Brett's past, he knew deep down that he had to. He needed to be able to defend himself against the deception, the darkness. It also meant that the sooner he did as Peter instructed, the sooner he could leave.

"Okay then," Azar said, walking over to Brett. Azar's heart was thumping in his chest. In a way, he was about to make physical contact with death.

"Now remember," Brett said softly, holding his hand up, palm facing Azar, "close your eyes and allow your mind to travel through your touch with me."

Azar took one final look at Brett before he closed his eyes. Then he raised his right hand and pressed his palm against Brett's. An energy suddenly rushed through his veins, and soon after he felt himself removed from his physical body, and was watching a scene unfold.

1839: Mortal Nation Forest

The trees barely stirred as Brett made his way along the dirt road. He had spent the day celebrating his eighteenth birthday alone at an isolated waterfall hidden within the seemingly endless forest of the Mortal Nation. It was a sweltering Autumn day, the sun beating down mercilessly. Brett had already dried, and could feel drops of sweat starting to fall on his brow. It had been a refreshing swim, but he wished he had someone to celebrate it with. His sandals crunched over the dry leaves. He was so entranced in thought he was oblivious to the sounds of travellers until a cart, led by an old, grey horse, slowly rounded the corner ahead. It wasn't uncommon to see people take the scenic route from the main village of Mintor to the far reaching towns. Thinking nothing more of it, he moved to the side of the trail as the cart rattled its way past. As it did so, Brett heard a woman giggling and glanced through the open window. The woman had blazing orange hair and piercing red eyes. They locked with Brett's and she suddenly sat bolt upright. Brett's stomach dropped, his legs almost buckling in horror as he realised what had just happened.

"Stop the cart, driver," Peacekeeper Serain demanded. It came to a halt. A man sat up and his face came into Brett's view. His messy grey hair spread across his forehead in sweaty streaks. Brett felt himself go numb, as if his blood was literally freezing in his veins.

"What is the meaning of this?" Orven asked irritably. The enemy of the Nations, the leader of the Pirates, the reason for Brett's Oklem existence.

"It's that boy. My love, he is an Oklem," Serain whispered in astonishment.

His senses kicking in, Brett immediately ran along the path in the direction he had been travelling, hoping to make it to the farmyards at the base of the mountain, or at least into a dense bushy area to hide. He was uncertain as to why the Fire Nation's Peacekeeper was with Orven, but he knew he could not be caught by the Pirate. His attempt, however, was futile. Suddenly a vine wrapped itself around his legs, and he toppled over, his towel flying off his shoulders and behind a shrub. His legs grazed, Brett rolled over to see Peacekeeper Serain and Orven standing outside the cart together. The vines had come from the Peacekeeper's body? Orven slowly paced towards Brett, crouching over the trembling boy.

"They did very well to hide you," he observed. Brett's heart was pounding.

"What do you want with me? Your plans were ruined by the doppelganger," he said, but his nerves prevented any real threat to support his words.

"Indeed," Orven replied softly. "But I now have the key ingredient to try again. You. However I must delay that mission, for I have a different need for an Oklem. Believe it or not, we will not be harming you."

The vines were wrapped tightly around Brett, meaning there was no chance he could break free from them. Orven picked Brett up, who offered no resistance, and carried him to the carriage. Brett knew he could not take either of them on. He stared glumly at the floor as the cart continued to rattle on. After a few moments of silence, he looked at Peacekeeper Serain.

"You're a treacherous Peacekeeper," he muttered. "I was warned about deception."

"That is frequently the case," Serain said with a humoured gleam in her wicked eyes. "Every time someone is exposed to the truth, they never have the opportunity to tell anyone."

"So you are going to kill me," Brett said.

"No, dear boy, we are not," Orven replied.

"We are sending you on an adventure," Serain added. It was now that Brett noticed two empty wine glasses lying against the door.

"An adventure," Brett repeated. Orven nodded.

"You see, things have unfortunately come to a stage where I need to look as if I've been 'dealt with'. So my lovely wife and I have worked the other Peacekeepers into thinking that the best punishment for me is not death but rather to be sent far away. Do you know much about the Supernatural Universe?" he asked.

"What? No I do not want a part in this," Brett said. He tried to move but the vines' grip tightened even more around his legs. Orven had called Serain his wife.

"Well, that is completely understandable,' Serain said, speaking slowly. "But I need some assistance. You see, I can send all the Pirates to the other side and close the path between the universes. The problem is that to reopen it, there has to be someone on both sides. Obviously we cannot send a Peacekeeper. But as we know, an Oklem can activate portals with their blood. So we will send you over to the Supernatural Universe, and whenever you want to come back, all you have to do is go to the portal and reopen it."

"You've become insane," Brett said, his eyes beginning to well up.

"Actually it's a very well thought out plan," Orven replied. "We will teach you everything you need to know. Then the power will be in your hands."

Brett did not say another word, realising he had failed his family. They had told him to never make contact with a Pirate and to try and avoid the gaze of a Peacekeeper. Now he had done both those things, and everything was about to change.

Chapter 35

Emma parked her motor scooter in her usual spot at the Whistle. She had initially tried to talk to Jake, but he had stormed past her and out of the building when she opened his bedroom door. She was quite astonished at his breakdown, and whilst she didn't know what was causing it, she assumed it had something to do with Azar. She still had slight suspicions over the Oklem and their secrecy, but right now her priority was finding out who owned the safe she was attacked in. The bank stored many of their files in a sector of the Whistle. Emma's status as the Peacekeeper's private investigator granted her access to the area she was after. She entered a small room with multiple computers in it. These computers contained a list of all the bank's safe owners, past and present. The name of the safe was fascinating. *Miring Seethe.* Emma went to the monitor labelled 'safe locator'. A basic machine where putting in a name would automatically reveal all known knowledge about the safe and owner that was stored within the database. The system searched the name for a long while, longer than usual, before the screen displayed the sign *no results found*. Emma sat back, frowning. There was not a trace of that name in the entire bank's system? Somehow that made sense. The safe was keeping the Queen of the Pirates hidden, so having a fake name would ensure nobody like Emma could track the owner, should that possibility arise. She thought back to the day she was there with Lux. And then the wheels of her mind began to turn. He was the one who found the safe. He had kicked open the door. The slightest memory flickered in her mind about that moment. The name badge on the door. She thought she had seen it move ever so slightly. As if...

"It was placed over something," Emma finished out loud. Placed over the real name, perhaps. She realised she would have to return to the bank, to the place where she had been poisoned by Tychun blood. Instinctively she clutched her left wrist as she stood up. Suddenly a pain shot through her body, and she looked down in alarm. Her skin was black, seared. The infection had come back.

Then just as quickly the pain vanished, and Emma found herself lying on the floor. Her skin was fine. Azar's blood had healed her, she thought. Had she been hallucinating? She stood up and left the room, pulling out her phone. As she tried to ring Jake, the call bounced back, indicating he was on the phone. Sighing in frustration, she walked back through the Whistle's hallways at a fast pace, trying to direct her focus onto the safe. She had never felt so unsure of what she was doing. Peacekeeper Drand had always kept her with a mission which she could confide in him. This time she was in charge and Emma felt a great pressure mounted on her shoulders. She returned to her scooter and headed for the bank. The trip was a blur, her mind racing a million miles an hour. The owner of this safe could hold many answers to Lara Sokolov's plans, to Jessani's, even to Lux's intentions. All these people would not be showing up now unless there was a reason for it. The bank had reopened to the public, however there was a much higher level of security present at the entrance as well as within the bank's halls. Emma went back down the corridor and arrived at the room where Lux had taken care of the traitorous guard. This time three guards sat together at the security desk. They all stood up as Emma entered, but relaxed when she produced her investigator's badge.

"What were you after today, Miss Flare?" one of the guards asked.

"I'm just retracing the steps the Pirates took on the day of the attack. I don't plan to enter any safes today," Emma lied.

Very well."

Emma went through the *Safes* door. For a moment she forgot how maze-like the area was, and worried she wouldn't find the safe. But soon she was on track, her boots clicking on the stone floor. The distant echo of another door closing bounced off the walls. As she neared her destination, she heard a sound behind her. Turning, she was looking at the fiery creature that had bitten her, saliva dripping from its mouth. She rolled out her whip, the electrifying crack signifying the weapon's readiness to strike. But she was alone. Something was messing with her. She shook her head and hurried to the safe. She approached the door and looked at the name again. *Miring Seethe*. It was written in bronze on a rectangular base. She ran her fingers along it, expecting to find a great deal of dust. It was clean, adding to her suspicion that it was a fake name that had been recently placed over the true owner. She applied some weight to it and felt it move slightly. But it didn't come off all the way. She pulled out her hair pin and placed it between the sign and the door. She could feel there was some sort of glue holding the sign in place. She scraped vigorously at it. Soon enough, the sign shuddered, then with one final shove of her pin, it fell away, clattering onto the ground. Emma glanced at the name and took a step back in horror. How was that possible? She suddenly had a million questions and for a moment she almost lost her footing and slumped against the opposing wall. The owner of the safe was Miriam Flare. Emma and Jake's mother. The last Emma had heard of her parents was when the twins were abandoned in the Earth Nation. Yet somehow her mother owned a safe hundreds of years old, one that kept hidden the Queen of the Pirates. Despite the sudden pain and fear she faced thinking back to her childhood, Emma wanted to know why.

Chapter 36

Supernatural Universe (10 Years Ago)

Another rumble. This time much stronger. The walls shuddered, the roof creaked. A howl echoed across the bare hills of the Supernatural Universe. Brett peered out the small diamond shaped window. Although he had been trapped there for so long, he still wished that one day he could see the sun light up the world instead of the two dim, red moons. He did have a choice though. The choice he always had, the one that Orven had given him before sending him through the portal. His Oklem blood could let him return to the Mortal Nation. But it would also let the enemy return. He looked around his small hut. This was all he had lived with for over a century, and it wasn't fair. He decided to go for a walk. As he put his shoes on, there was a knock at the door. Nobody ever knocked, he thought. Cautiously, he walked over and opened it. His stomach dropped a bit as he looked at the visitor.

"Where are we off to?" Lux asked, glancing down at Brett's shoes. Brett had first met Lux just after they had portalled from the Nations. Lux used his new found speed abilities to help take Brett to a safer zone of the universe. A small town created for mortals, protected by indestructible stone hounds. Although the town did not only house mortals like Brett. Witches, ghosts, and a wondrous mix of large and small creatures shared the area. It had become a home away from home, but Brett still longed for the life in which he felt he was supposed to live in Mintor. Lux had given Brett a potion he managed to retrieve before he had broken up with Jessani. A potion that stopped him from aging. Brett was eager to take it, because he knew that one day he would reopen the path.

"I'm clearing my head. I sense you're probably going to strike me, but I think I want to open the portal, for real this time," Brett said, closing his eyes and expecting a punch from his friend. It didn't come. He slowly opened one eye to see Lux grinning at him.

"Actually, I was going to suggest the same thing," he said.

"What?" Brett asked in surprise. Lux stepped aside to allow Brett to walk out. The two began to pace down the black soiled trail towards the centre of town.

"It's been ten years since I broke up with Jessani. More specifically, since I stopped loving her. I have made many connections with those who can still reach out to some living outside the Supernatural Universe. A lot has changed in the Nations. And it turns out I have someone over there that I need to see," Lux explained.

"So this is about you?" Brett said, slightly disappointed. A ghost train came screaming up the path, giving Brett no warning to move. He had learnt the hard way that despite it being a ghost, it could still blow one off their feet. Lux grabbed Brett and sped off, stopping moments later at a lava lake.

"Not just about me," Lux replied, eyeing Brett closely. Brett could feel his heart rate beat a little faster. He shook his head.

"Do you think it's been long enough? Surely the Pirates are no more, Peacekeeper Serain must have been removed by now," he said.

"I don't know," Lux said, lifting his shoulders. "Are you going to be okay? I mean you won't really have anybody waiting there."

Brett was aware of that. His family would have passed away a long time ago, there would be no reconnecting with them. It would be like he was starting a life from scratch.

"I'll have one friend," he said, looking at Lux with a sly smile. A slight flash of hesitation flickered in Lux's eyes before he replied.

"Yeah."

A small woman dressed in a black gown and pointed hat walked past, a bubbling green cauldron in her hands. Brett remembered Lux's story about how he had foiled Orven's plans, and was not surprised to see that the cauldron had impacted the boy. But Lux quickly shook it off, clearing his throat.

"Shall we go, then?" he asked. Brett took a final look over the lake, over the forever darkness he had gotten used to. Then he looked at Lux.

"Yes."

Moments later, Brett found himself standing outside the tall iron gates he had only ever seen once before, when he had first arrived. Immediately a figure appeared in front of him in a grey cloak, floating off the ground. They had a round, stone head and yellow eyes.

"The Oklem has arrived," it hissed, sending shudders down Brett's spine. Brett glanced behind him but Lux was nowhere to be seen. The gates opened slowly and Brett followed the creature towards a large stone castle. Orven had been busy, Brett thought. Brett was taken to a small foyer, where he waited until two large double doors opened. Jessani, the daughter of Orven, stepped through, her silky black hair down to her knees.

"It's about time," Jessani said. "I've been rather bored this last decade."

"You think I care about you?" Brett asked sourly. His anger at what Orven had done to him was starting to seep through.

"I don't think anybody here cares about anything to be honest," Jessani replied. Then she indicated with her head for Brett to follow her before turning around. They entered a large throne room, which was bare apart from a huge stone emblem of Skull on the back wall, and Orven seated on a glass throne below it.

"Ah, my boy, at last you have come," Orven said, his voice icy. As Brett neared him, the Oklem could see Orven's crooked, yellow teeth, and oily, stringy grey hair. Brett wasn't sure who was more hideous. The creature that had greeted him before or the leader of the Pirates. Brett did not reply to Orven, but he did not seem fazed by it.

"Now it is as simple to reopen the portal as you did to get us here all those years ago. Just step over to the wall," Orven said. Brett did as he was instructed. There was no turning back now. He was going home. It was unfortunate that he was bringing one nasty surprise back for the Peacekeepers. He had suffered enough, it was time to be free from this burden. Orven joined Brett and pulled out a small knife. Jessani watched on in silent fascination. The Pirate cut Brett's palm. Brett flinched as the blood began to run down his skin. Orven used a finger and swiped it along the blood, then used it to draw a circle on the wall. It was roughly the same size as Brett's hand span.

"Now just keep in mind where you want to go. Then press your palm into the middle of the circle and the portal will be created," Orven said enthusiastically, his eyes wide. Just then the doors opened and a line of Pirates entered. Brett realised they were all planning on coming through his portal. He looked away, there was nothing he could do. He imagined the Mortal Nation as he had last seen it, then pressed his palm in the centre of his blood circle. Immediately the wall vanished and a beaming circle of light took its place, bordered by Brett's red blood. The portal was open.

A silence filled the room before someone suddenly shot out of the line of Pirates. Lux stood just in front of the portal. He looked directly at Jessani, who had an expression of shock and hurt in her eyes.

"Hi sweetheart," Lux said warmly, full of sarcasm. Then he looked at Brett just long enough for Brett to see an expression of sorrow in those blue eyes before Lux dove into the portal. Jessani raced forwards, followed closely by the Pirate army. Brett lunged through the portal, and then the vision went black.

****

Azar opened his eyes. He was gripping Brett's hand tightly, to the point their palms were both red. But this time Azar wasn't sweating or short of breath. He looked around the Oklem ice cave and realised they were alone, Peter nowhere to be seen.

"So now you know the story," Brett said, stepping away from Azar.

"You were so innocent back then. What changed that? And what happened to your friendship with Lux?" Azar asked. He was surprised at knowing the truth, how Brett used to be. He had never shown that vulnerable side since Azar had met him.

"I came back thinking I'd at least be recognised for what I had done, the sacrifice I had made. But nobody knew me. The Peacekeepers were very quickly distracted with Orven's return. There was only one person who appreciated what I had done. That was your mother," Brett said, looking sorrowfully at Azar. Azar looked at the ground, understanding why Brett was so willing to work with Maree Geminus. But there was something else Azar had felt through the vision, and he knew he had to bring it up. "You had feelings for Lux," he said, not even posing it as a question. Brett looked at Azar with a certain hostility.

"Don't judge me for my choices," he said coldly. Azar was caught off guard by Brett's defensiveness.

"I wasn't judging you, Brett. It makes sense. And knowing Lux, I am guessing he didn't come and find you until recently. The one friend you had didn't come looking for you when you came back," Azar said, feeling a hint of pity inside his heart. Brett walked over the wall with symbols, which had changed into various shapes Azar couldn't understand.

"When your mother came to me, and I saw who she wanted me to get close with, I knew straight away you were a doppelganger,' Brett explained. "It wasn't hard to fall in love with you, but I lacked direction with everything. I screwed us up. I'm dead now, so there's no point in dwelling on it. Right now I want you to be safe and happy. Does Jake do that for you?"

Azar started to become suspicious of Brett. Why was he asking about Jake?

"Jake isn't perfect, there are a lot of secrets with his work," he replied cautiously.

"His betrayal is pretty serious. I saw the vision too," Brett said before Azar could ask.

"At least he didn't cheat," Azar replied.

"Were you hurt by his betrayal?" Brett asked, ignoring Azar.

"A little—"

"Does he make you feel safe?"

"Why are you doing this, Brett?" Azar finally snapped. "Are you still upset that we aren't meant to be? That you never got what you really wanted?"

Brett stormed over to Azar, who didn't flinch as he put his hands on Azar's shoulders and looked him dead in the eye. The touch sent chills down Azar's back.

"I'm asking because I want you to remember what you felt when you were truly in love with me. Do not sell yourself for anything less, because before our lives went to hell, you and I shared a real love. If Jake doesn't do that then he does not deserve to be with you."

Azar once again found himself in a state of silent astonishment. What does one even say to that? He didn't want to think about what Brett just said. Jake had not yet convinced Azar of his trust. Every time he takes a step forward, something is revealed that takes Azar's relationship with him two steps back. Azar started to feel angry. But at who? At Brett for giving him advice on love? At Jake for not giving Azar the confidence to defend him in moments like now? At himself for needing someone to make him feel better? Brett dropped his hands and Azar took a dazed step back.

"I'll come back tomorrow," Azar said slowly, rubbing his head before turning around and running back out of the cave. He ran towards the igloo town. He was suddenly exhausted. His cheeks flushed at the drop in temperature as he left the Oklem cave. He continued until he saw a larger igloo labelled *Diner*. Reena had said she would be waiting there for him. As he entered, he saw her sitting alone at a booth, holding a steaming mug. She looked up as Azar approached. "That was fast," she said. Azar had no idea what time it was, or how long he had been, but right now he didn't care.

"Is there any way I can contact someone in Mintor? There's got to be a way," he said, sitting opposite her. Reena cocked her head, exposing the blue veins in her neck.

"There is. And you're in luck, because the phone is in this diner. Go through that archway over there and you'll see the phone. Did you want me to order you anything?" she asked.

"Just a hot chocolate. Thank you," he said, realising he was sounding unappreciative of what Reena had already done for him. He found the phone in a small boxed room. It was called a *Special Landline*. A small step-by-step instruction manual was stuck next to a screen. *Step 1: Select the Nation you wish to contact. Step 2: Put in the number of the contact. Step 3: Enjoy your call.*

It seemed simple enough, Azar thought. He followed the rules and put in Jake's number. He stopped at the last digit. He had already memorised Jake's number. Was he taking things too quickly? Brett's words rang around the back of his head as he pressed the final number. The phone made multiple beeping noises before a ringing tone came through. The nerves crept through his stomach.

"Hello?" came Jake's voice.

"Jake. Hey," Azar said, his throat suddenly going dry. Azar could smell meat wafting from the kitchens, and his stomach churned in hunger.

"Azar? Umm, how…how are you?" Jake asked. His voice seemed pitchy, as if he'd been crying.

"I'm okay, I found the Oklem cave," Azar said.

"That's great, is there anything you want to tell me about it?" Jake replied.

Azar paused. He didn't know enough to tell Jake, and mentioning Brett would only start a drama.

"Actually no, but that's not what I wanted to talk to you about," he said slowly. He replayed Jake's vision in his head.

"I'm so sorry," Jake began, as if he was reliving the same moment.

"It's okay. I just want to know something," Azar said.

"Anything, I promise I'll tell the truth," Jake replied. Azar sensed Jake was being genuine.

"Why didn't you kill me? On that hill, you had been prepared for anything. But you shook my hand instead of doing your job. Why?"

A long pause followed, and Azar got increasingly worried about Jake's response.

"I believed you," came the reply. "I believed you were not dangerous. Maybe it was some gut instinct. I felt that killing you would have been worse."

Azar could feel the warm tears slowly rolling down his cheeks.

"I'm sorry I left the way I did. When I get back, we're going to sort everything out, I promise," he said.

"I'd like that, I want to trust you and I want you to trust me," Jake said with a sniffle.

"Done," Azar said.

"I love you, Azar."

"I love you too, Jake. Honestly, this call is really helping me clear my head. I'll see you soon." Azar hung up the phone. He stood there for a while afterwards. Some of the weight that had been bearing him down was lifted, and he could feel the difference. He needed to finish his work with Peter as quickly as he could tomorrow so he could go home. Ensuring his face was dry from the tears, he walked back out to Reena. He was looking forward to his hot chocolate, if anything to help thaw his fingers.

As he rounded one of the ice pillars which structured the interior of the diner, the front doors to his right opened with a jingle from a bell. Azar glanced towards the newcomer without much thought. Then he froze. He knew the face. The boy was about the same age as Azar, skinny, but with broad shoulders. His skin was toned, and he had dark hair slicked back with icy blue streaks running through it. His brown eyes locked with Azar's, and the Oklem finally realised where he had seen the face.

In the Fortune Caves, during the first vision Azar had as an Oklem, a third boy had appeared alongside Brett and Jake. Azar didn't know who he was, but his initial gut instincts weren't good.

"Wow bro, I was not expecting an Oklem with my order. My job just became a whole lot easier, aye?" the boy said with a smirk. Azar looked for Reena but she was not sitting at the booth. He began to feel the danger of the situation press down on him. He had seconds to decide what he would do. Stay and talk or run like hell.

Ingram Content Group UK Ltd.
Milton Keynes UK
UKHW020115300523
422450UK00005B/43